No Cry for Help

ALSO BY GRANT MCKENZIE FROM CLIPPER LARGE PRINT

Switch

No Cry for Help

Grant McKenzie

W F HOWES LTD

This large print edition published in 2011 by
W F Howes Ltd
Unit 4, Rearsby Business Park, Gaddesby Lane,
Rearsby, Leicester LE7 4YH

1 3 5 7 9 10 8 6 4 2

First published in the United Kingdom in 2010
by Bantam Books

A CIP catalogue record for this book is available
from the British Library

ISBN 978 1 40747 763 3

Typeset by Palimpsest Book Production Limited,
Falkirk, Stirlingshire
Printed and bound in Great Britain
by MPG Books Ltd, Bodmin, Cornwall

MIX
Paper from
responsible sources
FSC
www.fsc.org   FSC® C018575

For Karen and Kailey,
laughter and love.

And for Mum and Dad,
who allowed their odd little boy
to be an old little boy.

CHAPTER 1

Late.

That wasn't like her.

Not *this* late.

Wallace Carver glanced at his watch for the tenth time in the last half-hour. He tapped its crystal face to make sure it wasn't broken. The tiny second hand ticked mercilessly, keeping perfect time.

A gift from the bus company, it was a proper watch. Heavy. Expensive. A four-letter inscription on the back. Apart from his gold wedding band, it was the only jewellery he ever wore.

Alicia teased him that she was jealous. She wanted to be the only valuable thing hanging on his arm. As if she ever had to worry.

No precious metal or jewel could shine as bright as his wife; at least, none he had ever seen.

Why else would he be sitting at an uncomfortable table in the noisy Food Court of a busy shopping mall, bored out of his mind, with sticky fingers and a well-travelled book of crosswords?

Wallace lifted his paper cup of coffee to his lips and grimaced when the cold dregs crossed his tongue. He had forgotten it wasn't fresh.

He looked at his watch again. It was after six. His family – Alicia and his two young boys, Fred and Alex – was supposed to meet him at five.

They hadn't checked into their hotel yet. Alicia and the boys had been so excited about driving across the border from Canada and going shopping in Bellingham's Bellis Fair Mall that they – by a vote of three to one – had decided to shop first and check in at the Holiday Inn just before supper.

The hotel was only a short drive from the mall, and the Olive Garden restaurant next to it promised a menu stuffed with the boys' favourite pastas, all-you-can-eat breadsticks, fountain drinks and, mercifully, a decent house red for Mom and Dad.

Thinking about the restaurant made Wallace's stomach grumble. All he had consumed in the last few hours were two large cups of coffee and a giant cinnamon bun smothered in cream-cheese icing. Granted, the promise of a sticky, gooey cinnamon bun had been his main lure for agreeing to visit the region's largest indoor shopping mall. His bad leg made walking for hours a chore and he had all the fashion sense of . . . well, of what he was.

He often wondered if the reason he chose to drive a bus was because the job came with a uniform. He didn't have to think before he got dressed each day, just slip on the company's baggy TransLink blues.

He glanced at his watch. Six thirty.

The uncomfortable knot of worry in his stomach began to churn and turn sour.

Come on, Alicia. Where are you?

Originally, Wallace had wanted to take a different type of trip: leave the boys with family friends, Crow and Delilah; have Alicia all to himself; reconnect. It had been a while.

But Alicia knew how much the boys would love an adventure, even such a short one. Money had been tight of late and, despite all his promises, family vacations had been one of the first luxuries to go. Fortunately, things were looking up. He was back to work full time, Alicia had picked up steady part-time hours at a local florist's, and the damn insurance company was finally off their backs.

Guess he couldn't blame Alicia for wanting to blow off a little retail steam, but still . . .

Wallace unfolded his long legs from beneath the table, stood up, stretched his arms above his head to unkink his back and loosen his shoulders, and looked around.

Alicia would be easy to spot if she was nearby. A natural redhead with uncontrollably curly hair that swept past her shoulders in adorable ringlets, she stood out like a beacon in an unending ocean of bland blondes and dull brunettes. She also walked with a bounce in her step – like Tigger from *Winnie the Pooh*; her favourite book – as though she was twenty years younger than her recent milestone birthday would imply.

A faint smile crossed Wallace's lips as he thought of her. Even when they first met, when he had been younger and owned a gym membership that he actually used, Alicia had been out of his league. He knew he was nothing to brag about. What you saw was what you got: an everyday guy with a steady job on the buses that he happened to enjoy. Alicia, meanwhile, not only turned heads, she was smart as a whip, too.

In a box, somewhere in the garage or attic, there was even a nicely printed, but never framed, Bachelor of Fine Arts degree from the University of British Columbia.

When Wallace questioned what first attracted her to him, Alicia would smile coyly and say he knew just how to fill out a pair of blue jeans. He still did, although his waistband had expanded a notch or two.

At six-foot-two, two hundred and twenty pounds, Wallace was no pushover. But, truth be told, before the accident he had balanced the scales at a solid two hundred even. That extra twenty pounds was hanging around his middle like an anchor, forcing him to wear his T-shirts untucked to hide the flab.

The weight never seemed to bother Alicia, though. Then again, few things did. He was her Pooh Bear. She was his eternal optimist; his needle pointing North.

Wallace's smile faded. There was no sign of her.

Even if Alicia had found a to-die-for shoe sale,

4

she would have checked in on him by now, if only to hurriedly drop off the boys so she could sprint back to the sale with unencumbered focus.

Wallace moved to the edge of the Food Court. One corridor connected the bulk of the mall with the atrium-style eating area. The spacious corridor was lined with shops and dotted with island kiosks offering everything from cellphones to real estate. It was all on sale. If you had the money, a lousy economy was a shopper's dream.

Crowds had thinned marginally since he last checked, as the weary headed home to feed their kids or soak their throbbing feet.

Wallace climbed on to a low wooden bench to peer over the tops of people's heads. He hoped to see Alicia threading her way through the crowd, face flushed, apologetic expression, a boy clutched tightly in each hand, their faces full of delighted mischief.

But she wasn't there.

Wallace looked at his watch.

Seven.

He wished he had brought his cellphone. Alicia had talked about bringing them. They both owned one, but he had been worried about roaming charges. He had heard horror stories about people who received outrageous bills when they travelled across the border without the proper international phone plan.

Wallace hadn't wanted to take the risk, it was just for the weekend, but now . . .

He stepped down from the bench, ignoring the disapproving glare from a sour-faced shopper who was obviously wondering what he was doing up there in the first place. He started down the corridor at a slow pace, allowing the stiff joints in his left leg to loosen.

Commission salesmen from the island kiosks tried to coax him over to sample their wares, but Wallace ignored them. As a public transit driver, he had quickly learned how to tune out annoying people. It was one of the necessities of the job.

The corridor led into a large, circular hub. From the hub, three more corridors stuffed with shops and kiosks stretched into the distance. Discount stickers for thirty, forty and fifty per cent off littered every window display. There were so many signs it was difficult to tell what each store actually sold, just that it was on sale.

His family could be anywhere.

Wallace glanced at his watch and cursed under his breath. Twenty minutes past seven. This was getting ridiculous.

Alicia had a tendency to be easily distracted by the silliest of things. It was a quality Wallace found both adorable and annoying in almost equal measure. On the one hand, she had a unique perspective on the world and an ability to make him see wonder in the mundane. And on the other . . . well, sometimes a rock was just a rock.

But even when she became distracted – grocery stores and craft fairs being the worst – she rarely kept him waiting longer than ten or fifteen minutes. To be over two hours late went against everything he knew about her. And after ten years of marriage, Wallace was pretty sure he knew it all.

What if one of the boys had taken ill or been injured? He dismissed the thought. If Alicia couldn't reach him, she would have had him paged. Despite her sense of whimsy, Alicia had always been good in a crisis.

In the middle of the hub was a circular backlit sign that displayed the floor plan of the mall. Wallace crossed to the sign and studied the map. Every store was catalogued both alphabetically and by the type of merchandise it sold. A letter and number ID tag beside each listing corresponded with a location on the map.

Wallace found the one he was looking for. The map showed it was located a short distance down the B corridor on his left.

Stuffed between a T-shirt shop that specialized in rock bands Wallace had never heard of and a women's lingerie store, a narrow hallway led off the main thoroughfare. Halfway down, a plain white door was labelled *Security*.

Wallace knocked and entered without waiting for an answer. He had grown too damn worried to be polite.

Two men in white shirts, black pants and skinny black ties sat in wheeled office chairs behind an old wooden desk. An adjoining door was open to a second, slightly larger office that glowed with both colour and greyscale monitors displaying various parts of the mall.

Wallace had entered in the middle of a joke and the larger of the two security guards was near-choking on a mouthful of egg-salad sandwich.

'Wrong door, I think, sir,' said the smaller guard. He had sandy blond hair and a button nose that made him look awkwardly elfish.

'Isn't this Security?' said Wallace.

The larger guard swallowed and swiped a paper napkin across his mouth. He was mostly bald and his freckled forehead was large enough to rent out for advertising. He also wore three stripes on his sleeve, compared to his partner's one.

'It is,' he said. 'How can we help?'

'I need to page my family.' Wallace's jaw locked tight.

'Is there an emergency?' asked the younger guard.

'I don't know.' Wallace suddenly felt self-conscious and a little ridiculous. 'I can't find them. They're missing.'

'Missing?' the younger guard scoffed. 'It's a large mall, sir. You sure they didn't just lose track of time?'

'I'm sure. We were supposed to meet,' Wallace glanced at his watch, 'two and a half hours ago. Can you page them?' He unclenched his jaw and squeezed out, 'Please.'

The two guards exchanged a glance that spoke

volumes. They could have just as subtly twirled a finger at the side of their heads.

'Did you try Customer Service?' said the older guard. He sounded weary, as though chewing his sandwich had been enough of a chore for the day.

'No. I came here.' Wallace locked eyes with the senior guard, getting a read. He felt his worry turning to anger, but kept it in check. He had learned on the job that if someone was nice to him, he could be their best friend, let them know when the right stop was coming up or what connecting bus to catch. But when someone pissed him off, it was easy to make a mistake and drop the jerk blocks from his intended destination. 'You're the professionals, right?'

The guard puffed up his chest. His nametag caught the light: *Victor Schulz*.

'That we are,' said Schulz. 'But we don't normally—'

'I'd really appreciate it,' Wallace interrupted. His voice held a note of desperation and he allowed it to show. 'You must have kids? A wife? I'm really worried and you guys know this mall better than anyone.'

Schulz sighed. 'OK. What are the names?'

Wallace told him.

'Hold on.'

The guard spun his chair to face a small black microphone. He flicked a series of switches until a row of red lights glowed across the front of an outdated electronic Public Address system.

Glancing over his shoulder he said, 'When the mall first opened, we used carrier pigeons.'

Wallace didn't smile.

Schulz rolled his eyes in sympathy for the wasted joke and returned to the microphone. He hit a button on the main panel, waited for a burst of static to clear, and then issued the page.

'Attention shoppers. Would Alicia, Fred and Alex Carver please report to the security office in Corridor B. That's Alicia, Fred and Alex Carver. Your husband is worried. Thank you.'

The guard switched off the microphone.

'Can that be heard everywhere?' Wallace asked. 'In every store?'

Both guards nodded.

'What about the large department stores?' said Wallace.

The guards exchanged another glance. Schulz stuck a finger in his mouth to dislodge a chunk of something green and crunchy from a gap in his back teeth.

'Target and Macy's have their own systems and security detail,' explained Schulz. He sounded annoyed at this division of labour, as though a piece of his kingdom had been usurped. 'We're patched into Sears and JC Penny, though, so that's most of the mall.'

Wallace glanced at his watch. Seven forty. The mall closed in just over an hour.

'I'll wait outside,' he said.

Wallace exited the office and made his way

back down the short hallway. He stood between the T-shirt and lingerie stores and watched the flow of traffic, hoping to see an embarrassed flash of ginger with a hurried bounce in its step.

It never came.

At ten minutes after eight, he returned to the security office.

'Can you page them again?' he asked.

Schulz seemed about to say something contrary, but the look on Wallace's face made him swallow his words. The guard flicked the switch and broadcast the same message as before.

Wallace returned to his spot between the two stores. His head was like a lawn sprinkler, moving left to right and back again as he scanned the thinning crowd.

Twenty minutes later, Wallace returned to the security office for a third time.

When he opened the door, he was older. A year for every footstep along the hall. Eyes red, irritated and moist. Fingernails chewed to the quick, near bleeding. The worry no longer churned, it was boiling, gushing through his veins like an injection of hydrochloric acid to burn his nerves raw.

'Page them again.' His voice trembled, but only a fool would mistake it for weakness.

'Look,' said Schulz, 'maybe they've gone home. You know? They were looking for you, you were

11

looking for them. You missed each other and they—'

'NO!' Wallace ground his teeth and his eyes darted quickly between the two guards, but he was no longer seeing them. 'They would have waited.'

'Did you try calling them?' said the younger guard.

A violent hiss escaped Wallace's clenched teeth as his breathing grew shallow and his tone went dangerously flat.

'We didn't bring phones. We're visting from Canada. We haven't even checked into the hotel yet. They would have waited. Page them again.'

Every word was uttered as a separate sound with barely controlled enunciation.

'Look,' said Schulz, 'we've paged them twice and—'

Wallace's balled fists slammed on to the desk with such force that everything on its surface jumped and something deep within the wood splintered with a loud *crack*.

The younger guard leapt out of his chair and backed up against the far wall. His face had gone shockingly pale and his fingers twitched spasmodically above the leather holster at his waist. He looked like a nervous young gunfighter suddenly called upon to draw against Doc Holliday. He had all the training, but no real-world experience.

Wallace's eyes flicked to the ham-hock-sized butt

and menacing steel hammer of a large Smith & Wesson revolver nestled in the young man's holster. It looked big enough to be used as a club, but at that particular moment, Wallace just didn't give a damn.

'Page them again,' he demanded.

'OK, OK.' Schulz held up his hands to calm the situation. 'I'll page them.'

He issued the alert for the third time.

At nine o'clock, the stores locked their doors and the mall began to empty.

Wallace stood in the Food Court and watched everyone leave. Couples, singles, a few families. None of them belonged to him. After the final customer had left, it was the store employees' turn. Wallace stood alone, watching them go, his heart sinking deeper with every passing face.

The mall was empty.

His family was gone.

CHAPTER 2

When the police arrived, Wallace explained his situation.

The uniformed officers listened. Asked questions. Told him to calm down when he grew irritated that *they weren't doing anything*, and then radioed for a detective.

Two showed up.

'You're Canadian,' said the first detective. She was a hard-looking woman in a gunmetal grey pantsuit with short black hair in a Dorothy Hamill bob and a light olive complexion. She identified herself as Detective Stacey, stepping close to him, shaking his hand. Only later did Wallace realize she had actually wanted to look into his eyes and smell his breath; check for alcohol or the glassy signs of drug use.

'Yes,' said Wallace, 'but my wife is a dual citizen. She was born here. Well, south of here. California.' He was rattled, babbling, trying to keep it together. Failing.

My family is missing, how does it matter what bloody nationality we are?

'Does your wife still have family there?' asked the detective. 'In California?'

'What?' Wallace was confused by the question. 'No. Her parents died when she was just a kid. She moved to Canada to live with an aunt when she was eight.'

'Do you have a photo?'

'Of my wife?'

The detective chewed a wad of greenish gum and seemed disinterested to the point of insulting.

Wallace found himself fighting a reflex to raise his voice. From the moment he lost patience with the uniformed patrol, he had seen the cold calculations flow like ice water behind their eyes. He saw the same gears churning inside the two detectives when they took over.

A man ditched at the shopping mall by his wife and kids. Obviously, he must be an abusive asshole who had beaten her one too many times. She had simply taken the opportunity of a shopping trip to run away.

This kind of thing didn't happen to happy, loving couples, right?

Wallace wanted to scream that they had it all wrong, that he had never, could never, raise his hand to his family. But he felt powerless. If he showed his anger, they would only interpret that as proof he had done exactly what they already suspected him of.

'I don't carry a wallet,' said Wallace in answer to the detective's question. When you sit on your ass all day at work, a wallet is not your friend. 'But I have all our passports in the van. We needed them to cross the border.'

Detective Stacey turned to her partner. Detective Paul Petersen was a slim-built man with a hawkish nose and unusually bright hazel eyes. In his early thirties, the end-of-shift shadow showed he shaved his head for vanity. Otherwise he might be mistaken for a tonsured monk. The only stubble was on the sides.

'Go with him to the vehicle.' Detective Stacey snapped her vile-looking gum. 'I'll see what Security has to say.'

Wallace's green minivan stood alone in the deserted parking lot: a seven-year-old Dodge Caravan with British Columbia plates and a cracked rear bumper from the time Alicia had backed into a light pole at the boys' school.

Wallace dug out his keys and hit the remote button on the fob to disengage the locks. The van beeped and flashed its lights in compliance.

'The passports are in the glove box,' he said.

Detective Petersen yawned and scratched his cheek as Wallace slid into the passenger seat and opened the small compartment in the dash. He reached in and pulled out a plastic Ziploc bag.

Instantly, he knew something was wrong. Instead of four passports, there was only one.

He quickly opened the bag and yanked out the

lone booklet. When he flipped it open, his own horrid mug shot stared back at him.

This wasn't possible.

He pulled everything out of the glove box. There wasn't much: two roadmaps, registration and insurance papers, some extra fuses, an expired McDonald's gift certificate from the previous Halloween, and a Dollar Store plastic tyre gauge.

'Is there a problem?' Petersen asked.

Wallace turned to him, his face a blanched mask of disbelief. 'They're gone,' he croaked. 'The passports are gone.'

The detective narrowed his eyes and pointed at Wallace's lap. 'What's that then?'

Wallace glanced down at the slim navy blue-jacketed book. 'That's mine,' he said. 'But Alicia's and Fred's and Alex's . . .' He couldn't finish.

Detective Petersen frowned and moved around the van. He peered through the back window at the cargo space behind the middle seat. The rear seat had been folded flat to make room for luggage.

'You all just have the one bag?' he asked.

Wallace scrambled out of the passenger seat and moved to the large sliding door in the van's side. He threw it open with such force it nearly jumped its tracks.

Their luggage was missing, too.

Before they left home, Alicia had packed a back-pack for each of the boys so they could pitch in and carry their own clothing. She also liked to have her own suitcase, a small hard-sided model to make sure her clothes didn't get wrinkled. Wallace usually just tossed underwear, socks, bathing suit and an extra shirt into whatever duffle Alicia left out for him.

The only piece of luggage in the back of the van belonged to him.

The detective eyed Wallace with renewed suspicion.

'Their luggage was here,' said Wallace. He knew he sounded desperate, but what else could he say?

'Uh-huh.'

'Somebody must have stolen it.'

'But left behind *your* bag and *your* passport?' Petersen struggled not to roll his eyes.

Wallace snapped. 'FUCK!'

He slammed the van door closed with enough force to rattle the window and spun on the detective. The muscles in his neck bulged from the strain and his face flushed crimson as a flood of adrenalin made his blood pressure shoot off the charts.

'They didn't leave me!' He was gasping, his words barely coherent. 'Something has happened. You need to believe me.'

Petersen took a backwards step and held up one hand. His other hand drifted down to the weapon on his hip. 'Let's just take it easy,' he said. 'No one's accusing you of anything. We're still investigating. OK?'

Wallace couldn't speak. His breathing was out

of control. A sharp pain stabbed into his chest, and then he bent over and vomited on the ground.

The detective jumped back in disgust. He lifted his radio and called for a uniformed officer.

'Let's talk about this back in the mall.'

While Wallace clutched the side of the van and struggled to breathe, Petersen's eyes never looked away and his hand stayed close to his weapon.

CHAPTER 3

Inside the mall's compact security office, Detective Stacey listened to her partner's report. After he was done, she told Wallace to sit in the chair facing her.

Detective Petersen rested his hip on the nearby wooden desk, while the uniformed officer who had helped escort Wallace in from the parking lot stood in the doorway. The two security guards had moved into the adjoining room where they were scanning through surveillance footage on the wall of monitors. So far, they hadn't turned up anything out of the ordinary.

'You know how this looks, right?' Detective Stacey said. 'You've got quite the temper.'

Wallace sighed. His throat was raw, but his panic was under control, replaced by a cold, aching dread. He cleared his throat. 'I know you think I had something to do with this, but I didn't. I don't know how to prove it to you, but my family really is missing. They're in trouble and I need you to help me find them.'

Stacey scratched her nose and snapped her gum. 'You said you crossed the border today?'

'Yes.'

'What time?'

'Just after two. We had a late start.'

'We could check that,' Petersen interjected.

Stacey turned to her partner and raised one eyebrow. 'You still dating that blond hunk at Border Patrol?'

'I wouldn't exactly call it dating,' Petersen said drily. His lips curved in a smile.

'He working tonight?'

Petersen nodded.

'Call him,' said Stacey. 'Ask for a favour.'

As Petersen flipped open his cellphone and stepped into the hallway, Stacey turned her attention back to Wallace.

'Every vehicle that crosses the border is automatically photographed at Customs,' she said. 'Our tax dollars at work. If we can get proof that you're not bullshitting us—'

'I'm not,' said Wallace.

'Good.' She turned her head and spat a wad of spent gum into a nearby trashcan. Before it finished bouncing off the sides, she had replaced it with a fresh piece. It was small and square with a white candy shell. She didn't offer to share.

Petersen stepped back into the room.

'Ten minutes,' he said.

Fifteen minutes later, the detective's cellphone rang. He answered and listened.

'Do we have email here?' he asked.

Schulz cleared his throat and entered from the

adjoining room. He pointed at a small monitor, mouse and keyboard sitting off to one side of the PA system.

'We have email on the company computer,' he said.

Stacey snapped her gum and told Schulz to give her partner the address.

Two minutes later, the computer's Inbox showed the arrival of a new message with an attached file.

Stacey clicked on a tiny paperclip icon and waited while a new window opened and the enclosed image filled the screen.

The photo was large and the detective had to scroll down to see the central part of the image.

Wallace moved to look over her shoulder and his breath caught in his throat.

This wasn't possible.

The photo showed Wallace in the driver's seat of the van. The passenger seat beside him was empty and nobody occupied either of the seats behind.

Except for Wallace, the van was empty.

Wallace staggered away from the computer and collided with the desk.

What was happening? How? Why?

He couldn't make sense of it.

Detective Stacey read aloud the message attached to the photo.

'Lone driver. Identified by Canadian passport as Wallace Gordon Carver. Crossed Peace Arch

22

border at fourteen twenty-two today. Zero passengers. Border Patrol has no record of Alicia, Alex or Fred Carver entering the United States of America.'

Wallace's mind reeled.

Photographs don't lie.

But this one did.

It had to.

CHAPTER 4

Crow Joe slapped the steering wheel of his '97 Ford pickup in rhythm to the music and laughed at the lyrics. Man, he loved Country music. Those dumb-ass cowboys were always getting themselves into hilarious shit – and that was only the stuff they could sing about on family radio.

The cowpunks he'd known on the rodeo circuit had stories that would curl your toes and make your stomach roil. The clowns and bull riders were the worst. Those boys were downright insane.

Back then, Crow thought he had what it took to ride the lightning and get all the pretty girls cheering. His damn-near Hollywood good looks gave him every advantage: bronzed skin; proud nose and chin; hair the colour of raven's wing, braided into two thick ropes and held in place by his grandfather's traditional Orca headband.

All he was missing was talent and the sheer buck-stupid lack of self-preservation it took to make a living in eight-second increments on the back of a 1,800-pound Brahman that wants nothing

24

more than to step on your skull and spray your brains in the dirt.

He got bucked off so many times that the only purse he ever took home was Delilah. Short, sassy and with a dimpled smile that could part clouds, Delilah nursed his bruises, knit his bones and made his body tingle. Later, she bore him two beautiful daughters, neither of whom had even seen a real Brahman bull, never mind tried to ride one.

The biggest beast Crow straddled now was the padded driver's seat of a 28,000-pound, forty-passenger, diesel-electric bus.

Crow slapped the steering wheel of his pickup again and raised his voice to sing the chorus of Joe Nichols' 'Tequila Makes Her Clothes Fall Off'. Mercifully, he was riding alone.

Before his off-key rendition could shatter glass and assault the night air, it was interrupted by the vibration of his cellphone.

He dug the small silver phone out of his shirt pocket, glanced at the Caller ID and winced. He switched off the radio and answered the call.

'Hey, baby.'

'Where the hell did you run off to?'

'Didn't you get my note?'

'I got your damn note. Here, let me read it to you. "Gone out." What kinda note is that?'

'Short and sweet. Just like you.'

'Don't . . .'

Crow heard it in her voice. The tiniest pause;

25

the smallest rumble of laughter. Delilah wasn't as angry as she was making out. He guessed he should have talked to her instead of leaving a note, but the girls were acting all moody and whispery and had trapped their mom in the bathroom for some big powwow over something they didn't want him to share in.

'Look,' he said, 'I'm sorry, but you and the girls were in some big discussion and I didn't know how to help and—'

Delilah laughed. 'Do you know what we were talking about?'

'Well, no, but I knew it was probably something girly and—'

'Menstruation.'

Crow blanched. 'Oh.'

'Yeah, *oh*.' Delilah's imitation of him made Crow sound like Fred Flintstone. 'One of the girls' friends had an embarrassing accident at school, and they're both getting to the age when they need to be prepared. At least the school seemed to handle it with some sensitivity, which makes me happy. In my day—'

'We should have had boys,' Crow interrupted. Not that a discussion of reproductive cycles made him squeamish – he had been in the delivery room with her both times, and that kinda kills squeamish for ever – it was just, well . . . he loved that Delilah was a woman, for all the obvious reasons, but he didn't really need reminding of all the ins and outs that entailed.

'Uh-huh. You think boys would have been easier?'

Crow shrugged, then remembered Delilah couldn't see him.

'Maybe not easier,' he said, 'but less—'

'If you say gross, I'll scream.'

'Complicated,' said Crow, sounding defensive. 'I was gonna say complicated.'

'And you think teenage boys jerking off in their bed sheets twenty times a day is less complicated?'

Crow cringed. 'Now who's getting gross?'

Delilah laughed again. She had always loved to make him squirm. And she was a master at it.

'Where are you anyway?' she asked.

'Wallace asked me to look after the house.'

'Wallace? I thought they were only going away for the weekend?'

'Yeah, but there's been a stray cat hanging around the garden shed and the dummy wants to make sure it gets fed. He didn't want to leave food out 'cause the raccoons would get it all.'

'What's he need a cat for? Aren't two boys enough?'

'Beats me,' Crow said. 'I told him he should take the garden hose to it, but you know these white men. All soft in the head.'

'But not white girls, right?'

'Well, now that you mention it—'

'Hey!'

Crow grinned. 'You know it's your forked tongue that kept me on the Rez.'

Delilah nearly purred. 'Well, why don't you turn the truck around and we'll put that to the test.'

Crow grinned wider. 'I'm almost at Wallace's. Let me feed the damn cat and then I'll head straight home.'

'Wake me if I'm asleep.'

'Count on it.'

Crow hung up the phone and turned off the main road into the quiet cul-de-sac where his best friend had lived for the last ten years.

An unexpected sight caused him to slam on the brakes. The front tyres squealed in protest and the old Ford's chassis shuddered.

Four police cars blocked the way, their red and blue flashers near-blinding in the dark.

CHAPTER 5

Wallace rode alone in the rear of a four-door cruiser that smelled of strong disinfectant and the lingering remains of violently disgorged stomach acid.

A welded tubular steel barrier separated him from the uniformed driver and his olive-skinned passenger.

The barrier was overkill.

Wallace's hands were cuffed behind his back and every nerve in his body still trembled from the sharp, muscle-numbering jolt of the patrolman's hand-held Taser.

His throat was raw from arguing, from demanding that they do their damn job and find his family.

Fuck the photo.

Fuck how it looked.

Fuck—

That's when the patrolman had stepped in with a paralyzing 50,000-volt dose of shut-the-fuck-up.

Bellingham now lay behind him.

Ahead, dark sky and empty road.

The officers' jurisdiction had ended miles back,

but Wallace knew better than to broach the subject.

Detective Stacey turned around in her seat and moved her gum from cheek to cheek, pressing it against the walls of her mouth with her tongue.

Wallace met her gaze and held it. He refused to blink or turn away.

He figured she'd probably enjoyed it when he collapsed on the floor of the security office and writhed in agony as his nervous system went into arrest. From her deductions, she believed he deserved it – and more.

Christ, if he thought it was the truth, if it was even remotely possible that he could harm his own family, he would have told her to keep pressing that button, keep sending those volts, make this killer's heart explode.

But it wasn't the truth and she had no idea what true torture was. He'd be damned if he let her see him crumble again.

Stacey broke the silence.

'Think of this as a courtesy,' she said. 'One friendly nation to another.'

Wallace didn't speak, but his unblinking stare spoke volumes.

'Your family isn't in the United States,' she continued. 'I don't know what you're running from or what you've done and, frankly, I don't care. It's not my jurisdiction and it's not my problem. You're no longer welcome here. Once you're back across the border, you can file a missing person report with the RCMP. I'm sure they'll be happy to investigate or get you the help you need.'

She paused, waiting for a response.

One didn't come.

She blinked rapidly and the wrinkles around her mouth deepened in annoyance.

'If you try to return, you'll be arrested and imprisoned for criminal mischief, wasting police time and making a false report. Simple as that. Your passport has been flagged and my report will be attached.' She snapped her gum. Loud. 'Bottom line: don't come back.'

The car crested a hill and the lights of the border appeared a short distance ahead. The driver followed the road into Peace Arch International Park and pulled off to one side. He stopped less than two feet from the painted boundary line that straddled the 49th parallel and marked the longest undefended border in the world.

Off to their left, an impressive white stone archway stood in the middle of the sixteen-hectare park that, on a clear day, could steal your breath with its ocean vista upon a crown of steep bluffs.

The iron gates on the giant archway were kept open as a symbol of peace between two great nations. On the American side, an inscription read: *Children of a Common Mother*. On the Canadian side: *Brethren Dwelling Together in Unity*.

Until today, Wallace had actually believed the lies.

On either end of the park stood another set of gates. These were not kept open. They were patrolled day and night by members of the Canada Border Services Agency and US Customs and Border Protection. Despite the symbolism of the white monument, every vehicle entering either country had to pass through proper inspection.

The patrolman switched off the engine, climbed out and walked around the cruiser. He opened the rear passenger door and motioned for Wallace to join him outside.

Wallace struggled out of the seat and finally made it to his feet. His legs were wobbly, the muscles still in spasm, but he managed to stand tall. He was two inches taller and more than a few pounds heavier. The officer smirked, unafraid, and motioned for him to turn around. When Wallace complied, the officer unlocked the cuffs.

Detective Stacey walked up beside Wallace and placed one hand on the crook of his elbow. Her thumb hovered over a nerve cluster, the threat of pain cocked but held in check.

'Don't do anything stupid,' she said. Her voice was quiet but direct. 'You're still on American soil and our justice is swift.'

Before Wallace could formulate a response, his green minivan pulled in behind the patrol car. Detective Petersen climbed out of the driver's seat and moved towards them. A purple vein pulsed on one side of his egg-shaped skull, as if driving the van had been an indignity.

'Keys are in it,' he said. 'And you need a tune-up. It runs like shit.'

Detective Stacey released Wallace's arm.

'You should go now,' she said. 'I wouldn't want you to see me when I get angry.'

Wallace rubbed his wrists and walked to the van. He wished he could leave them with some scathing remark, but the only thought that raced through his mind was playing on an endless loop: *What do I do now?*

He climbed into the van, adjusted the seat for his longer legs, and glared out at the cops.

He wasn't given a choice.

He drove the van across the boundary marker into Canada. Fifty metres ahead, Customs waited to check him through.

CHAPTER 6

Crow eased up to the police barricade, shut off his engine and stepped down from the cab. The four cruisers were empty, their occupants busy somewhere within the residential cul-de-sac, but two Royal Canadian Mounted Police constables had drawn the short straw and stood guard in front.

The uniformed constables – black storm jackets and forage caps, the distinctive yellow headband and gold badge reflecting the cruisers' flashing lights – eyed him with suspicion.

Crow flashed an easy grin and held his hands open by his sides to show they were empty. It was a reflex he had learned the hard way when youthful exuberance had mixed with political naivety and he stubbornly believed defiance and civil disobedience could save an old-growth forest from the loggers' saw.

He called out, 'Is Marvin Joe working tonight?'

The constables exchanged a glance; the question was unexpected.

'He's inside the house,' said one of the constables. He was young, barely into his twenties, with a pinched nose and skin the colour of rye bread. His tone turned cautious. 'He know you?'

His partner was roughly the same age, but white skinned with a dimpled Kirk Douglas chin and light baby-blue eyes.

'He's my cousin.'

That was another lesson he had learned. Let the fascists know you were, in some small way, part of the extended family and sometimes things went a little bit smoother.

Crow walked closer, straining his neck in an attempt to peer beyond the pulsating strobes to see which house the cops were investigating. He couldn't smell smoke, so at least Wallace hadn't left the coffee pot on or anything stupid like that.

Perhaps, he reasoned, one of the neighbours had become the victim of a marijuana grow-operation. Potent BC Bud was a huge cash crop all over the province and more than a few absent landlords had been devastated to find their rental homes stripped to the studs and infested with harmful mould after a gang made its quick profit and left the unsuspecting owners in the lurch.

Crow couldn't see what was going on beyond the blinding bars of light, so he asked.

'What's going on?'

Blue Eyes looked Crow up and down. Fleece-lined, red-and-black checkered lumberjack shirt; loose Haines T-shirt over washed blue jeans and a ratty pair of dirt-brown cowboy boots that had actually done some of the shit-kicking they were designed for. Crow wasn't as handsome as he had been in his lean-bodied youth. Soft living and a dark period before the girls were born, when liquor made a damn good attempt at curdling his soul, had definitely left their mark.

Blue Eyes curled his lip in disapproval. 'You live here?'

'No, but—'

Blue Eyes snorted. 'Then it's none of your damn business, is it?'

'I have friends on this street,' said Crow. 'No need to get nasty.'

Blue Eyes puffed up his chest like a rooster. He stepped forward and aggressively sniffed the air.

'This ain't band land, Chief. You been drinking?'

Crow immediately took a step back and held his hands up in mock surrender. *Racist paleface motherfucker.* He shook his head in disgust, but kept his anger in check. No point getting into it. Only one side lost in a clash between redskins and police, and it was never the police.

So much for being part of the family.

Crow returned to his truck and opened the door. Before climbing in, he stopped and turned to the dark-skinned constable.

'Can you at least tell me the number of the house you're investigating? Just so I don't have to worry.'

'Twenty-eight oh five,' the constable said before his partner could stop him.

Blue Eyes glared across the gap with his lips

curled in a mocking sneer. 'That your friend's house?'

Keeping his face immobile, Crow shook his head again. He climbed into the truck and made a U-turn. Once he was back on the main drag, he drove another three blocks before pulling into the empty parking lot of a small daytime bakery. He threw the truck into park and yanked out his cellphone. His palms were sweating as he stabbed number two on the speed dial.

Wallace's cellphone went straight to voicemail without ringing, which likely meant it was switched off.

Crow chewed his lower lip as he scrolled through the phone's built-in contact list until he found his cousin's number.

The phone was answered on the fourth ring.

'Marvin,' said Crow without preamble, 'are you at Wallace's house? What's going on?'

There was a pause. 'That you, Crow?'

'Yeah. I was outside and saw the roadblock. Some racist dickhead with an ass for a chin wouldn't let me through.'

'You know where Wallace is?' Marvin's voice was tight, as though he was trying to talk without moving his lips.

Crow could hear him walking through the house, then the opening and closing of a sliding door. The background noise changed. It became more open, airy. Marvin had moved outside, probably to the back yard.

Crow had helped Wallace build the large deck his cousin was now standing on. Red cedar with a circular stone fireplace at one end for kids' wiener roasts and the only good thing white men had ever brought to a campfire – S'mores.

Crow had a bad feeling, so he didn't hesitate to lie. 'I've no idea where he is. What's happening there?'

Marvin sighed heavily, trying to shift a burden. 'You would tell me if you knew, right?'

'Course I would, Marv, we're family. Now come on, spill. This is my buddy we're talking about. You're making me nervous.'

Marvin sighed again. The burden hadn't moved. 'OK,' he said finally, 'but this stays between us.'

'Course.'

A long pause followed until Crow was ready to reach through the phone and grab his cousin by the neck. Marvin had always been a cautious one. Straight-laced, bookish, afraid of girls, and always the first one to squeal to the elders when the older kids tried to make the younger ones swallow worms like baby birds. It was no wonder he had joined the red jackets.

'Now come on,' Crow growled impatiently, 'tell me.'

Marvin relented. 'The detachment received a call from a concerned neighbour,' he said. 'The caller said a cat was howling at Wallace's door. It sounded like the thing was dying, so this neigh- bour went over to check. While he was there, he saw the front door slightly ajar and smeared blood on the handle. That's when he called us.'

Crow frowned. There wasn't supposed to be anybody at home. The whole family had gone down to the States for the weekend.

'Is anybody hurt?' he asked.

'We don't know,' said Marvin. 'That's the weird part. Inside, we found evidence of more blood on the floors. A lot of it. It appears someone made an attempt to clean it up. We found the mop in the garage.'

Crow shook his head in disbelief. There was no way. Not Wallace. They had worked together for fifteen years. He was godfather to Crow's two girls; Crow was godfather to his sons. Wallace was a goddamned hero. The mayor awarded him a special medal. He didn't have an enemy in the world.

'There's been a mistake,' said Crow.

'It's not just the blood,' said Marvin.

Crow felt his head spin and his stomach churn. *Don't let it be the boys. Please.*

'There are no bodies,' continued Marvin as though reading Crow's mind, 'but all of Alicia's things are missing. Same with the boys. All their clothes, toys, toothbrushes, shoes, everything. There are no school photos or drawings on the fridge. It's like they were never here.'

Crow couldn't comprehend what he was hearing. 'How is that possible?'

'Wallace's stuff hasn't been touched,' Marvin

said. 'His clothes are hanging in the closet, his toothbrush is by the sink. All perfectly normal . . . if he was a bachelor. Add that to the blood on the floor and you've got a real messy situation.'

The colour drained from Crow's face and his mind reeled at the unimaginable possibilities.

'Wait a minute,' he said. 'You're saying Wallace did . . . did what? You think he killed his family?'

'Killed them, dumped the bodies and erased all signs of them living here is what it looks like.'

Crow snapped his teeth together. 'That's bullshit! Wallace lives for those boys and he would never harm a hair on Alicia's head. He loves her, loves *them*. He wouldn't just snap. No way. They're his goddamn life.'

'When did you see him last?' asked Marvin.

'Yesterday. We were working the same shift.'

'He seem OK?'

'Yeah, he was fine. Crackin' his usual lousy jokes.'

Crow remembered Wallace talking about going to Bellingham with his family for the weekend. The boys were stoked because the hotel had a swimming pool, and Alicia was looking forward to finding some bargains at the mall.

'And you haven't noticed anything odd in his behaviour,' Marvin pressed. 'Depression, anger, hitting the bottle, anything like that?'

'Nothing.' Crow snapped his answer, not liking the question. It felt like he was being grilled and and . . . *when had Marvin grown a pair?*

40

'When was the last time you saw Alicia and the boys?' Marvin went on.

Crow hesitated, tried to think. He knew that Delilah saw Alicia all the time. They talked just about every day.

'Last weekend,' said Crow.

'You sure?'

'Yeah, we all went to the park. The boys were kicking a soccer ball around. The girls played on the swings.'

'Huh.'

Crow cringed. He hated that type of vague response. It was so . . . cop-like.

'Wallace just has the one vehicle, right?' Marvin asked.

'Yeah, the minivan. Is it around?'

'No, it's missing.'

'Huh.' Give him a taste of his own medicine.

'So why were you coming to see him? It's late.'

Marvin's tone had changed and Crow knew he was no longer talking to family. He was talking to a cop.

'I went out for a drive,' said Crow. 'Too much oestrogen flowing at home, so I thought I'd see if Wallace was still awake and we could play a couple games of pool. He has a table set up in his garage.'

'I saw that.' Marvin's voice had grown distant as Crow's apparent usefulness faded.

Crow heard the sliding door being pulled open and Marvin's heavy footsteps slap the linoleum of

Wallace's kitchen floor. For some reason, it caused a shiver to run down his spine.

Why was there blood on the floor?

Were Alicia and the boys OK?

Was Wallace?

Crow chewed his bottom lip again. *Marvin was fucking useless*. He didn't have any answers, just questions, and Crow didn't like the direction they were going.

'If Wallace gets in touch, call me,' said Marvin. 'It would be better for him if he comes to us rather than gets picked up on a warrant. We're issuing that now.'

'If he calls,' said Crow, 'I'll—'

Crow hung up without finishing. It would have been another lie anyway. He rubbed his hands across his face while he processed what Marvin had told him. But the more he thought about it, the less he believed.

Marvin may be family, but Wallace was his brother. Not through blood or marriage or drunken indiscretion. By choice. And the people you choose to bring into your life, to share your heart and your home, those were your *real* brothers and sisters. They became part of your soul, your spirit. To doubt them was to doubt yourself.

CHAPTER 7

Wallace cleared Customs without incident, his emotions too numb to explain his living nightmare to the officer in charge. Where would he begin? How do you explain something that even the police believe is a lie?

No, he had nothing to declare. Yes, it was a miserable night. Thanks, same to you.

Back on the road, he pressed the accelerator hard, speeding north-east along the rural back roads of Surrey with a plan to connect with the TransCanada highway before turning west towards North Vancouver – and home.

Home? The evocation brought him up short. Home didn't exist without Alicia and his sons.

Tears sprang to his eyes, a salty trickle that quickly became an unstoppable flood until a powerful tsunami of suppressed emotion broke over him all at once. Lethal debris churned in its wake, slashing at his soul and kicking his tortured mind with steel-toed boots.

Wallace gasped, drowning beneath the suffocating weight.

He couldn't breathe.

He couldn't see.

A painful realization: *What was he doing?*

He had to go back.

An agonized howl erupted from deep within his core as he cranked the wheel too aggressively for the van's speed. The ungainly vehicle reacted badly. Near-bald tyres howled as the brakes screeched and smoked; something deep within the steering column *snapped*. The wheel was torn out of Wallace's grasp as the rear tyres lost their grip on the slick tarmac and the van slid out of control.

When it hit the gravel shoulder, its top-heavy frame tilted precariously before two of the tyres blew and forced the metal rims to chew across a narrow grassy verge.

Wallace held on for dear life, praying to survive and wondering if he had foolishly wished this upon himself. A way to end the pain of losing everything that mattered.

The van lost its battle to stay upright as it slammed into a deep trough. The passenger window exploded inward, spraying Wallace in a shower of blunt-edged fragments.

He gasped as the glass was followed by a surge of cold, rank water.

Then it was over.

The van settled on to its side in the waterlogged ditch where its engine sputtered and died.

Wallace hung precariously by his seatbelt, barely scratched despite the non-deployment of air bags.

He punched the roof in frustration, bruising his knuckles, and struggled against his bonds. The buckle was jammed and the seatbelt cut deep into his waist every time he moved.

To calm his racing pulse, Wallace closed his eyes, listening to the burst radiator hiss and the strained engine tick as it cooled. Above the mechanical sounds, a cacophony croaked from a puddle of angry frogs.

He breathed deeply. He was a better driver than that. What the hell was he thinking?

The answer was simple: he wasn't thinking, he was reacting. Blindly. Stubbornly.

He contorted his body again and attacked the belt mechanism with both hands.

This time the lock snapped open and Wallace fell, his body twisting uncontrollably as gravity took hold. His feet flew skyward, his bad leg smashing painfully into the steering column while his arms vanished through the shattered opening of the passenger window to sink into the murky, foul-smelling ditch beneath.

He panicked as his head and shoulders quickly followed. Grimy brown water filled his mouth as he thrashed around, trying to find a purchase on something solid. His hands slipped across sunken roots and submerged grass while his fingers sunk into deep loose clay and his lungs began to burn. He flailed his feet, but that only pushed him deeper into the suffocating murk.

Desperate, he realized it was impossible to fight his way back into the van. Instead, he twisted on to his back, grabbed hold of the broken side mirror and yanked himself forward. His body slid barely two feet, his shoulders and back squelching into a layer of thick clay. The weight and angle of the van seemed to push him deeper into the dank and he suddenly wondered if he had just made his perilous situation even worse.

He scrambled to grasp the slippery hood, but his fingers failed to find a grip. Blind and frantic, his lungs on the verge of collapse, he tucked in his knees and felt his feet hit the edge of the broken window.

This was it. Last chance.

He braced his feet against the window edge, wincing slightly at a sharp pain in his left leg, and pushed with all his might. A loud, internalized sucking noise filled his ears as his shoulders fought against the vacuum of mud.

His mouth opened in a silent scream as the vacuum popped and he was suddenly launched like a loosed torpedo. Scrambling, desperate, he squeezed around the van's front bumper and clawed his way skyward.

His head broke the surface just as his lungs gave out. He gulped in air and spat out slime, cursing his own damn stupidity.

After crawling out of the ditch, Wallace slopped off as much of the mud and rotting vegetation as he could. He looked like hell, but didn't care. That was the least of his worries.

He started walking, his limp more pronounced but the pain manageable.

He needed to find a phone.

CHAPTER 8

Crow answered on the first ring. Sleep had proved impossible. His thoughts too troubling. His answers too few. If he still drank, it would have been a bad, bad night. When the phone rang, he silently thanked his ancestors for helping him stay strong.

On the other end of the line, Wallace said, 'I need your help.'

Crow sighed with relief. 'Where are you? What's happening? Is everyone OK?'

'Something's happened. Can you pick me up?'

'Yeah, of course. Are Alicia and the boys with you?'

Crow heard the catch in his friend's throat. 'I can't talk on the phone.'

'Hang tight,' said Crow. 'I'll be right there.'

Wallace gave him the address.

Crow's clothes were in a heap on the floor beside the bed. All he had to do was step in and zip up.

Delilah didn't stir.

Twenty-five minutes later, Crow pulled into a twenty-four-hour gas station in Surrey and

48

spotted Wallace sitting on a plastic bench out front.

He was alone and he had spoken true. He was a mess. His clothes were ripped and soiled with a mixture of mud and blood from numerous shallow cuts and scrapes.

Wallace limped over to the truck and climbed inside. His shoes squelched and his eyes revealed a roadmap of sorrow and pain. He had a difficult time meeting Crow's questioning stare and Crow felt his heart sink.

'I need to get across the border,' said Wallace.

Crow hesitated. 'I thought that's where—'

'You know people, right?' Wallace interrupted. He dragged filthy nails across the edges of his teeth, breaking off tiny slivers and spitting them on the floor.

'What do you mean, *people*?'

'I can't use my passport.'

'Why? Did something happen—'

Wallace interrupted again. 'I'll also need a gun.'

Crow raised one eyebrow.

The pain that racked his friend's face was palpable. He was struggling to keep his composure, but his body trembled with all the fragility of a featherless bird fallen from its nest. Wallace had aged a decade since Crow last saw him and he smelled as though he had recently bathed in a sewer.

With his requests delivered, Wallace lowered his head and focused on the floor mat. A sudden tremor coursed through his body, making his shoulders twitch and his legs jerk in uncontrolled spasms. He looked ashamed, destroyed, but also in the latter stages of shock.

Crow switched on the truck's heater and aimed the dashboard vents towards his passenger. He studied the blood on his friend's clothing. There wasn't a lot of it, but still . . .

Before he went any further, he had to know. 'Where's the van?'

'In a ditch,' Wallace mumbled. He didn't look up. 'A few miles back. I . . . I lost control.'

Crow swallowed, suddenly afraid as every dark thought, every dark question that he had tried to suppress bubbled up to the surface. 'Where're Alicia and the boys?'

Wallace inhaled deeply and his mouth struggled to form the words. 'I . . . I . . . don't know.'

'But they're alive?'

Wallace jerked, his eyes suddenly wide with horror, his voice incredulous. 'Why would you ask that?'

Crow had no choice. He told Wallace about the police at his house and the blood on the floor. The discarded mop and concerned neighbour. He told him about Marvin. And finally, about the missing clothes and toys.

Every detail landed like dirt on a coffin lid. There was no way to fake it. Unless the man sitting beside him was a different Wallace than the one Crow had known for over fifteen years, he hadn't known about any of it.

'The police think I killed my family?' Wallace said.

Crow nodded. 'They've issued a warrant for your arrest. They'll be looking for the van.'

'And the photograph cements it.' Wallace shook his head in disbelief. 'It makes this shopping trip look like a stupid cover-up.'

'What photograph?' asked Crow.

In one breathless soliloquy, Wallace recounted the hours at the mall, the missing luggage and passports, and the damning photograph.

'See?' Wallace's voice verged on hysteria. 'I'm not just a murderer. I'm a stupid fucking one, too. No luggage. No passports. And a bloody picture of me driving alone across the border.'

'How is that even possible?' asked Crow.

Wallace shook his head and an icy glaze covered his eyes. 'You don't believe me, do you?'

'No, I do,' Crow said quickly, trying to hide the quiver in his voice. 'It's just so . . . hard to imagine. Somebody's gone to a lot of trouble, but why?'

Wallace released a heavy sigh. 'I don't know.'

Crow almost didn't want to ask, but before he could stop himself, the words tumbled out. 'Do you think Alicia and the boys are OK?'

Wallace flinched before wiping away some of the mud that had streamed down his cheeks.

'I have to believe so.'

CHAPTER 9

After Crow's truck pulled away, a black-on-black Lincoln Navigator SUV drove into the gas station and parked beside the middle pump on the island farthest from the Plexiglas-enclosed cashier.

The Navigator's lone occupant climbed out, swiped a credit card through the pump's electronic reader and began filling the vehicle's fuel tank with mid-grade unleaded.

Although he stood with his back to the late-night attendant locked inside the brightly lit kiosk, he easily observed the sloth picking his nose and thumbing through a glossy magazine in the reflection of the Lincoln's heavily tinted glass.

If the bored clerk happened to take an interest and look outside, he might wonder if he was looking at an empty silhouette – an echo – rather than the man himself. A charcoal two-piece suit draped seamlessly over an ebony shirt and a minimal Western-style shoestring tie. Even the piercings in each ear were invisible: black metallic tunnels in the same circumference as a .45 shell.

If the driver closed his gloriously bright eyes and

sucked bruised plum lips inside his mouth, he could almost disappear.

The cashier wiped sticky fingers on one of the magazine pages before turning it, causing a visible shudder to run down the driver's back.

Observing was a force of habit, as natural as breathing. And, at times like these, it was a curse, especially when he was forbidden from bringing any undue attention to his presence.

More the pity.

The clerk was disgusting. A poorly shaved monkey with an IQ no larger than his waistband, he was one of those useless specimens whom nobody would miss and whose only benefit to the planet would come when he stopped consuming its limited resources, especially oxygen and water.

With his gloved left hand engaged with the gas nozzle, the driver's bare right palm glowed purple from the screen of his personalized cellphone. Although to call the slender, touch-screen device a phone was a tragic misnomer. Boasting military-level encryption and specialized apps, the phone was the closest thing to secure communication since the Navajo Windtalkers stumped the Japanese.

While texting with only one thumb slowed his overall speed, it was only a slight impediment as the phone's artificial intelligence had a surprisingly good record of correctly auto-completing his words.

When his latest message was composed, he hit

Send. The phone's software automatically encoded all of his outgoing messages and decoded his incoming. It did it with such alarming speed, it was virtually invisible.

Like him.

The driver returned the nozzle to its housing. Before pocketing the printed receipt, he glanced at the customer name gleaned from the credit card: Darius Black. He didn't care for the Christian name, but the surname was surprisingly delicious.

He could enjoy being Mr Black.

Before getting behind the wheel, Mr Black endured one last unobserved glance at the sloth-like attendant. The young man's skin was the colour of ash under the booth's harsh fluorescent lights. His milky eyes were already dead to the dim future of his existence.

Spilling his blood would be a blessing, but such things were no longer that simple.

It was better before. Much better.

Inside the vehicle, Mr Black placed his phone in its dashboard cradle and activated the tracker application. A detailed map appeared on the phone's generous high-resolution screen.

A pulsating red dot, like a single drop of blood, showed him exactly where to go.

CHAPTER 10

When Crow turned off the main road on to the quiet side street that led to his home, Wallace finally emerged from his self-imposed cocoon.

Crow had glanced over numerous times during the trip, wondering if his friend had fallen asleep. But every time, he saw Wallace's eyes staring blankly through the windshield, seeing nothing.

Or perhaps, thought Crow, seeing too much.

He hadn't pushed, even though the heavy silence made him nervous. The time to talk would come.

Wallace stirred and took in his surroundings. 'What are we doing here?'

'The people whose help we need don't appreciate drop-ins,' Crow explained. 'It's best I give them a heads-up first.'

'I thought they were family.'

'They are, but that doesn't make them any friendlier.' Crow wriggled his nose. 'Besides, you could do with a shower and a change of clothes.'

When they were within two blocks of the house, Crow eased up on the gas and flicked on his high beams. The street ahead looked the same as it always did – a harsh commingling of pride and neglect with the self-respecting owners holding a narrow lead over those who had given up trying to stand on their own two feet – but still . . .

'Marvin was at your house,' Crow said, thinking aloud. 'He knows we're tight. Bringing you in would look good – maybe earn him a pat on the head.'

Wallace leaned forward and peered through the windshield. 'You think he would stake out your place?'

Crow shrugged. 'He's one of them now.' He paused; chewed his cheek. 'Although if you wanted to turn yourself in. Explain everything. He would treat you all right.'

Wallace's eyes flashed with anger as he shook away the suggestion.

'I need to get back down there.' His jaw was clenched so tightly, the words could barely squeeze through. 'Find Alicia and my sons. The cops get me now, I could be locked up for days.'

Wallace's eyes hardened and Crow felt his gaze on a physical level. It burrowed into his skull with the force of a dentist's diamond-tipped drill.

'I don't want to get you or Delilah into trouble,' Wallace continued. 'If you think you need to turn me in, drop me off now and I'll be on my way.'

Crow slowed the truck further and turned a small dial beneath the headlight switch. The lights in the dashboard went dark until only a green luminescence remained to show the vehicle's decreasing speed.

'It disables the interior light,' explained Crow.

Wallace turned away and reached for the door handle, but as he did so, Crow grabbed his shoulder and squeezed.

'This is just a precaution,' he said. 'I'll see you at the house.'

Crow pulled into the driveway and wished his garage wasn't so stuffed: summer gear for the kids, winter gear for hunting and snowmobiling. If they weren't such pack rats, he could just drive inside and close the door.

Instead, he parked in the driveway beside Delilah's compact, four-passenger Focus and switched off the engine. As soon as he opened his door, a powerful flashlight cut through the darkness to blind him.

'You alone, Crow?'

'Nope,' said Crow. 'You're here.'

The beam moved to illuminate the truck's interior. When it found the cab empty, the beam travelled the length of the open truck bed before returning to Crow.

'Kind of late for another drive.'

'Kinda early for a visit, too,' answered Crow. 'I don't remember making plans to go fishin'.'

Marvin's sigh of exasperation crossed the dormant lawn like a golf ball on the moon.

'Did you see him?'

'Who?'

The vexed sigh again. 'You know who.'

Crow scratched his chin. 'I'm not gonna lie to you, Marvin. I talked to Wallace.'

'Damn it, Crow.'

Crow held up one hand. 'Now hold on a minute and listen.'

Crow moved his hand slightly to block some of the flashlight's intensity. He could see Marvin standing behind it. He was dressed in regular street clothes, which told Crow that he was alone and unofficial.

'I gave Wallace your offer about turning himself in,' Crow continued. 'But he has a slight problem.'

'What's that?'

'He's innocent.'

'He tell you that?'

'He did. And I believe him.'

A third sigh. 'How did he explain the blood?'

'He doesn't know how it got there.'

'Then where're Alicia and the boys?'

'He doesn't know that either.'

Marvin snorted. 'Listen to yourself. How could he not know where his wife and kids are?'

'It's complicated.'

'It's not. Where is he?'

'He's gone looking for them.'

'Bullshit. Where is he?'

Crow shrugged. 'I don't know. I told him not to tell me.'

Marvin ground his teeth in frustration. 'Dammit, Crow. I could have you arrested.'

Crow narrowed his eyes and held out his wrists. 'That would look good on your record, Marvin. Locking up family members for leaving the Rez and talking out of turn.'

Marvin bristled. 'It's called aiding and abetting. Wallace is wanted—'

'Fancy words for the same thing,' interrupted Crow. 'I haven't done anything except deliver your message to a friend. Arrest me and you'll just be trying to prove how white you can be.'

'Fuck you.'

'No, Marvin, fuck you. If you want to be the goddamn sheriff then do some of the work. Wallace said he didn't do anything and I believe him. That should mean something to you, too. Has your department even tested the blood to make sure a crime was actually committed there?'

'It's not just the blood, Crow. You know that.'

'First things first. Find out whose blood it is and then we'll see about the rest. If the blood belongs to Alicia or the boys, I'll hunt Wallace down myself and bring him to you.'

'That's not how this works,' said Marvin. 'The evidence points to Wallace and we need to talk to him.'

'Well, you can't. He's gone. You do some bloody work and maybe he'll come back.'

Marvin shook his head. 'You watch too much damn TV, Crow. DNA takes a long time to

59

process, plus there's nothing left to match it to. He got rid of everything, remember? No toothbrushes. No hair brushes. No soiled clothes. Pretty convenient, you have to admit.'

Crow hesitated. In this arena, as with the rodeo bulls, he was clearly outmatched.

'Just test it, Marvin,' he said dismissively. 'It might be something.'

Marvin switched off his flashlight.

'You're an embarrassment, Crow,' he said from somewhere in the dark. 'Always have been.'

Hell, thought Crow as he walked up the path to his front door, with his family history it was impossible not to be.

CHAPTER 11

Crow found Wallace standing in wet, grubby socks in the middle of the kitchen at the rear of the house. He had removed his muddy shoes and jacket at the back door before slipping quietly inside. All the lights were off except for the perpetual glow of the microwave's digital clock and its electric blue hue turned his pale flesh a zombified grey.

His resemblance to the living dead was further enhanced by sodden clothes and mud-streaked hair. If Delilah had heard him enter and had gone to investigate, she would have screamed at the top of her lungs.

How the hell would Crow have explained that to Marvin?

'Why did you tell Marvin we spoke?' asked Wallace.

Crow parried his friend's suspicious tone with an easy grin. He hadn't known Wallace was listening to their conversation.

'He'd know I was lying if I hadn't,' said Crow. 'Then he would hang around and try to catch me meeting up with you. This way, he thinks I warned you and you're gone. I'd have to be a fool to meet up again.' Crow grinned wider. 'Marvin knows I'm a lot of things, but I ain't that dumb.'

Wallace attempted to return the smile, but the muscles around his mouth were unable to co-operate. He shifted from foot to foot like an old boxer who's suffered one too many blows.

'When do we move out?' he asked.

'I'll make some calls,' said Crow. 'You grab a shower, I'll find some fresh clothes and we're gone. Sound good?'

Wallace nodded and padded his way out of the kitchen and down the hall. He left wet footprints in his wake, the arches flat, carrying a heavy load.

The shower brought new life. Wallace felt its warm spray easing the sore muscles in his back, the deep bruises on his legs and hips, and the cuts, chinks and scrapes that pebbled nearly every inch of his flesh.

The crash had rattled his bones more than he'd realized, but he knew it could have been much worse. The passenger side of the van was crushed. If Alicia had been with him, or the boys . . .

He pushed away the blackness, allowing the steam to seep into his mind and shift the muddled clouds that were interfering with his brain, slowing him down, making him unable to think. Despair was a slug that curled inside your head, growing fat upon worry and regret. But Wallace knew he

62

had to keep it at bay. His life, and the lives of his family, was forfeit if he allowed it to feed.

As he shampooed his hair, picking out chunks of dried mud and broken twigs, he heard the bathroom door open and, a short moment later, close again. He rinsed, shut off the water and pulled back the vinyl curtain.

A fluffy towel lay atop a pile of fresh clothes folded neatly on top of the toilet lid. Wallace dried himself and dressed. Crow's clothes were a close match. The pant legs were two inches too short, but they fit in the waist and were comfortable. The T-shirt was short-sleeved and loose, just the way he liked it, and the fresh socks were warm and perfect.

He returned to the kitchen, but stopped short when, instead of Crow, Delilah stood in a fluffy housecoat and fur-lined sheepskin moccasins, frying a pan of bacon on the stove.

She turned when she heard him and her face radiated everything that Wallace was trying so desperately to keep bottled up deep inside.

She ran to him and wrapped her arms around his waist, squeezing so tight he could hardly breathe.

'Crow told me about Alicia and the boys,' she said. 'Who would do something like this? Why?'

'I don't know . . .' Wallace had to fight not to break down then and there. He wanted to drop to his knees, bury his face against her stomach and collapse into a blubbering mess. Instead, he gently pushed her away and wiped at his eyes. '. . . but I aim to find out.'

Delilah stepped back and looked up into Wallace's face. His pain was etched too deep to be hidden. She studied his eyes for a moment, then gently patted his chest and returned to the stove.

'I'm making you boys breakfast to go,' she said. 'You'll need your strength.'

She turned to take in his clothes and nodded her approval.

'Crow's feet are smaller than yours,' she said. 'Your shoes are in the sink. I washed all the gunk out of them and stuffed them with newspaper, but they won't have had time to dry.' She pointed to a deep drawer beside the fridge. 'Take two grocery bags, slip one over each foot before you put on your shoes. That'll work for now.'

'Thanks.' Wallace made another attempt at a smile. It was weak, but it softened his face just enough. 'I appreciate all you're doing.'

Delilah's eyes watered and her lower lip twitched as if she wanted to say something more.

'It's OK,' said Wallace. 'I may look it, but I'm not going to break.'

Her voice was quiet. 'This may sound odd.' She hesitated. 'But do you ever look at Alicia's Facebook page?'

'Facebook?' Wallace was puzzled. 'That thing on the computer?'

Delilah nodded. 'It's a social networking site. It's

64

how all us moms communicate now. You know? The kids are in school, who's free for coffee? When? Where? Alicia and I love it. She wrote about going to Bellingham. Then about finding a great deal on a new skirt at the mall. She even posted a photo of it.'

Wallace held up a hand to stop her. 'How did she post something from the mall?'

'From her cellphone. Most of the new ones can connect directly to the Net. You can Tweet about where you are, what you're doing, everything. Alicia was always doing it.'

Wallace shook his head. 'Alicia didn't take her cell. I was nervous about roaming charges.'

'But she must have,' said Delilah. 'I saw the photo.'

'Can you show me?'

Delilah led the way out of the kitchen to a small alcove in one corner of the informal dining room that housed a compact all-in-one computer. This was Delilah's only private area in the house and it offered her no privacy at all.

Delilah wiggled the mouse to bring the monitor to life and then launched a web browser. Facebook was her default home page and she quickly logged in.

There were a dozen status updates from friends posted on the main page, but the one that instantly caught Wallace's eye was Alicia's.

Posted beside a small photo of her smiling face was her last update. It had been posted at four twenty-two p.m. and it read: DfGDKqjk CvTrhG.

'What does that mean?' asked Wallace.

'I don't know.'

'Why would she post gibberish?'

Delilah's voice was strained as she fought back tears. 'I don't know. That's what I wanted you to see.'

Wallace rubbed his brow in frustration. It made no sense.

'Can I use your phone?' he asked.

'Of course.'

Delilah quickly crossed the room and returned with a small cordless phone.

Wallace dialed Alicia's cell. A thick lump of phlegm was stuck in his throat, blocking the airway. He tried to swallow, but it wouldn't budge.

When the phones connected, Alicia's cell went straight to voicemail. If she did have it with her, it was now switched off. Wallace listened to his wife's voice, the joyful lilt that told him she was happy when she recorded the message. When the beep sounded, Wallace's voice struggled to squeeze through the blockage in his throat as he said, 'I'm coming, babe. Hold on.'

He hung up and handed the phone back to Delilah. 'Show me her other posts.'

Delilah clicked on Alicia's photo and the screen switched to her personal profile.

Wallace was startled to see Alicia had over one hundred and fifty friends listed. How could she possibly know that many people? Not that Alicia ever had a shortage of friends. People were naturally drawn to her. She exuded joy; just being around her made everything and everyone feel better. It was one of the reasons why he looked forward to coming home after a hard day. Just to see her face. Hear her voice. Secure in the knowledge that no matter what, everything was OK.

Without her, he would only ever be half a man.

And yet he hardly recognized any of the names and faces posting updates on her virtual wall. Had he been that out of touch?

If he had a Facebook page it would probably show Crow, maybe one or two other bus drivers and a couple of old friends from back in the day, but there would likely be no more than six people in total.

Underneath Alicia's garbled message was her previous post. Delilah clicked on the photo's icon to enlarge it.

The photo showed Alicia standing in front of a full-length mirror. She was holding a pleated skirt in one hand, while taking the photo on her phone with the other. She looked happy, carefree and enjoying her shopping adventure.

Wallace studied the photograph carefully. There were no other shoppers in the frame and nothing to indicate the store was specific to the Bellis Fair Mall. It couldn't be used to prove that Alicia and the boys had been with him in the US when they disappeared.

Wallace looked at the time stamp on the update.

It had been made less than ten minutes before the garbled post.

He tried to think. He hadn't known Alicia had brought her cellphone with her, which meant she likely kept it tucked out of sight inside her purse. He didn't know why she thought she had to hide it from him. If taking it had meant that much, he wouldn't have denied her. It was only money. And not that they had much of it, but compared to Alicia's happiness, it truly meant nothing.

He thought about her being grabbed by a stranger. The stranger had no face, for Wallace still couldn't comprehend why this was happening or who was behind it. Alicia's first instinct would be to cry for help, but if someone had the boys, if he threatened to harm their sons, Alicia would go quietly. She would die for those boys.

But she had her phone. She had just posted a message about the skirt. What if she reached into her purse and attempted to send another message? If she couldn't see the letter keys, the text would be a garbled mess.

Wallace looked at the message again. Its meaning was clear: *Find us*.

CHAPTER 12

Driving one-handed in the dark, Crow wiped breakfast crumbs off the front of his shirt and then unclipped a three-inch folding knife from his belt.

He handed the knife to Wallace.

'Not to criticize your fashion sense,' he said, 'but maybe you could trim the ends of thosebags. My cousins already think white men are strange. They don't need any more encouragement.'

Wallace accepted the knife, unclipped his seatbelt and leaned down to trim the vibrant yellow plastic bags that stuck out from his wet shoes to flare around his ankles.

'It was a clever idea,' he said. 'My feet are still dry.'

'Just don't tell Delilah,' said Crow. 'She's always stuffing black garbage bags in my glove box in case I have to change a tyre in the rain. If you encourage her, she'll have me trading my old hipwaders for a pair of leaf-bags.'

'Those waders do have a distinct stench to them,' said Wallace.

69

'Don't you start,' said Crow. 'It's that hard-earned musk that makes the fish take the bait. You ever see me come home without a catch?' He answered his own question: 'Never.'

Wallace finished trimming the plastic bags and handed back the knife. Crow clipped it to his belt.

The traffic light in front of them turned red, but Crow didn't slow down. Traffic was non-existent; the sun yet to rise. As he drove through the four-way intersection, Crow glanced in the rear-view mirror and checked both side mirrors.

'No flashing lights,' he said casually. 'That's something.'

'You expecting Marvin and the Mounties?' Wallace asked.

'Marvin's a keener,' said Crow. 'Could be dangerous. Especially where we're going.'

'Your cousins don't get along?'

Crow smiled. 'Two different paths. You haven't met this cousin before. He's a big believer in the old ways. In their day, the Squamish people had a purpose for everyone. Unlike the white men, the band didn't try to mould and shape people into what they needed. Instead, tasks were given based on a person's natural abilities. There were the elders, the fishermen, the warriors—'

'Bus drivers,' said Wallace.

Crow grinned wider, but continued with his story. 'Some of these warriors, by today's standards, would have been called psychopaths. There are tales passed down that still give children nightmares. Food was scarce in the winter and we were a warlike race, so there was a place for these men. They earned everyone's respect.'

'And this cousin we're going to see,' said Wallace, 'he's a respected man?'

'Very much so,' said Crow.

Two miles later, the road came to an abrupt end. Behind them, the sprawling residential neighbourhoods of North Vancouver reached all the way to the bustling maritime shores of Burrard Inlet. Ahead lay the dense forested slopes of the North Shore Mountains.

The road formed a T-junction, but instead of turning either left or right, Crow engaged the truck's four-wheel drive and kept going straight. The truck bounced and swayed as it descended into a steep ditch, climbed out the other side and crashed through a weedy copse of brush and small trees.

Wallace held on to the door handle to stop his head from smashing into the roof with every bone-jarring bump.

'You sure you know where you're going?' he asked.

Crow shrugged. 'My cousins change the route all the time to allow new foliage to grow, but this is the only path I know.'

'Must make mail delivery a bitch,' said Wallace.

Crow grinned. 'We use smoke signals. Much easier.'

After the truck bounced through another small grouping of trees, the ground levelled out slightly into two shallow ruts that resembled the off-road trails enjoyed by recreational quad-bikes. Crow attempted to increase his speed, but the truck shuddered in protest.

'I thought your people were fishermen.' Wallace gripped the seat with both hands and his face took on a sickly green hue. Even if his body hadn't already been tender, the ride would have been rough. 'Flat land. Cool streams.'

'Hunters, too,' said Crow. His face was alight, enjoying every bump. 'Whatever it takes to survive.'

The ruts followed the mountainous terrain and used a series of nausea-inducing switchbacks to climb to higher elevations. The truck's headlights could only illuminate a short distance through the thick foliage and Wallace fought a sickening dread in the pit of his stomach that the trail would lead them right over the edge of a cliff.

Finally the ruts converged with a slightly wider, hard-packed mud road that led through a tunnel of pine, fir and cedar to an unexpected tubular-steel gate. The heavy gate looked solid enough to stop most vehicles smaller than a Leopard tank, and the heavy forest on either side made driving around it impossible.

'Slide over and take the wheel,' said Crow. 'I'll get the gate.'

'Stay there. I can get it.'

Wallace moved to open his door, but Crow grabbed his arm to stop him.

'You can't,' he said. 'Trust me.'

Crow opened his door and climbed out. Inside the cab, Wallace slid over into the driver's seat. The sun was just beginning to rise, turning the sky an impressive shade of blush. Crow walked to the gate, stopped and held up one hand at shoulder level. He waited silently.

Wallace attempted to peer through the gloom ahead to see what or who Crow was waiting for, but the trees were too thick and the light too dim. He couldn't see a thing.

After several seconds, Crow lowered his hand and punched a combination into a keypad on the gate's handle. It appeared to take some shoulder grease to lift the heavy bar out of the ground, but Crow soon had the gate pushed open wide enough to allow the truck access.

After Wallace drove through, Crow relocked the gate and returned to the truck. Wallace slid over to the passenger side again as Crow climbed back inside.

'What were you waiting for out there?' asked Wallace. 'I couldn't see a thing.'

'Just making sure we were still welcome.'

'And how did you know?'

Crow shrugged. 'They didn't shoot me.'

The truck rolled into a small clearing and came to a stop in the middle of a rough circle surrounded by a series of raised wooden huts. It was too dark and too sheltered for Wallace to make out the size of each hut, but some appeared to be for living, while others seemed large enough to be used as warehouses.

Wallace went to open his door, but jumped back when a pair of glowing green eyes appeared at his window.

The owner of the eyes laughed loudly before removing a pair of night-vision goggles. He looked like a younger version of Crow: Same incredibly deep-set eyes, strong nose and sharp cheekbones that threatened to slice through skin as smooth and supple as tanned leather. Unlike Crow, however, this younger version lacked the bulk to handle the weight of such features. His face had matured before his body caught up.

The young man was dressed in camouflage army fatigues and had a large, semi-automatic rifle slung over his shoulder. Unlike a regulation soldier, however, his thick hair was pulled into a luxurious ponytail that reached to the middle of his back. A wide blood-red headband wrapped around his forehead completed the look.

Still laughing, the young man opened Wallace's door.

'Should've seen your face, dude,' he said. 'Priceless.' He sounded about as native as Keanu Reeves in the *Bill & Ted* movies.

Crow walked around the truck and slapped the

74

younger man on the shoulder. He looked in at Wallace.

'This is my young cousin. Everyone calls him JoeJoe.'

''Cause my first and last name is Joe,' said JoeJoe. 'Lazy-ass parents, what can I say?'

'Joe Joe?' said Wallace.

'You got it, dude.'

Crow squeezed his cousin's shoulder. 'Is your brother ready for us?'

'Yeah, I'm to take you straight there. I'm told this ain't a social call.'

Crow lowered his voice. 'What name is he using now?'

JoeJoe rolled his eyes. 'Cheveyo. It's Hopi and means "spirit warrior" or something. I don't get it, we're not Hopi.'

Crow shrugged. 'Basil doesn't exactly inspire fear. You ever think of taking a new name?'

JoeJoe grinned. 'Bro threatened to call me Teetonka, which is Sioux for "talks too much". But what a mouthful. Nah, I'll stick with what I got.'

Wallace climbed out of the truck and JoeJoe quickly led the way to one of the smaller huts. A thin column of fragrant wood smoke rose from the chimney and an armed bodyguard stood outside the door.

The guard was the size and shape of a shaved bull and even without the semi-automatic rifle clutched in his hands, he was an intimidating sight.

75

He moved to block Wallace's progress.

'He's with me,' said Crow.

The guard moved his massive head from left to right. Once. 'Cheveyo sees you alone.'

Crow looked at Wallace apologetically.

Wallace shrugged. 'Must be my shoes.'

CHAPTER 13

Mr Black sat in his vehicle at the base of the North Shore Mountains and studied the stationary red dot on his phone's screen. It hadn't moved in over twenty minutes and, according to the tracking data, it had stopped in the middle of unmapped territory.

He switched to satellite view and zoomed in on the dot's location, but all he could see from space was the same thing he saw out his own windshield: trees. Lots and lots of trees.

Entering the forest in pursuit did not seem logical. He had no scouting reports and didn't know what dangers may be concealed within the dense undergrowth. To make matters worse, according to the map there weren't any roads that led to that location. Without local knowledge, it would be very easy to break an axle or worse on the rough terrain.

He smiled thinly and without warmth. Wallace Carver was proving more unpredictable than expected. After crossing the border, he should have headed directly home. If he hadn't foolishly crashed the van, Carver could be in RCMP custody by now and trying to explain away the horror of a hastily covered crime scene.

Unfortunately, Carver hadn't even driven by.

Mr Black studied the satellite map again. If Carver had decided to hide out from the RCMP while he plotted his next move, he had chosen a good location. But without supplies, he couldn't stay in the woods for long.

The decision was simple: he would wait. Mr Black was very good at waiting.

CHAPTER 14

In fluffy housecoat and moccasins, Delilah padded down the hallway to the front door. Her eyes were puffy and her mouth was uncomfortably dry. She lifted her hand in front of her face and huffed. The rankness of her own breath made her cringe. She needed toothpaste and coffee. Lots of coffee.

An impatient fist thudded against the door frame for a third time, causing her teeth to grind and a shiver of irritation to march down her spine. She tempered her annoyance with a note of caution. It was too early for church recruiters or foolhardy salesmen.

At least the doorbell was broken – one of Crow's handyman I'll-get-to-it-soon promises still lingering from last winter – or whoever was outside would likely be ringing that, too.

'Hold on,' she called out, trying not to raise her voice and wake the girls, 'I'm coming.'

She felt more tired now than when she had first woken. Her conversation with Wallace and her fear for Alicia and the boys had made it impossible to fall back to sleep after the men left.

She kept getting up and checking on her sleeping girls.

Just to watch them breathe. Just to be sure.

Delilah opened the door and glowered up at the four men on her doorstep. All dressed the same. Hats and handguns. Official, pompous and intimidating, they excreted testosterone. Which meant they weren't there to deliver good news.

'Shit, Marvin,' she groaned at the only one of the four men she recognized. 'You know what time it is?'

'Is Crow here?' asked Marvin.

Delilah blinked, then crinkled her nose playfully. 'You sound all grown up when you get direct like that, Marvy. Your voice is kinda growly. It's nice.'

Marvin's cheeks reddened slightly.

'Is Crow here?' he repeated.

Delilah looked left and right before shaking her head. 'He went out somewhere. Didn't even leave a note.' She inhaled, her ample bosom straining against the soft, over-washed cloth, and let it out with a sigh. 'Typical man.'

'Has Wallace been here?'

'Who?'

It was Marvin's turn to sigh. 'Wallace Carver. Your husband's best friend.'

Delilah waved her hand dismissively. 'Crow's always making friends. All his passengers love him, you know? His regulars memorize his schedule just so they can get on his bus. He's too damn sociable, I say.'

Marvin held up a piece of paper. 'I have a warrant.'

'Uh-huh.' Delilah narrowed her eyes. 'For what?'

'To search your house.'

'What for?'

'Wallace.'

Delilah straightened her shoulders and her voice turned screechy. 'You think I'm hiding a man under my bed while my husband is away, Marvin? Is that what you think of me?'

Marvin glanced at the three men standing impatiently behind him. He lowered his voice.

'We just want Wallace,' he said. 'Hand him over and I'll do my best to keep you and Crow out of it.'

Delilah sneered. 'You wake my babies and I'll have your badge. You ain't coming in here.'

'We are,' said Marvin firmly. 'We have a warrant.'

Delilah was shoved aside as the four RCMP constables moved past her and into the house.

'Don't think I won't tell your mother about this, Marvin. I'll chew her bloody ear off.'

One of the constables sniggered, but Delilah couldn't tell which one. They all looked the same in their black jackets, gold-striped pants and jangling belts stuffed with pepper spray, handcuffs and handguns.

As the constables entered the kitchen and small living room, Delilah headed down the hallway to her daughters' room. Better she wake them than have the storm troopers do it. No sooner had she entered the girls' shared bedroom when Marvin called from the kitchen.

'Delilah! What's this?'

Delilah tried to think what they could have possibly found. And then it dawned on her. Crap.

She returned to the kitchen to see Marvin holding up a grubby pair of pants and a torn shirt that he had removed from the trash. Delilah had briefly considered washing them after Wallace left, but the crash had left large rips in both items of clothing. She threw them out instead.

'There's blood on this shirt,' said Marvin.

'It's Crow's.' Delilah lowered her gaze, portraying embarrassment. 'I haven't been honest with you, Marvin.' She looked up with glistening, newformed tears in her eyes. 'This trouble with Wallace made Crow fall off the wagon. I don't know what he got into, but he came home in those filthy, torn clothes and reeking of booze. I think he was wrestling a cougar in a ditch somewhere.'

Marvin shook his head slowly, not buying it.

'I saw Crow just a few hours ago. He was sober and clean.'

Delilah swallowed. 'I wondered what it was that pushed him over the edge.' Her voice hardened and her eyes turned cruel. 'You did this to him. One minute he was my husband and the next he was opening a bottle and running out the door.'

Her voice rose in anger and her hands curled into fists. 'Look at my face. Do I look like a woman who's slept peacefully or one who's been trying to wrestle her husband out of the goddamn bottle you drove him into?'

Marvin kept his composure, but the other constables stared at him. Unsure and unsettled.

'So where is he now?' said Marvin.

'I dragged him home, got him out of his clothes and into bed, but I must have dozed off. When I woke up, you were at my door and he was gone again. Thanks a lot.'

Marvin stared at Delilah. His gaze was hard, penetrating. His mouth twisted and he shook his head.

'No,' he said. 'Crow was never a good enough cowboy to escape your lasso. If you tied him down, he stayed tied down.' He passed the clothes to one of the other constables. 'I'm taking these with us.'

Marvin turned to a second constable. 'Issue an alert on Crow's truck. We find him, we find Wallace Carver.'

Delilah tried to keep the emotion off her face, but it was too raw not to seep into her voice. 'You're making a mistake.'

'We'll see,' said Marvin. 'Once we have them in custody, we can talk further. But as of this moment, Crow is as much a wanted man as Wallace is.'

Delilah followed the constables to the front door. Marvin was the last to leave.

'I'm still going to tell your mother,' said Delilah.

Marvin hesitated and appeared about to turn around, but then he shook his head and kept walking.

CHAPTER 15

Crow exited the hut with JoeJoe by his side and quickly descended a flight of wooden stairs to reach Wallace.

'Do you still have a credit card?' he asked.

Wallace patted his front pocket. The only items he left the house with each morning were an emergency credit card, driver's licence and enough pocket money for continuous coffee refills plus the bus driver's pension scheme: twice-weekly lottery tickets. He had abandoned his now-useless passport and change of underwear back in the overturned van, but these meager necessities had stuck with him even through a change of clothes. He nodded.

'Good,' said Crow. 'Cheveyo is ready to take you across the border, but he needs you cleaned up first.'

'Cleaned up?'

'Less redneck,' said JoeJoe. 'You look too much like a fugitive in borrowed clothes. He wants you looking smart. More American.'

Crow nodded in agreement. 'JoeJoe will take you to the mall for new clothes and then over to the Peace Arch.'

There was a pause and Wallace could feel the unspoken tension.

'You're not coming with me?' He tried to hide the hurt in his voice, but knew he couldn't disguise the raw desperation. The thought of being alone, not knowing how to proceed, frightened him to death.

Just as Crow was about to answer, his cellphone rang. He pulled it out of his pocket and listened.

'It's OK,' he said into the phone. 'I'll be home soon. Don't worry. It'll be fine.'

Crow hung up and squeezed the phone so tightly in his hand that his knuckles turned white. He had trouble meeting Wallace's gaze.

'That was Delilah,' he said. 'Marvin's just been to the house and found your bloodied clothes. They've issued an alert on the truck and a warrant for my arrest.'

'Ah, Christ.' Wallace ran his fingers through his hair, digging the nails into his scalp, finding too many tender spots in tight, knotted muscles.

Crow kicked at the dirt. 'If it was just me, I'd be backing you up one hundred per cent. You know that, right? But I can't leave Delilah and the girls, especially since we don't know what the hell is going on. What if . . . ?' He hesitated, unwilling to put his thoughts into words.

'It's OK.' Wallace infused his voice with grit, hoping it was enough. 'I understand.' He gnashed his teeth, hating his own selfishness and the position he had placed his closest friend in. 'Christ,

Crow, if *anyone* understands, it's me. The girls come first. Go to them.'

'Yeah, I know, but I still feel like shit. Those are my godsons out there.'

A heavy silence passed between the two men.

JoeJoe broke the tension. 'This is sweet an' all,' he said, 'but we've got, like, other things to do.' He grabbed at Wallace's arm. 'We gotta go, dude.'

Crow squeezed Wallace's other arm. 'I'll wait here until JoeJoe gets back and I know you're across the border,' he said. 'That way if the cops arrest me, it'll be too damn late.'

CHAPTER 16

JoeJoe led Wallace at a hurried pace behind the huts to a semi-circular metal barn that housed a dozen ATV quads and trikes. The roof of the barn was covered in camouflage netting, which trapped fallen needles and leaves.

As Wallace's vision grew accustomed to the ghostly gloom, he saw at least a half-dozen other barns hidden beneath the forest canopy. He doubted they all contained recreational vehicles.

Inside the barn, a mechanic in pristine blue coveralls with the nametag *Clarence* embroidered over his breast pocket had pulled two of the vehicles into the centre and was giving them a quick final inspection.

JoeJoe handed Wallace a plastic helmet and a pair of goggles before straddling one of the two-seater trikes.

'Climb on, dude. We need the head start.'

Wallace had just settled himself on to the narrow seat when JoeJoe tilted his head back and released a loud whoop that had all the earmarks of a war cry. In the same breath, he twisted the accelerator to the full-on position. The trike's front wheel lifted off the ground for an instant before the back wheels dug in and they roared off into the woods.

Before the huts vanished in a blur behind them, Wallace caught a glimpse of two native men climbing on to the other vehicle.

Wallace held on for dear life as JoeJoe thundered through the forest. He used previously laid ruts and cleared bush as general guidelines rather than broken trails, preferring to make the trike leap over fallen logs and threaten to flip end over end as they careened up the sides of narrow gullies and down steep ravines.

Branches whipped across Wallace's face, making him glad for the helmet and goggles. He just wished JoeJoe had also given him a jock and protective cup for the hard landings.

After a final leap that crossed a small mountain stream and sent Wallace's stomach crashing against the back of his teeth, JoeJoe landed the trike in a rough clearing that acted as a parking lot for two black 4x4 Toyota trucks and four large bone-white Yukon Hybrids.

Two armed guards appeared from two different directions as JoeJoe killed the ignition and yanked the helmet off his head. JoeJoe waved at the guards and turned to Wallace. His face was split in a grin that stretched from ear to ear.

'Now that was cool, dude. You stoked?'

Wallace tried not to vomit all over his shoes.

★   ★   ★

The only store open that early in the morning was a Wal-Mart Supercentre, but it carried everything Wallace would need.

JoeJoe instructed him to go 'paleface casual': beige slacks, a golf shirt, comfortable shoes and a light wind jacket in a dull colour. JoeJoe also told him to stop by the electronics department and pick out a digital camera.

'Nothing too small,' JoeJoe said. 'The bulky ones are cheapest anyway. Get one of those.'

Wallace did as he was told. When he returned to the truck, he was dressed in his new clothes. He had discarded his ruined shoes, but bundled the clothes borrowed from Crow into a bag under his arm. JoeJoe promised he would return the clothes to Crow when he got back to camp.

JoeJoe had changed his appearance as well. Instead of army-surplus fatigues, he wore a simple pair of dark blue jeans and a black T-shirt. Even tucked into jeans, the T-shirt hung loose around his skinny frame.

JoeJoe gave Wallace the once-over. 'If I looked like you, dude, I'd kill myself.'

Wallace frowned. 'Is that good or bad?'

JoeJoe grinned, displaying a disturbing array of crooked teeth. Without another comment, he threw the truck in gear and aimed for the border.

CHAPTER 17

Instead of staying on the highway straight to the border, JoeJoe took the 8th Avenue exit off the traffic circle and drove to 172nd Street. There, he turned south, skirting the Peace Portal Golf Course, and west again when he reached Zero Avenue.

The houses running along this stretch of rural suburbia were separated from their American neighbours by nothing more than a small ditch, border markers and an occasional line of decorative rock.

Wallace looked across the invisible border, so close he could touch it. Alicia, Fred and Alex were somewhere on the other side. Needing him.

He had been there when both boys were born. Feeding Alicia ice chips, feeling helpless and scared and in awe of it all. He had been there when each boy started school, despite the ribbing from his boss and co-workers when he booked the mornings off.

Both times, he and Alicia had lingered outside the classroom with the other parents, finding it more difficult to leave than it was to be left. A part of him didn't want his sons to be growing up and yet his heart filled with pride that they were.

He had been there when Alicia's father died. When she needed him to stand strong and just hold her.

And they had all been there for him when he needed them most.

It seemed ridiculous that he couldn't just sprint across the narrow patch of ground separating the two countries. Neighbourhood dogs did it on a regular basis, but a series of hidden ground sensors combined with video surveillance made human crossings a risky proposition.

JoeJoe drove to the end of the avenue and parked the truck on scenic Peace Park Drive. The ocean was stormy; dark clouds in the distance rolling towards shore.

'Dude?' JoeJoe snapped his fingers to get Wallace's attention. 'Now we walk.'

Wallace followed JoeJoe down a grassy knoll into Peace Arch Park. When they reached the bottom, Wallace found himself standing by the side of the road where Interstate 5 became Highway 99. It was practically the same spot where the Bellingham detectives had given him back his van and told him never to return.

JoeJoe pointed at the large white monument glistening with dew in the middle of the groomed green lawn.

'You're already on the US side,' he said. 'Now you just need to stay here.'

A lanky figure crossed in front of the monument

and headed towards them at a leisurely pace. He was definitely native, a hard-scrabble life etched deeply in the shadows and lines under his eyes, but his hair was cut short and he possessed a similar build to Wallace.

'Two people walked down the hill to look at the park,' said JoeJoe. He waited until Wallace's face registered confusion before continuing. 'But nobody cares, dude.' He grinned. 'So long as two people walk back.'

JoeJoe nodded to the south where a public washroom was nestled in a stand of trees.

'Go in there. Wait five minutes, then head east. Walk easy. Put that cheap-ass camera around your neck. There's a parking lot for American tourists. Transportation will be waiting. Don't panic. Don't rush. And everything will be cool.'

'That's it?' asked Wallace.

JoeJoe laughed. 'This ain't *Mission Impossible*, dude, and you're not a truckload of weed. Why would anyone think a paleface like you needed to sneak across the border?'

Wallace bumped JoeJoe's extended fist with his own. 'Tell Cheveyo I appreciate all he's done.'

JoeJoe's smile faltered and he lowered his voice. 'Between you and me, dude, I'd forget you ever heard that name. Cheveyo did a favour for Crow. Normally, he wouldn't lift a finger for a white man.'

Wallace nodded in understanding, then turned and headed for the washroom.

★ ★ ★

93

Wallace was inside less than a minute before the washroom door opened and the man he had seen walking past the monument entered. He had sad brown eyes and his cheeks and chin were pitted from a bad case of childhood acne. Combined with his height, the scarring gave him a threatening presence.

Wallace gulped, suddenly wondering if something had gone wrong. What if Cheveyo had made a secret deal with whoever abducted his family to deliver Wallace in exchange for leaving Crow out of it?

Wallace braced himself, preparing to fight, but the man simply nodded to him, washed his hands in the sink, and exited without a word.

Three minutes later, Wallace followed.

Outside, Wallace was surprised to see an attractive native woman leaning against a tree. She was young and lean with an angular face so perfectly proportioned it would have made Michelangelo itch to pick up a chisel. Her hair flowed past her shoulders and made him think of spilled ink, flashes of indigo glistening within the midnight strands.

As soon as their eyes met, she flashed him a dazzling smile and rushed over. She wore a playful silk blouse above a smart pair of tight, riding-style pants and polished boots. Before he could react, the woman wrapped her arm in his, squeezed it against her body and stood on tiptoes to peck his cheek.

Wallace tensed. The woman's soft lips burned into his stubbled cheek with the heat of fresh embers. Her kiss felt like an invasion, a hammer against glass, the brief intimacy a betrayal of his missing wife. He struggled not to recoil, knowing this stranger couldn't possibly understand how fragile a simple kiss made him feel.

'Relax,' she said. 'It looks better as a couple. Not so obvious.'

She steered him, arm in arm, along a landscaped white gravel path towards the parking lot on the Washington side.

Sweat trickled down the back of Wallace's neck as they moved further away from the Peace Arch headquarters of US Customs and Border Protection.

Despite its recent makeover, the two-storey building still looked tired as it squatted on a tarmac island in the middle of the incoming and outgoing traffic. The money it was promised to beef up security prior to the 2010 Winter Olympics had been compromised by a government that inherited a financial sieve rather than a bucket.

There was little activity visible on this side of the building. Most of the officers were on the far side, facing the ocean, screening five lanes of slow-moving, bumper-to-bumper traffic. The outgoing vehicles weren't their concern; they would all be handled by Canada Customs at the north end of the park.

'They're busy,' said the woman, 'looking for

95

drugs and nervous tourists sneaking a personal stash of Cuban cigars. Don't worry.' She squeezed his arm. 'And don't stare. It's not polite.'

She grinned up at him, but Wallace didn't smile back.

He couldn't.

Soon, the building vanished from sight as they strolled by a stand of tall cedars. No one called out for them to stop or fired a warning shot into the air.

When they reached the parking lot, the woman led the way to a midnight-blue Crew Cab truck.

'Get in,' she said. 'I'm ready for breakfast.'

Wallace wiped the nervous sweat off his brow and climbed into the passenger seat. He was relieved to be back in America and one step closer to finding out what had happened to his family.

CHAPTER 18

Mr Black sipped a cup of hot tea and munched on a breakfast sandwich consisting of a circular slice of lightly spiced sausage atop a rubbery preformed egg patty and served inside a cheese-infused biscuit. Despite the greasy, powdery texture, he found it oddly satisfying.

His cellphone chirped and the screen switched to the tracking program. The red dot was on the move.

Mr Black placed the phone in its dash-mounted charging cradle and watched as the red dot descended the mountain via a different route than the one it had taken to ascend.

Curious.

He wondered why Wallace Carver and his companion were being so cautious. They had no reason to suspect the RCMP had any clue as to their current location.

Not that it mattered. If he still cared when the time came to eliminate them, perhaps he would ask.

Mr Black continued to watch the red dot's progress as it slowly wound its way down the mountain, moving closer to civilization and his own static position.

CHAPTER 19

Wallace and the woman he had learned was named Laurel sat in a small family-owned diner that overlooked Blaine Harbor. With moorage for nearly six hundred boats, the harbor also boasted waterfront trails plus clear views of the Peace Arch border and the Canadian seaside town of White Rock nestled a short distance beyond.

Laurel ordered a full breakfast of eggs, bacon, sausage, hashbrowns and a green salad in place of the proffered biscuits and gravy. Wallace ordered coffee, but before the waitress walked away, Laurel asked her to also bring him an order of toast.

'You have to eat,' Laurel said.

'I'll eat when I'm hungry,' Wallace snapped and instantly regretted it. He hadn't meant to be rude, but his body chemistry was in turmoil. One moment his heart thumped so hard it threatened to break free of his ribcage, and the next, he wondered if it had stopped beating. He had never felt so helpless or so completely out of control in his life.

He also hated waiting, but Laurel assured him that final arrangements were being made to get him the supplies he requested. She didn't have an address to give him until she heard from Cheveyo.

Wallace turned to stare out at the boats bobbing on the waves. Most of them were covered in blue and green vinyl tarps, locked down for the oncoming winter. A few elderly locals, bundled in waterproof jackets, had risen early to stroll the boardwalk and their cheeks glowed with the bite of a salty wind.

The promising red sky had turned a menacing grey and the threat of rain dragged the clouds so low they became part of an encroaching fog that wavered a short distance from shore.

'The weather's turning nasty,' said Wallace.

Laurel glanced out the window and shrugged. 'It does what it does.'

Wallace twisted a paper napkin between his hands as if wringing the neck of a chicken.

'Why are you helping me?' he asked.

'Cheveyo requested it.'

'Why?'

'Because Crow asked him.'

'Do you know Crow?'

Laurel nodded. 'We're family. Cousin-of-a-cousin stuff, you know? Although I haven't seen him in years, not since before I went to Iraq.'

Wallace raised his eyebrows. 'Iraq?'

'Mmmm. I did two tours as a field medic there, plus a stint in Afghanistan.'

Wallace couldn't hide his surprise. 'You don't look old enough.'

Laurel grinned. 'Good genes.'

Wallace's lips twitched. 'Crow says something similar when he steals the last doughnut and then criticizes me for gaining weight.'

Laurel smiled wider. 'You've been friends a long time.'

'Fifteen years,' said Wallace. He changed the subject, not wanting to measure time. He already felt it flowing too quickly. 'Are you still in the military?'

'No. Soon as I paid Uncle Sam back for the training, I got the hell out. It wasn't what I expected, but it gave me what I needed.'

'Which was?' Wallace probed.

'Let's just say it opened my eyes to who and what I really wanted to be. I bought a small plane, a modified Beechcraft with low hours, and I'm able to travel from Rez to Rez, conducting clinics and offering medical help where I can.'

'Noble,' said Wallace.

Laurel bristled. 'I wouldn't call it that. Some of those reservations make the city slums look like luxury housing. These tribes were conquered, practically wiped out, and it shows. America is so busy trying to buy friends in developing nations, that it's forgotten the very people whose land *its* nation is built upon. It's not noble, it's vital. And with the help of friends, I do what I can.'

'Friends like Cheveyo?' asked Wallace.

'You're one to judge.'

Wallace flinched, but Laurel didn't notice. Her eyes were sparking fire and her face had hardened.

She continued without a pause. 'I'm proud of my heritage, but it sickens me to see what some of us have become. Yeah, our land and our livelihoods were stolen and it sucks, but that doesn't mean we stop living. As a people, we're better than that. Even Cheveyo, in his own screwed-up way, understands and wants to help. If we want to survive, we need to pull together and adapt. Too many of us just can't see it.'

She took a deep breath, cooling the anger in her voice. 'You ever get embarrassed for your own people?'

'Every time I watch Jerry Springer or Dr Phil,' said Wallace.

Laurel's mouth froze in mid-response, as if she had been expecting an entirely different answer, before she suddenly chuckled and relaxed. Wallace did the same.

'I get what Crow sees in you,' she said.

Wallace turned serious again. 'But do you believe my story?'

Laurel shrugged. 'I don't need to.'

'But I want you to,' said Wallace. 'It's important.'

Laurel steepled her fingers beneath her chin and focused her full attention on him.

'Tell me again,' she said. 'From the beginning.'

CHAPTER 20

When Laurel's breakfast arrived, she looked it over with eager anticipation. 'You sure you don't want some?'

Wallace shook his head. He couldn't even stomach the thought.

Laurel dug in, breaking one of the egg yolks with a strip of crisp bacon and sliding it into her mouth.

Wallace watched in silence, his mind churning over everything he had just told Laurel, exploring every detail, filtering out the distractions, the white noise.

Finally he said, 'Do you know where they made their mistake?'

Laurel looked up in confusion. 'Who?'

Wallace's eyes flashed anger. 'Whoever took my family.'

Laurel carefully wiped her mouth and fixed her gaze, returning her full attention to Wallace.

'Go on.'

'The photograph,' said Wallace. 'It was the final piece of evidence needed to convince the police that I was out of my mind. Without that photo, the detectives might have listened to me and launched a real investigation.'

'So why was that a mistake?' asked Laurel, playing devil's advocate. 'It obviously worked.'

Wallace leaned forward. 'But I know the photograph was a lie. Which means someone had to plant it.'

Laurel raised her eyebrows. 'Who?'

Wallace closed his eyes and thought back to the previous day. The boys had been curious about the border, chattering excitedly when two of the guards stepped out of the office to walk a pair of handsome German shepherds up and down the rows of waiting vehicles.

Fred, his youngest, had called out from the backseat, 'What are they looking for, Dad?'

'Probably drugs,' Wallace answered. 'The dogs can smell them. They've been specially trained to pick up the scent.'

'What if the drugs are wrapped in plastic?'

Wallace looked at his wife and grinned. 'A dog's nose is more sensitive than a human's.'

'They can smell through plastic?'

'Yes.'

'What if the bad guys sprayed the drugs with perfume?'

Wallace turned to his wife again, but Alicia wasn't offering any help. She was engrossed in a *Crafts* magazine that promised to reveal all the secrets of felting old wool clothes into handsome modern covers for your cushions.

'I'm sure that's been tried,' Wallace said. 'But the dogs must be able to smell the drugs even under perfume, otherwise they would stop using them.'

Alex joined the conversation. 'You said "probably drugs", Dad. What else do the dogs look for?'

Alex was older than his brother by eleven months, but they were almost mirror images – opposite, yet alike. If you gave Fred a toy, he would tear it apart within days. He loved to see how things worked, but only so far as the components within. He didn't smash the toys, but very carefully deconstructed them, piece by intricate piece. Alex, on the other hand, liked to put things back together. He was always picking up Fred's scattered bits and rebuilding them. The thing that impressed Wallace the most, however, was that Alex rarely built the same toy that the parts originally belonged to. Instead, he would combine parts from different toys to build something new and unique – until Fred took it apart again.

Wallace didn't know where the boys inherited their mechanical skills from. He had certainly never impressed anyone in shop class and Alicia wouldn't have the linear patience to make sure the correct nut went with the right bolt. If you gave Alicia a box of Lego, she would be more likely to grab a hot-glue gun and turn the pieces into buttons or earrings rather than a futuristic fort for toy spacemen.

'Some dogs are trained to sniff out explosives,' Wallace said in answer to his son's question.

'Like bombs?' asked Fred.

Alicia flashed Wallace a warning glance, but it was too late.

Both boys looked at each other and gushed in unison, 'Cooooooool.'

Fred pushed his face against the window as the dogs walked past the van with their noses pressed to the ground. After they were gone, Fred bounced in his seat.

'We made it,' he cried. 'No drugs or bombs.'

Wallace rolled his eyes.

When they finally arrived at the checkpoint, Wallace handed the guard their passports.

'What's the reason for your visit today?' The guard's tone was clipped, almost a snarl.

'Pleasure,' said Wallace. He tried to smile, to appear relaxed and pleasant, but it did nothing to appease the guard's demeanour.

'Your destination?'

'We're going to Bellingham,' said Wallace. 'A little shopping, a little weekend R&R, you know?'

The guard glared at him. 'You mean you'd *like* to visit Bellingham?'

He emphasized the word 'like' to let them know that whether they were allowed to cross the border and visit the neighbouring town was entirely within his control.

Wallace bristled and his first, unuttered thought was, *You fucking jerk.*

He had crossed the border numerous times in the past. Sometimes he lucked out and landed a friendly guard, but he had definitely encountered his fair share of assholes, too. He didn't know if it was part of their training, some psychological trick to make civilians nervous about trying to sneak forbidden items across the border, or if it was just the type of personality that was attracted to an authoritarian role.

He had often found the same arrogance in encounters with security guards, the military and police. If bus drivers were allowed to carry weapons to protect themselves against unruly passengers, there was a good chance they would likely attract the same type, too.

Instead of rising to the bait, Wallace controlled the impulse and simply replied, 'Yes, sir.'

His sons could sense the tension and instantly went quiet the moment he supplicated to the guard. Thinking back on it now, Wallace didn't like the lesson that taught.

He pictured the guard's face in his mind. He wasn't good with guessing the ages of people, but he would place him in his early to mid thirties. His hair could be mistaken for blond, but it was actually white. It was buzzed short at the sides and spiked on top. There was definitely product in his hair to hold the look.

The prick was handsome, too, if you liked your men looking like they belonged on the cover of a bodybuilding magazine. His eyes were so light they were almost colourless and his jaw was square enough that he could use it as a carpenter's level. The sleeves of his shirt had been tight to show off muscular arms, and the button on his collar had been loose beneath the tie because his neck was too thick.

Had there been a tattoo? Wallace couldn't remember, but there had been something just beneath his left ear. A dark mark, almost like a forked lightning bolt. It had caught Wallace's eye but failed to make a lasting impression.

If the guard hadn't been such a jerk, Wallace wouldn't have remembered if he was black or white. It just took that one moment, that brief challenge to his masculinity, forcing him to bow his head and back down in front of his wife, in front of his sons.

In that Darwinian moment, he looked into the guard's unpleasant eyes and memorized his face, subconsciously tucking it away in case they ever met in different circumstances where the man's authority no longer held any power.

Wallace opened his eyes and stared at Laurel. She hadn't moved. Her remaining breakfast lay untouched.

Wallace recalled something else: a brief conversation between the detectives when he was sitting in the security office at the Bellis Fair Mall.

You still dating that blond hunk at Border Patrol?
The blond hunk had emailed the false photograph to the detectives.

He was the weak link.

CHAPTER 21

Mr Black watched the blinking red dot move to within a mile of his location before he slipped into traffic. From there, it only took a few minutes to arrive at a side street that crossed paths with the truck's main route.

He timed it perfectly. The light facing him turned red just as he pulled up to the crosswalk with a clear view of the busy four-way intersection in front.

He glanced at his phone, watched as the red dot approached, and then looked up to get a visual on his prey.

Unfortunately, instead of driving straight through the intersection and delivering a clear side-on view of its occupants, the truck seized the opportunity of a brief gap in oncoming traffic to quickly turn west. It vanished behind a closed curtain of vehicles before Mr Black could fully observe its interior.

But with that brief glimpse his thin smile faded, taking with it the delicious tingle of hunger and power that a game of cat and mouse always delivered. Unless it was a trick of the light, the passenger beside Crow appeared too small and his hair was tied back in a long, stark ponytail.

Mr Black glanced at the map displayed on his phone. The truck's destination was clear. Crow's home was located a mere three blocks away.

When the light turned green, Mr Black pressed the accelerator hard. He needed visual confirmation before his targets disappeared inside the house.

CHAPTER 22

Laurel's cellphone buzzed with an incoming message.

She pushed her plate away and read the text. When she was done, she looked over at Wallace with sad eyes.

'I hope everything works out for you,' she said. 'You're going?'

She nodded and handed over a single key on an electronic fob, then she copied the directions from the text message on to a blank business card.

'The keys are for the truck,' she said. 'I have my own car parked nearby. The directions are to a dealer that Cheveyo trusts. It's best I don't know too much about that.'

Laurel dug into her other pocket and pulled out a second blank card. She hesitated for a moment, then wrote down a phone number and added it to the pile.

'That's my number,' she said. 'I don't expect you to use it, and I may not answer if you do, but just in case.'

Wallace looked up at her with gratitude in his eyes.

'Thanks.' It wasn't much, but it was all he could think to say.

Laurel smiled, stood up and pressed a hand to his shoulder. She squeezed, lightly, and then was gone.

Alone, Wallace made his way out of the restaurant and down the block to where Laurel had parked the blue truck.

Every step felt heavy, as though his shoes were soled with lead, but at least he had a destination.

He thought of the blond guard. His sneer, his muscles. First, he would get a gun, then he would track down the son of a bitch. He would get him to talk, to tell him where his family was and why they'd been taken.

And if he didn't talk . . .

Across the street, a marked Sheriff's patrol car snuck up on soft tyres, catching Wallace by surprise. It drifted past slowly, not in any hurry, but the mere sight of it quickened Wallace's heartbeat and brought a nasty lump of phlegm to his throat.

His first instinct was to lower his gaze and turn his head, but he fought the impulse. Better to keep moving, not to falter in his step and bring unwanted attention with a suspicious display of guilt. He had seen enough junkies scurrying along East Hastings to know what not to do.

The uniformed deputy gave Wallace a quick but casual once-over before turning his attention back to the rain-slicked road.

Wallace watched him drive away, waiting breathlessly for the sudden flash of brake lights, followed by the squeal of rubber and pierce of siren as he spun around. It didn't happen, but Wallace was still drenched in sweat by the time he climbed into the truck and started the engine.

So much for being a tough guy.

Wallace followed Laurel's written directions a short distance inland from Blaine. He compared the route to the truck's built-in GPS system, impressed by its uncanny accuracy until he almost missed his turn. The potholed gravel road that led to an unmarked private acreage wasn't on the truck's electronic map.

After two miles, the country road swallowed its last sprinkle of gravel and became little more than a deep-rutted mule trail before it dead-ended at a dense barrier of old growth forest. Wallace had to flick on his high beams to spot the narrow break in the trees that served as an unwelcoming driveway. If it hadn't been for the bullet-ridden *No Trespassing* sign, he may have missed it completely.

When his truck finally broke through the dark tunnel of trees, the grey sky opened upon a rough square of cleared land that had a distinctly inherited feel about it.

The current owner had allowed a once impressive Victorian-style home to fall victim to cruel weather and neglect. And what had once been a perfect circle of smooth lawn was now pockmarked with a rusting menagerie of the discarded engines and corroded chassis of at least a dozen trucks. All of the wrecks were peppered with bullet holes in a wide assortment of sizes.

Wallace parked the truck and climbed out just as a half-dozen hound dogs, baying as if they had been kicked in the nether regions, came bounding around the side of the house. Foamy tendrils of slobber flew from their dangling jowls.

Wallace froze, but he was no stranger to dogs. Despite the excited barks, every tail was wagging. He held out his hands and allowed the large animals to catch his scent. After they each had a good sniff, the dogs quickly calmed down and lay panting at his feet.

Shortly after, as though it had been a test, the porch door creaked open and the dogs' owner stepped out of the house. He was shirtless and barefoot, his lanky frame draped in a baggy pair of denim dungarees that were at least six inches too short at the cuffs.

He wore an off-white turban, unusual enough for a Caucasian, but it was the unkempt mass covering his face that made him look like the long-lost cousin of Jed Clampett from *The Beverly Hillbillies*. His salt-and-pepper blend of prickly hair sprouted from every pore, so that it became difficult to ascertain what was actually ear hair, nose hair, chest, shoulder or beard. Given a few more years, his unibrow would join the mix and some hunter would likely mistake him for a starving Sasquatch.

The man pointed a slim finger at Wallace and grinned through a set of baked-bean teeth.

'You he?'

'I . . . I guess so.'

Wallace cringed. He had hoped to sound more confident, but his voice betrayed a total lack of experience in such matters. He felt as awkward as a teenager buying his first dime bag of weed and hoping it wasn't oregano.

The man looked him over and wrinkled his nose before slipping a hand inside his dungarees and scratching his groin.

'Who sent you?' he asked.

'Cheveyo.'

The man winked to show he had delivered the correct password and widened his grin. The contents of his breakfast were trapped in the sides of his mouth for later enjoyment, making Wallace suddenly glad he hadn't eaten.

'I'm Randolph Phineas Gage. What d'you need?'

'I was told I could get a gun,' said Wallace. When the man didn't blink, he added, 'I also wouldn't mind a pair of good binoculars and a spare canvas tarp if you have one.'

Randolph stuck his hands in his pockets and

stepped off the porch. He moved like he had a song stuck in his head, all hips and shoulders.

'Follow.'

The dogs stayed put as Wallace followed the man around the house to a double garage that had been built in a matching Victorian style but had suffered the same neglected fate. Randolph moved to the near side and yanked open a flimsy screen door that was barely hanging on to its hinges.

Behind the thin screen, however, was a second door. This one was solid steel and could have easily been rescued from a bank vault. Randolph used two keys, which he turned simultaneously, to unlock it.

Inside, the room looked nothing like its owner. Everything was displayed and organized in a spotlessly clean, temperature-controlled environment. One wall showed an assortment of over twenty different handguns, while the rear wall held long guns of every action: bolt, hinge, lever, pump, semi-auto, and some that looked like they could take out a tank.

The third wall contained a series of heavy-duty shelves that housed crates of ammunition, explosives and various other pieces of lethal ordnance. The only item that seemed out of place was a red plastic rain barrel stuffed with highly polished wooden baseball bats with the name *Phineas* stencilled in fancy script on each one.

Randolph turned to Wallace. 'You do much shootin'?'

Wallace shrugged. 'A bit of hunting with friends; mostly just targets.'

Randolph moved to the rear wall and grabbed a sleek satin-black shotgun. He pumped it twice and peered down the barrel before tossing it over.

Wallace caught it in both hands and held it as awkwardly as if he had been thrown a dead fish.

'That's a Winchester Super X Defender: pump-action, twelve-gauge, with five-shot magazine. Eighteen-inch fixed cylinder choked barrel for wide patterning. Best weapon for someone who don't know what they're doin'. Just pump, point and shoot. Shoot low, you'll cripple 'em. Shoot high and they'll be missin' a head. Basically, if you're close enough, you can't miss.'

Randolph studied Wallace's reaction intently before adding, 'That's one scary gun. Point that at someone and they'll be shitting themselves before you even pull the trigger. It's unloaded, so play with it, get comfortable. It's got a nice weight. You run out of ammo, it also makes a hell of a club.'

Wallace pumped the action and lifted the gun to his shoulder. He peered down the length of the barrel.

Randolph grinned. 'See. Perfect fit.'

He turned to the other wall, opened a crate and pulled out a box of thumb-sized slugs. He tossed those to Wallace, too.

'You've got six shots; five in the magazine and one in the chamber. If you need to reload, it's too

big to kill. At that point, I suggest runnin' away.'
Randolph grinned, enjoying his own joke.

He returned to his shelves and found a pair of binoculars still in the box.

'I don't get much call for this regular stuff, but I like to be prepared. These are Nikon glass, military grade, real beauties.'

Randolph handed them over and moved his gaze to the shelf of explosives. He raised his unibrow enquiringly.

'I just got a new supply of Paleface Barbecue Lighters.' He chuckled when Wallace looked confused and explained, 'White phosphorous grenades. Hard to come by, but I'll give you a good deal.'

'I want to get someone to talk,' said Wallace nervously, already feeling too far out of his depth, 'not blow them to bits.'

Randolph clapped his hands together and flashed his stained browns again. 'Then let me give you a present. Free with every purchase.'

He moved to the rain barrel and selected a baseball bat. Its lacquered coat had a sleek bluish finish.

'I make these myself,' he said proudly. 'Got a woodshop out back.'

He held it out patiently until Wallace shifted the shotgun to his left hand and accepted the bat in his right. It was surprisingly heavy.

'I core out the centre with a honeycomb drill and fill it with a patent-pending molten blend,' said Randolph. 'But I still manage to keep the balance, you know? You can swing a home run or shatter a man's knee with one blow. If it was legal, every major leaguer would use one.'

Wallace didn't know what to say. He remained quiet and hoped he didn't look as overwhelmed as he felt.

'Anything else?' Randolph asked.

Wallace cleared his throat and asked about the canvas tarp.

'I've got one in my woodshop,' said Randolph. 'It's a bit messy, paint splatters and woodchips and such.'

'Sounds perfect.'

Randolph led the way outside and locked the steel door behind them. He loped off behind the house to his workshop, while Wallace returned to his truck with his new supplies.

The dogs had moved off the lawn and were sprawled across the front porch of the house. Each one of them yawned in turn as Wallace walked by.

At the truck, Wallace laid the shotgun on the rear seat and covered it with a blanket. He placed the baseball bat on top and the binoculars beside it.

When Randolph returned, he dumped the tarp in the back of the truck and shook Wallace's hand.

'Nice meetin' you, fella,' he said. 'I'll send our friend the bill and forget I ever saw ya. 'Preciate the same in kind.'

If someone had told Wallace two days before that he would be buying illegal firearms while trespassing in a foreign country, he would have checked their veins for track marks. It wasn't difficult for him to agree to never speak of it again.

CHAPTER 23

Mr Black sped down the quiet residential street, acutely aware that any hope of remaining inconspicuous was rapidly fading.

Even if he wasn't speeding, the large and expensive Lincoln stood out. Despite its incredible view of Burrard Inlet and the glistening office towers of downtown Vancouver on the far shore, this segment of the city was built on native reserve, which protected it from the get-rich-quick developers who would have stuffed it with million-dollar condos for white and Asian yuppies.

As such, the newest vehicles parked in driveways and on the street were from the previous decade. Anything newer was small and cheap and bought with gas mileage in mind.

But if Mr Black's suspicions were confirmed, being inconspicuous was the least of his worries.

Crow's truck loomed less than half a block ahead and Mr Black closed the gap in a hurry. Two figures were inside the cab. Talking. Oblivious.

He moved closer still. Reckless. Uncaring.

He eased up just as the Lincoln's chrome grill

came within inches of the truck's rusting rear bumper.

Both Crow and his passenger – a young native with a thick cotton headband the colour of ox blood – looked back in alarm.

Mr Black bared his teeth and twisted the steering wheel to the left. His foot pushed the accelerator to the floor, making the large vehicle growl.

The Lincoln jerked to the left and shot through an impossible gap between Crow's truck and a parked van. The gap proved too narrow and Crow's side mirror snapped off at the base in a shower of broken glass and twisted metal.

Mr Black sucked air through his nostrils to expand his lungs in an attempt to circulate every last drop of precious adrenalin. This is what he lived for.

Once the Lincoln cleared the nose of the truck, Mr Black tugged the steering wheel to the right and slammed on the brakes – blocking the road.

He twisted in his seat and braced himself. Through the passenger window he watched Crow's truck screech in agony, its rear-end fish-tailing as ageing brakes desperately tried to bring the clapped-out hulk of iron to a halt.

The rush was razor sharp.

To its credit, the truck stopped with barely an inch to spare. Smoke poured from its wheel wells and a thick cloud of steam exploded from beneath its hood.

Mr Black exhaled and opened his door. He

walked around the front of the Lincoln, preparing his mind and body as he moved. He knew the passenger would be the first to exit the truck. The young native looked physically lean and cocksure, and his anger wouldn't be tempered by the relief of having miraculously avoided an expensive collision.

Mr Black wasn't disappointed. The young man's face was practically purple with rage.

CHAPTER 24

The grocery clerk eyed Wallace's colourful Canadian currency with unbridled disdain before reluctantly allowing him to exchange it for a prewrapped sandwich, two chocolate-dipped granola bars, four cans of a caffeine-loaded energy drink with a Freudian name, and a large bottle of artesian tap water.

Back in the truck, Wallace tossed his groceries on the seat beside him and studied the dash-mounted GPS. By zooming out the map, he was able to scout the area around the border without accidentally displaying his hand and setting off any 'suspicious vehicle' alarms.

It didn't take long to find a spot that appeared perfect for what he had in mind.

Following the GPS directions, Wallace kept to the east side of the interstate. At 6th Street, he turned north and then west again on C Street. There, he drove into a seldom-used parking lot behind a large rectangular warehouse with a corrugated-steel roof.

The gravel lot was bordered by a shallow grass verge that overlooked the I-5 and offered a clear view of the border patrol headquarters.

Wallace slowly turned the truck around and reversed into an out-of-the-way spot under a neglected huddle of trees on the edge of the grass.

He stayed parked for a while with his back to the view. His palms were sweating and the back of his neck itched with the need to turn around, to locate the guard, to get some answers.

He fought the impulse and stuck with his plan, sitting in silence to make sure his presence didn't warrant any undue attention. If a nosy patrol car came by, he would need to move fast.

Fortunately, there didn't appear to be anyone working inside the warehouse or patrolling its grounds. On the far side, where gravel turned to tarmac and the lot butted on to 2nd Street, cars came and went at a large Pac Can Duty Free, but everyone there was too focused on a last chance for discount liquor even to glance in his direction.

Before today, Wallace's biggest crime had been disobeying company policy and refusing to pick up certain unstable passengers with a track record for violence. The courts may have ruled those individuals still had a right to ride the bus, but when a fellow driver could no longer do her job because of the severe beating she'd received over a 25-cent shortage in fare, Wallace – and most of the other drivers – believed the judges could go fuck themselves.

Alicia had worried about him, about the increasing violence that made driving a city bus more dangerous than most people realized. He had always tried to assure her that he could handle himself. And he had.

But how were they to know that danger would arrive through a different door? A door that neither of them even knew existed.

Wallace rubbed his face. He didn't want to think any more. He needed to act.

After sliding out of the cab, he quickly moved his supplies into the open-air cargo area and lowered the tailgate. Next, he unfurled the canvas tarp and draped it over the truck bed, anchoring it on each side to a series of welded hooks. He left the rear flap hanging loose. When he was done, he took one last look around, lifted the flap and crawled underneath.

The truck bed became a hunter's blind, cold and damp but perfectly disguised by its normalcy.

If he'd had more cash, Wallace would have bought a sleeping bag and waterproof mat. With the RCMP looking for him, and his illegal status on this side of the border, his credit card was useless. But, then again, with comfort came sleep. And he couldn't afford to close his eyes – even for a second.

Lying on his stomach and using his elbows for support, Wallace lifted the skirt of the tarp and focused powerful binoculars on the rear entrance to the border headquarters situated less than eight hundred feet to the north.

On the far side, out of his line of sight behind the building, border guards questioned their share of the 250,000 people who wanted to enter the

United States from Canada every day. If they suspected anyone of trying to smuggle contraband across the border, or they just wanted to be jerks, they sent them to the search and seizure stalls on Wallace's side of the building.

Wallace was assuming the guards took turns at each station to avoid boredom and that sooner or later his blond guard would appear on one of the search crews. Not that it mattered. Even if his guard stayed on the far side of the building, Wallace had chosen this spot because it offered a clear view of the staff parking lot. That meant he should easily spot him heading home at the end of his shift.

Wallace watched the guards working for a while before grabbing a sandwich and energy drink from the grocery bag. The sandwich disappeared so fast, he became worried he hadn't taken the time to remove all of the packaging and had simply inhaled the Styrofoam liner along with whatever the processed meat was supposed to be. He contemplated eating a granola bar, too, but a sudden sharp pang of guilt stopped him.

He thought about his sons and wondered if they were being fed. At home, they were constantly eating and yet still complaining about being hungry, and they weren't even teenagers yet. Alicia kept saying they would soon have to start going to all-you-can-eat buffets each evening to let the boys graze before they ate them out of house and home.

Wallace didn't know where they put it all. Both boys were lean like . . . well, Wallace patted his stomach, like their father used to be.

When he complained to Crow about the pounds he had put on in the time he was off work, Crow had laughed and told him the extra weight suited him.

When Wallace questioned what he meant by that, Crow had said, 'You're settling down, becoming comfortable in your own skin. Even when you were bitching about the physiotherapy you had to do on your leg, your outlook was changing. Day by day, I watched you become happier than I've ever seen you. Frankly, I was a little jealous.'

Wallace stared straight ahead, lost in thought as though a movie was being projected on the flapping canvas. He wiped a stray tear from his eye.

He had been happy. At the time of the crash, he had been sure he was going to die, but to survive that only to have something even more terrible brought down on his family . . . It just didn't make sense.

Why would someone take his family? There'd been no ransom or demands of any kind. In fact, it was the opposite. Someone had gone to a lot of trouble to get him completely out of the picture.

'And why not just kill me?' Wallace whispered aloud. 'If the bastards want nothing from me, why *didn't* they kill me?'

Wallace drained his energy drink, feeling the

caffeine and sugar buzz filter through his brain, and turned his attention back to the binoculars. He focused on the busy guards and devastated bystanders whose vehicles had drawn the short straw. He knew the blond guard would relish being part of the wrecking crew, to wield the immense power of the Patriot Act like a sledgehammer wrapped in the Stars and Stripes. He scanned each guard's face, desperately trying to find him.

And then he did.

Blond. Smug. Muscles bulging as he wrestled the middle seat out of a minivan while a young olive-skinned couple and their three children looked on in horror and confusion.

'If this fucker doesn't talk,' Wallace told himself, 'I hate to think what I'm going to do.'

He heard another voice from deep within his brain say, *Don't worry. He'll talk*. And before he could question it, the voice told him why: *Because you're not a nice man. Not any more.*

CHAPTER 25

JoeJoe threw open his door and rushed out of the truck. His lean frame was electrified with anger and his hands automatically curled into tight fists. He wished he had thought to pack a gun, but when he bummed a ride into town with Crow, the last thing he had been expecting was trouble. Any other time and he would have made the fuckin' idiot really crap his pants. The jerk had almost killed them and now he was—

Grinning?

JoeJoe's step faltered under the intensity of the man's unapologetic stare – coffee-brown orbs within an elliptical pool of startling white. He moved with alarming speed and purpose, every muscle seeming to know its place, its connection to the others. His face reflected stone-cold sobriety with a hint of glee rather than the expected fear or remorse.

'Dude, are you fuckin' crazy?'

The man's right hand slid across his belt and suddenly there was a flash of curved silver.

JoeJoe unfurled his hands to protect himself,

but the black man rushed in so close, so quickly—

JoeJoe fell to his knees, warm blood gushing from between his fingers as he clutched at his torn throat.

Crow released his white-knuckled grip on the steering wheel and stepped out of the truck.

His legs felt wobbly as he walked around the rear of the vehicle and saw—

The black driver, his right hand dripping with blood, was staring down at JoeJoe, watching him die.

Crow gasped, 'Jesus.'

The black man cocked his head.

'Where's Wallace Carver?'

'Jesus,' said Crow again.

And then Crow did the only thing he could think of. He turned and ran.

Mr Black cursed and launched himself in pursuit, but he had been standing too close to JoeJoe's draining corpse and his left foot slipped in the expanding puddle of blood.

Even as he tumbled to the tarmac, Mr Black did a quick calculation of Crow's speed. He rolled and regained his footing, making the move look fluid, before deciding he was better off giving chase in the Lincoln.

Without another glance at the dead youth

slumped in the middle of the road, Mr Black leapt into his vehicle and screeched the tyres as Crow turned a corner and headed down a back alley.

Within seconds, the Lincoln entered the mouth of the alley, chewing up any advantage that Crow's head start had given him. The alley had been a poor choice. It was high-fenced, filled with locked gates and chained animal-proof garbage containers. It gave Crow nowhere to hide.

At the time, however, it had offered the only thing that mattered – it took Crow's pursuer away from Delilah and the girls.

Crow fumbled with his cellphone as he ran. He glanced over his shoulder. The Lincoln bore down. Its huge front grill was the size of a bar piano and projected an unspoken promise of major pain and irreparable damage to whatever it struck.

Crow stabbed at the tiny plastic keys of his phone with his thumb. Number one on the speed dial.

His lungs burned as the cellphone rang and he was panting like an overheated dog. The real agony, however, was in his stomach. It had twisted into a knot and was trying to exit his body.

He glanced from side to side as he ran. The alley was too narrow, the fences too high. He was going to be crushed.

He thought of his youth: Indian Days at the rodeo; the insane clowns distracting the angry bulls so they didn't crush the fallen braves.

He reached back his hand, felt it skim hot metal. One chance. He kicked up his heels and leapt skyward at the first kiss of steel.

A voice answered the phone. Delilah.

But it was too late.

Mr Black cursed and slammed on his brakes as Crow was carried over the Lincoln's grill. The large native dented the metal as he rolled the full length of the hood and flattened briefly on the windshield before momentum squirted him on to the roof and away.

When the Lincoln finally screeched to a halt, Mr Black tore out of his seat and ran back down the alley. He needn't have hurried. Crow was lying face-down in the gravel and dirt, his leap to safety anything but.

Mr Black rolled Crow on to his back. His face was bloody, clothes ripped and torn to expose raw patches of skin. His proud nose was bent at an awkward angle and his eyes were closed. Mr Black checked the man's pulse and breathed a sigh of relief. His heartbeat held strong and steady.

Eliminating Crow's young passenger had been an unnecessary indulgence, but it would have been a major mistake to lose the only other person who knew Carver's location.

He unlocked the rear hatch of the Lincoln and, with some sweat and effort, dumped Crow inside.

The rear third of the vehicle had been equipped for transporting private security guard dogs and as such was separated from the rest of the interior by a reinforced cage of powder-black steel bars.

Mr Black had never liked dogs. Not even as a child. He found the domestic breeds too neurotic, as though bred by insecure sadists to continually pine for human interaction and approval. The trained breeds were no better. They always killed too quickly, seeming to take more pleasure in ripping out someone's guts than listening to them beg.

He had respect for their handlers, though. He enjoyed that gleam of madness behind the eyes. They reminded him of the explosives specialists he'd worked with in the sand. They were crazy fuckers, too.

The owner of this vehicle had been no different. The dogs hadn't turned on him until the third slice, when he held his liver in his hands and his voice took on a whiny pitch. The dogs hadn't liked that pitch.

Mr Black closed the rear hatch and climbed back behind the wheel. Now he just needed a quiet place to talk. Somewhere he wouldn't be disturbed until he had all the answers he needed.

CHAPTER 26

Wallace dropped his bottle of water and refocused the binoculars. The blond guard was leaving the stalls and walking quickly towards the main building.

Moments earlier, Wallace had watched him answer his cellphone. Instead of lifting it to his ear, the guard had read its tiny screen. He only hoped it wasn't a text message request to work overtime.

Holding his breath, Wallace waited in silence, his binoculars focused on the rear entrance to the customs office. After a few minutes, the guard reappeared. He was still in uniform, but had swapped his navy blue and white-lettered US Customs and Border Protection jacket for a plain civilian number in black leather.

'This is it,' Wallace said, needing to hear a reassuring voice, even if it was his own.

Forcing himself to remain calm, he kept the binoculars trained on the guard, watching as he made his way through the staff parking lot. Wallace didn't move a muscle until he knew the make and model of the guard's vehicle – then he exploded into action.

Grabbing the binoculars and shotgun, he scrambled out from under the tarp, slammed the tailgate closed to trap the fabric, and climbed behind the wheel.

Dust and gravel flew from the rear tyres as Wallace floored the accelerator, sending the truck flying across the empty parking lot, past the busy duty free, and on to 2nd Street. From there, his GPS showed it was a straight path to the D Street underpass.

It took less than two minutes to reach the onramp that connected with the freeway, but for those agonizing seconds Wallace was completely blind.

If the guard had turned into Blaine, Wallace would have missed him, but if he stuck to the interstate, heading south towards Bellingham, his bright orange Camaro muscle car with twin gunmetal grey sport stripes running down its hood and flank should be easy to spot.

Wallace took the onramp for the freeway and accelerated again.

He needn't have panicked. The Camaro appeared in front of him within moments and Wallace quickly snapped up the binoculars to confirm the blond guard was driving.

Satisfied, Wallace eased off the gas and followed at a comfortable distance. There were enough vehicles on the road to avoid suspicion and the car's unique colour made it easy to keep in sight.

As the tension eased, a chill shivered through his body. His skin was cold to the touch and his clothes were damp from lying in the back of the truck. He turned on the heater, absorbing its soothing warmth.

The simple act made him think again of his sons. He hoped they were somewhere warm and dry. Alicia, especially, hated the cold. Last winter she had tried to convince him to join her at sweat yoga – a programme where bendy folks exercised in a steam room. It wasn't for him, but Alicia loved it, despite what it did to her hair.

He smiled to himself. He loved her hair, especially in the mornings when it resembled a tumbleweed of copper wire and there was nothing she could do to tame it.

After twenty minutes, the Camaro left the interstate at Exit 539. Wallace felt his stomach twist into a knot of eels as he glanced over his left shoulder towards the Bellis Fair Mall – the last place he had seen his family.

He tried to remember the last words he said to Alicia. The last expressions on the faces of his sons. They were happy. The boys had pocket money burning holes in their jeans; Alicia had sale signs dancing in her head, and Wallace could already smell the sugary overdose of fresh cinnamon buns being removed from the oven.

It had felt so normal. So right.

And then. Just like that. It wasn't.

The Camaro headed west and the busy mall fell

behind. Wallace stared into his rear-view mirror, his focus straining as he was suddenly overwhelmed by the irrational feeling that he should turn around and search again.

What if it had all been a mistake? What if Alicia and the boys were waiting inside, eating junk food and wondering where the heck he had run off to?

He shook away the feeling and concentrated on the task ahead. Driving in front of him was the only link he had to his family. And no matter how hard he wished it wasn't so, he had to accept that.

CHAPTER 27

Crow opened his eyes and groaned. His body oozed pain as if it was one giant, tender bruise. His nose and the left side of his face were on fire, the skin torn and bloody and peppered with chunks of gravel from his forcible face-plant in the alley. He tried to move his arms, but they were pinned rigidly behind him. He was tied to a wooden chair: tight, unforgiving rope around his ankles, wrists, lap and chest.

He moved his head and surveyed his surroundings. He was in a home garage. A bare 60-watt bulb burned above his head. The garage was drywalled and showed signs of recent wear and tear, but apart from an old oil stain on the poured concrete floor it was empty. A collection of DIY wooden shelves anchored to the far wall were bare; there was no clutter, just cobwebs and dust.

The sound of running water came from behind. It made him want to pee.

The water stopped.

A whistle, previously hidden beneath the water noise. Soft, melodic. Frightening.

A shuffle of feet.

The whistling stopped.

The silence became even more frightening.

'Do you know why our president banned water boarding as a means of interrogation?' asked an unfamiliar voice.

Crow's puffy eyes grew wide and he instinctively struggled against his bonds. Useless. Whoever tied them knew what he was doing.

'You can talk.' The unseen voice was calm, unthreatening. 'We're just chatting.'

Crow wanted to speak, to ask what the hell was going on and why this son of a bitch had butchered JoeJoe. But he feared that if he started, he might never be able to shut up again. Instead, he stared straight ahead, his lips knit together in brave defiance.

'Water boarding,' continued the voice, 'is so effective that trained CIA operatives who subjected themselves to the torture lasted, on average, fourteen seconds before caving. One report said that al Qaeda's toughest prisoner, Khalid Sheik Mohammed, won the admiration of his interrogators by lasting nearly two and a half minutes before begging to confess. Part of that is bullshit, of course. No American worth his salt would admire that terrorist son of a bitch no matter how long he lasted.'

Crow felt an uncomfortable tremor run through his body.

Warm breath tickled his ear and the voice said, 'We're about to get very intimate.'

Crow locked his jaw and stared straight ahead again.

'Fourteen seconds,' said the voice, 'can be an eternity.'

Without warning, a sheet of Cellophane was pulled tight across Crow's eyes and nose and his chair was tilted backwards to rest on a makeshift sawhorse. He stared up in wide-eyed disbelief at the unknown black man who had chased him down the alley. The man twisted the plastic into a knot behind Crow's head so that he could hold it with one hand. With his other hand, he scooped a plastic pitcher out of the water-filled sink behind him.

'My name is Mr Black,' said the stranger. He smiled. 'I straightened your nose again, by the way. You're welcome.' The smile dimmed. 'Question number one: where's your friend Wallace Carver?'

Crow tried to scream, but—

Mr Black poured the water into his mouth and over the plastic in a continuous, unrelenting wave. Crow gagged as his body convulsed and his lungs fought with his stomach to crawl up his throat in a desperate search for air.

He was drowning on dry land and there was nothing he could do.

Before unconsciousness or death could claim him, the plastic was pulled away and air rushed into his lungs with such force he could barely contain it. He vomited and convulsed, his throat and chest burning with a series of wheezy coughs.

'That was eight seconds,' said Mr Black. 'Bet it felt longer.'

'P-please,' Crow gasped. 'I don't know what any of this is about. What do you want with Wallace?'

'My reasons are none of your concern.'

Mr Black moved out of sight again.

'I'll ask again. Where is Wallace Carver?'

Before Crow had a chance to answer, the plastic wrap engulfed his face again and his chair was thrown backwards. He shook his head in frenzied panic, trying to ward off the oncoming assault, but it was too late. Mr Black was already pouring the water.

Crow was racked with sobs as he swallowed air in lumpy chunks. His body was turned inside out, every nerve on fire, every muscle petrified and drained of fluid. It was as though his body had died, yet his brain remained alive just to feel unbearable pain.

Despite an incredible sense of shame, he told the man everything he knew. It really wasn't much.

Mr Black listened with an intensity that suggested he was weighing each spilled word to see if it held truth or lie. When Crow was finished, Mr Black moved behind him and pulled the plug out of the sink. Crow heard the water gurgle down the drain, the sound filling him with relief.

'If I was a good man,' said Mr Black, 'I would make this quick.'

Crow strained his neck and tried to yell for help

as a thick band of grey duct tape was sealed over his mouth.

Mr Black moved in front of him and slipped a small, circular knife off his belt. As it caught the light, the knife resembled a tempered-steel claw from a giant mechanical bear. A hole in the grip was designed for the wielder's thumb so that it fit comfortably in the hand with the two-inch blade curving upwards.

The lethal blade had a sharp point and serrated, diamond-cut edge and Crow knew exactly what it was for: skinning the tough hide off slain elk, moose and deer.

Crow's own flesh would offer no resistance to the knife and he began to whine like a wounded dog. His whining exploded into a howling shriek as the cold blade touched his bare stomach.

The first nip of penetration threatened to take him into blackness and his muffled shrieks grew in intensity until they were suddenly accompanied by a piercing scream.

Crow tried to open his eyes, to focus on the source of the unexpected scream, but the fear and pain were too much.

His eyes rolled back in his head and blackness claimed him.

CHAPTER 28

The orange Camaro slowed and turned into a lazy maze of inner-city placidity.

Unlike outlying suburbs where a design plan was put in place to make sure individual taste and identity was unable to flourish, here the staggered rows of homes were keenly mismatched. Squat bungalows with drafty ill-used lofts nestled beside vast family homes that had once overflowed with rambunctious look-alike children.

The lots were large and displayed their owners' stubborn longevity with thick, old-growth vegetation, over-crowded gardens and stout wooden fences that might afford a little privacy.

At first glance, the neighbourhood exuded a sense of community pride and prosperity, but a closer examination soon exposed the cracks of hard-working people living too long in one spot with an income headed in the wrong direction.

Patchy lawns needed reseeding, exterior walls ached for fresh paint, and clogged gutters and drainpipes struggled to keep a grip on tired, weather-weary roofs. It was a place where an

146

injection of fresh blood and disposable income could do everyone good.

Wallace kept his distance, trying not to fall too far behind, but also nervous that he had now lost the cover of steady traffic.

Fortunately, the Camaro's driver didn't appear to notice. After all, the guard had no reason to suspect he was being followed. As far as he was concerned, Wallace never was, and never would be, a problem.

Upon reaching a small community park, the Camaro made a quick turn without signalling and pulled to a stop beneath a canopy of tall, broadleafed trees.

Caught off-guard, Wallace quickly pulled over to the kerb and parked. Grabbing his binoculars, he leapt out and rushed blindly across the road. His view of the Camaro was blocked by a two-storey house on the corner, but he also used this to his advantage. The guard couldn't see him either.

When Wallace reached the sidewalk, he hopped a small hedge, dashed across a short lawn and flattened himself against the house's painted wood siding.

Puffing from the unexpected exertion, Wallace carefully peered around the corner. He didn't need the binoculars. The Camaro was only two houses away.

The guard had parked in front of a quaint postwar bungalow that sat on a generously large treed lot. The location was surprisingly peaceful as the front of the house looked across the road on to a quiet, well-maintained park. The bungalow's owner was clearly in the middle of a major renovation and a large green dumpster in the driveway was filled with old drywall, roof shingles and rotted chunks of wood. A red wheel-barrow rested beside it, its latest load already dumped.

A new porch had recently been added to the front of the house to take advantage of the serene view. Not yet painted or stained, the fresh wood glistened like honey in the late-afternoon light.

Wallace watched the guard slide out of the Camaro and stretch his back as though he had just finished a gruelling six-hour drive instead of a scant thirty minutes.

The door to the house opened and a slender man with a shaved head stepped on to the porch. Detective Petersen.

Wallace bit back a bitter growl that threatened to burst from his throat. *Was he in on it, too? Why?*

He shook away the questions. The only thing that mattered was one of them had to know where his family was.

The guard's lips curled into a thin smile as he walked up the garden path. The detective met him halfway and immediately pulled him into a heavy liplock, which the guard cut short, looking around as though embarrassed by the possibility of drawing attention.

Petersen laughed, linked his arm with the

muscle-bound guard and dragged him across the porch and inside the house.

Wallace froze the scene in his mind – *especially the laugh* – and used it to stoke an intense white-hot fire that burned deep within. He fanned the flames, encouraging them to turn any doubt or trepidation to ash. He glanced back towards the truck, thinking of the various tools and implements within.

The inner voice returned: *We'll get them to talk.*

'Hell,' Wallace snarled, 'I'm ready to make them fucking scream.'

CHAPTER 29

Cheveyo lifted one corner of the yellow tarp and forced himself not to recoil at the sight beneath. The average human body holds eight to ten pints of blood, and his young brother had spilled every last drop.

'Any idea who would do this?' asked Marvin.

From his crouched position, Cheveyo looked up at his cousin, dressed impeccably in his RCMP uniform. The sight of it – oppression wrapped in starched, crisp lines – made him shudder inside, but he didn't allow it to show.

His cousin wasn't alone. Far too many unfriendly eyes were glaring at him from the uniforms that guarded the perimeter. His proximity to the police also made his warriors nervous, as they were forced to stay outside the flimsy barrier of crime-scene tape.

'I have enemies,' said Cheveyo in answer to Marvin's question. 'You know that.' He shook his head. 'But this . . . this isn't the Angels, Big Circle or Sanghera. Too personal. Too professional. An odd mixture, no?'

'Professional?' said Marvin.

'One cut.'

Cheveyo turned to stare over at his largest warrior, the one he had renamed Kuruk, a Pawnee name for bear. Kuruk was pressed against the yellow tape, arms folded across a barrel chest, biceps bulging. Two constables stood nearby, no doubt praying he wouldn't step over the line and force them to act.

Cheveyo raised his voice. 'It would take even a strong man a lot of practice to do such a thing. The cut is savage, but clean. This skill would not go unnoticed if he was available for hire.'

Kuruk nodded in understanding and immediately began working his phone.

'We don't think JoeJoe was the intended target,' said Marvin. 'This isn't about you.'

Cheveyo took one last look at his dead brother before gently replacing the tarp and standing up. He glanced over at Crow's truck, taking in the twisted remains of the smashed side mirror.

'You think it was about Crow?'

'He's missing,' said Marvin. 'We've posted two constables at his house, just in case. But no, we think it's about Wallace Carver.'

'The white man?'

Marvin nodded.

'The white skin didn't do this,' said Cheveyo.

'Oh?' Marvin raised both eyebrows. 'How do you know?'

Cheveyo allowed a thin smile to cross his lips. 'You need lessons in subtlety, my cousin. But

151

you already know it wasn't him.' He looked around at the crowd and the number of police cars blocking off the neighbourhood. 'What do the witnesses tell you?'

Marvin sighed and looked over his shoulder to where a small gaggle of senior officers were in deep discussion. He lowered his voice.

'Several witnesses saw a tall black man in a large SUV. He cut off Crow's truck, killed JoeJoe with one cut like you said, and then chased after Crow in his vehicle.' Marvin indicated a nearby alley. 'They went down there. We found a broken cellphone and some blood, but not enough to suggest he wanted Crow dead. At least not right away.'

'And this black man is what? Searching for Wallace, too?'

'We don't know.'

'But you believe my brother is simply collateral damage? Wrong place, wrong time?'

Cheveyo lowered his head before Marvin could answer, not wanting to hear the karmic truth.

Crow had asked for a simple favour to transport his friend across the border and Cheveyo had been happy to oblige. Crow had earned that loyalty. He was not only a cousin, but a childhood friend who had stood shoulder-to-shoulder with him when the skinny white boys at school had drunk their fill of bravery and decided to teach the unwelcome Indians a lesson in mob rule. It was a lesson *they* didn't forget.

But now that favour had cost him the life of his cherished brother.

Despite Cheveyo's attempts at running an equitable camp, with all members receiving a fair share in the band's profits, it had been difficult to disguise his biased affection for his young brother. JoeJoe was never the most reliable or hardest working, but he brought a joy and lightness to Cheveyo's life that few others could either appreciate or understand.

And now he was gone.

Why?

Cheveyo looked up at the sudden sound of screeching tyres as several patrol cars left the area with full lights and sirens. He saw Marvin running to his own patrol car and yelled after him.

Marvin turned his head slightly as he slid inside. He mouthed the words so perfectly it may as well have been a yell: 'We've found Crow.'

CHAPTER 30

Back inside the truck, Wallace quickly practised how to load the shotgun's magazine and the simple pump action required to eject the spent shell and load a fresh one into the chamber.

With spare shells stuffed in his pocket, he slipped out of the truck and moved towards the bungalow. His only lessons in stealth came from his childhood, playing Cowboys and Indians or Commandos and Nazis, where sticks became rifles and a mortal wound could be healed by a simple tag from a friend.

As he did then, Wallace avoided the sidewalk and stuck close to the homes. The neighbourhood was quiet and no one seemed to notice as he quickly cut back across lawns and ducked beneath windows.

After he hopped the last hedge to flatten himself against the side wall of the detective's bungalow, Wallace's heart was pounding at close to two hundred beats per minute and acrid sweat dripped off his brow. He glanced around nervously, but the neighbourhood remained quiet.

He dropped to a crouch and quickly scuttled underneath a large picture window that brightened the bungalow's main room. When he reached the other side, he popped up and glanced inside.

The room beyond the glass was empty.

Taking a deep breath to slow his racing heart, Wallace stepped on to the porch and moved to the front door. The new porch was solidly built, each floorboard screwed down tight. His footsteps barely made a sound.

A new screen had been hung in front of the original wood door. Its hinges were oiled and fresh. Silent. Wallace eased it open and tried the handle.

The door was unlocked.

If he wanted to turn around. Now was the time.

Wallace hesitated, knowing that both men inside were likely armed and definitely better trained than him.

But what choice did he have? They had taken his family; only he could get them back.

Wallace opened the door and crept into the house. Inside, he moved to the right, the shotgun held firm against his shoulder, leading with the barrel and scanning the room for any movement.

The room was barely furnished, the plaster walls showing recent signs of having been stripped of wallpaper. Large splotches of different-coloured paint were daubed on the surfaces, as though the owner was still deciding on his best combinations.

Wallace moved through the room and entered the adjoining dining area. Apart from a disposable

Formica-topped table and two green vinyl chairs, this smaller room was empty. The carpet had been ripped up to expose once-beautiful hardwood floors. The process of restoration hadn't yet begun here.

From the dining area, an arched doorway led into the kitchen. Wallace listened for any obvious sounds of occupation, but he didn't hear a thing. He wiped the sweat from his brow, repositioned the heavy gun against his shoulder and moved into the kitchen.

It was empty, too.

A shadow appeared in an opposing doorway and Wallace swivelled towards it, his breath trapped in his throat, eyes bulging. His finger moved to the trigger.

The shadow flapped and rustled, exposing itself as nothing but a sheet of heavy plastic covering a hole that led down to an old dirt basement.

Wallace gasped and instantly withdrew his finger from inside the trigger guard. He choked back a foul stream of abuse, desperately trying to turn his fear into fuel. His mind was alive with negative chatter, every base instinct telling him to flee. He bit down on his lip, drawing blood, fighting with one of the only weapons he had: rage.

Crossing the room, his shoes left footprints in a thick blanket of white plaster dust. A second doorway led into a narrow hall. Three more doors beckoned, but only one of them was closed.

After quickly checking the other two rooms and

finding them empty, Wallace pressed his ear to the closed door.

The sound of exertion vibrated through the wood. Inside the bedroom, somebody was grunting; working up a sweat.

Wallace gripped his shotgun tightly and inhaled.

His inner voice asked, *Are you ready?*

Wallace didn't bother answering as he turned the handle and rushed inside.

CHAPTER 31

In the middle of the large bedroom, the blond guard struggled with the limp detective.

His back to the door, the muscular guard stood on a wooden chair. His lover's slack body was slung haphazardly over one shoulder. With his free hand, the guard was busy attaching a purple silk cord to a secured metal eyebolt in the ceiling. The other end of the short cord was tied in a hangman's noose and strung around Detective Petersen's neck.

To make the scene even more disturbing, Petersen was dressed in women's lingerie: a padded black bra, matching lace panties, silk hose and garter belts. His face was painted with garish crimson lipstick, powdery blush and royal purple eyeshadow that was a close match to the cord.

The unexpected sight caught Wallace by surprise.

'What the fuck?'

The guard spun at the sudden intrusion. He was bare-chested with sloppy lipstick kiss marks dotting his smooth, swollen pecs. The marks betrayed a playful beginning to a deadly game.

The guard's eyes widened in disbelief as Wallace, armed and confused, filled the doorway. But then, without any regard for the limp form upon his shoulder, the guard released his hold on the detective and leapt off the chair.

In Wallace's mind, time slowed.

The guard seemed to float, his body twisting as he aimed for the bed and a leather holster resting on the nearby nightstand. In the same moment, Petersen's inert body dropped towards the floor.

'Don't!'

Wallace's shotgun boomed, the noise deafening, tearing chunks of plaster from the rear wall above the bed and causing an enormous cloud of white dust to explode outward. The dust was so thick that it wrapped itself around the guard like a wizard's cloak of invisibility.

'Don't move! Don't move!'

Wallace tried to rush forward, to stop the guard from reaching his gun, but his way was blocked when the noose snapped around Petersen's neck, stopping his fall with a violent jerk.

The detective's eyes sprang open in fearful panic, the pupils rolling, unable to focus, and a guttural, choking screech escaped his lips. His throat turned purple, his face red. His feet thrashed wildly, but his hands were bound behind his back and he had no way to stop himself from being hanged . . .

Wallace hesitated. If he lowered the gun to help . . .

The decision was taken from him as Petersen's

flailing feet miraculously found purchase on the wobbly wooden chair.

Wallace's attention immediately swung back to the guard whose hunched and ghostly form within the cloud of dust was circling around the detective's swaying body in preparation to attack.

'Don't fucking move,' Wallace screamed. He pumped the shotgun for emphasis, proving it was loaded. 'There's no place to run. I only want my family.'

The guard did two things simultaneously.

He freed his gun from its holster.

And he kicked the chair.

Petersen's feet instantly lost purchase with the tumbling chair and his body swung free again to block Wallace's line of sight. If he fired, the shotgun's wide spread would cut the hanging man in half.

The guard didn't face the same dilemma. He opened fire.

Wallace hissed in pain and stumbled backwards. The inside of his arm burned and he lost his footing. A piece of the wall exploded beside his ear as his feet slid out from under him. On the way down, his skull cracked against the door frame and a flash of starry darkness blurred his vision. When he hit the floor, his finger tightened on the trigger and his shotgun boomed for a second time.

Another, even thicker cloud of plaster filled the room as a huge chunk of the ceiling gave way and the detective crashed to the floor.

Cursing himself and knowing he was in mortal danger, Wallace shook off the pain and quickly scrambled back to his feet.

His choices were simple: retreat or move forward.

He chambered another round – the menacing sound of the shotgun unexpectedly making him feel slightly less vulnerable. The thick plaster dust made it impossible to see. It was like standing in the middle of heavy fog.

Another gunshot filled the room and something small, hot and lethal brushed Wallace's hair. He yelped in surprise and dove to one side, hitting the floor again and rolling with the shotgun clutched to his chest.

Two more shots followed to puncture the wall where he had just been standing.

Wallace kept rolling – under the bed where all scared children fled – only he didn't stop. On the other side of the bed he rose up on his knees.

The air cleared noticeably in front of the bedroom window where the single-paned glass was shattered in such a way it resembled the guillotine teeth of a Halloween pumpkin.

Wallace saw the guard's broad shoulders through the cloud of dust. He was moving cautiously towards the door, gun extended, to where he had last seen Wallace fall.

Knowing he was outmatched, Wallace didn't shout a warning or try to fight fair. With an internal roar, he reversed the shotgun in his hand

and sprang to his feet. Before the guard could react to his onrushing footsteps, Wallace slammed the butt-end of the gun into a tender spot above his right ear.

Bone cracked and flesh split, but the guard only dropped to one knee. No stranger to physical pain, he shook off the devastating blow. Wallace gulped in disbelief as the guard turned and lunged. His teeth were bared and his fingers had curled into eye-gouging claws.

Wallace took one step back, fighting against every natural impulse to turn and run, to take his chances with the broken window. Instead, he raised the shotgun again and slammed the guard square in the face with every ounce of strength he had left.

There was a sickening crunch as rubber-sheathed metal met bone and the guard's eyes rolled into the back of his head before he collapsed to the floor and lay still.

CHAPTER 32

Cheveyo entered the hospital with five warriors in tow and went directly to Emergency. When they pushed through the doors, a dark-haired nurse with all the curves of a blackboard eraser strode forward and held up both hands.

'Stop right there, boyos,' she growled. 'Where do you think you're going?'

Cheveyo fixed her with a steely glare. 'My cousin was just brought in by ambulance. I need to see him right away.'

The nurse didn't bat an eye. 'That's not going to be possible now, is it? You'll have to wait. There are chairs in the hall.'

Cheveyo rolled his shoulders and glanced at Kuruk. With arms crossed, he was as immobile as the old wooden drugstore Indians once used to advertise pipe tobacco. The only difference was in the eyes. Kuruk's never stopped moving. Even in a hospital, he trusted no one.

One word from Cheveyo and the nurse would be swept aside, but that wouldn't get him the answers he needed.

Cheveyo changed his tone. 'Could you tell Constable Marvin Joe that his cousin would like to speak with him?'

The nurse nodded. 'I can do that. Now wait out in the hall.'

Ten minutes later, Marvin pushed through the Emergency doors into the waiting area and approached the six men. Cheveyo stood and the two cousins walked a short way down the hall to a refrigerated vending machine. Neither man bothered to dig in their pockets for coins; Marvin appeared jittery enough to have already consumed more than his share of the caffeinated beverages within.

'How is he?' asked Cheveyo.

'Better than you would expect. He got lucky.'

'Lucky?'

Marvin sighed. 'I don't know all the details yet. We were called to the scene by a distraught realtor. She was showing an empty house to some clients when she heard a noise in the garage. When she opened the door, she saw an unknown black man cutting into Crow's stomach. She screamed and the suspect fled.' Marvin's voice trembled slightly. 'Crow had been tied to a chair and tortured, but if the realtor hadn't shown up, it was about to get real gruesome.'

'Did you get a better description of this man?' Cheveyo asked.

'No. The realtor is in shock. She was barely

coherent.' Marvin ran a tongue across dry lips and plucked nervously at his left eyebrow. 'What the fuck is going on? If you know anything—'

'I'm as much in the dark as you are,' said Cheveyo. 'What about Crow? Has he said anything?'

'The docs kicked us out so they could sew him up, but I'm going to talk to him as soon as they're done.'

'We'll wait,' said Cheveyo. 'I need answers, too.'

As Marvin turned to leave, his cellphone rang. He flipped it open and listened for a moment before hanging up. A frown creased his forehead and his pace quickened as he returned through the doors to Emergency.

Crow looked as if he had been dredged out of a watery grave and dumped on to the metal bed for autopsy. His skin was grey, but the nurses had bundled him up under a large pile of over-washed hospital blankets and a more natural colour was already beginning its return to his sharp-boned cheeks.

Marvin pulled up a chair beside his bed. 'The docs say you were lucky. Nothing important nicked. Just a deep puncture in that spare tyre of yours.' Marvin tried to smile. 'You could say it was all those Tim Horton doughnuts that saved you.'

Crow didn't return the smile. 'I don't think that was the plan,' he said solemnly. 'He wanted me dead.'

'Who?'

'He called himself Mr Black.'

'What did he want?'

'Wallace.'

Marvin raised an eyebrow. 'Why?'

'He didn't say.'

Marvin sighed. 'But you know, right?'

'Honestly,' said Crow, 'I have no idea.'

Marvin sighed again. 'So where is Wallace?'

Crow winced. 'That's all *he* kept asking. And do you know what the worst part is?'

Marvin waited.

'I don't even know,' said Crow. 'Not for sure.' He tried to smile, but it melted upon his lips. 'The stupid son of a bitch killed the wrong fucking Indian.'

CHAPTER 33

Standing over the body of the unconscious guard, Wallace surveyed the scene as the plaster dust settled. It looked like a home-made bomb had gone off – something that packed a punch but was just plain messy.

He stepped over the guard and knelt by Detective Petersen. As he loosened the silk cord from around the man's neck, he felt something warm and wet flowing down the side of his own body, underneath his left arm. When he touched it, his hand came back covered in blood.

One of the guard's bullets had scored a hit, but Wallace was so pumped up on fear and adrenalin, the pain had yet to kick in.

He shook his head in disbelief, knowing he was so far out of his depth it was a miracle he was still alive.

He wiped the blood on his shirt and felt for a pulse at the detective's neck. It was shallow but steady. He glanced up at the ceiling where his shotgun had blown a hole clean through to the rafters.

Petersen was damn lucky to be alive, too, and

Wallace doubted he would cause any trouble for a while.

He quickly surveyed the room again and moved to the bedside bureau. Inside the top drawer, lying beside the detective's shield and gun, Wallace found a pair of steel handcuffs.

In the next drawer down, he found a second pair. Unlike the regulation cuffs, however, this off-duty pair was made of lighter steel and wrapped in pink fur. They were nestled beside a red rubber ball gag the size of a clown's nose and some kind of odd stainless-steel plug that resembled a child's old-fashioned spinning top.

Wallace went back to the guard and used the first set of cuffs to lock his hands securely behind his back. He used the fur-lined pair around the man's ankles. He also decided to use the gag, slipping the rubber ball into the man's slack mouth. The guard had a large, melon-shaped head, but the gag's leather strap fit him without any adjustment.

When he was finished, Wallace dug his hands into the guard's armpits and attempted to drag him across the floor.

His lower back went into spasm at the dead weight and the wound under his arm flared into white-hot existence.

Wallace released the body and cursed. Time was slipping away. *Think.*

He left the room and moved to the front door. It was still ajar from when he had first entered – a moment in time that now seemed a lifetime ago. With a deep, calming breath, he moved on to the front porch, expecting to find a mob of curious neighbours wondering what all the noise was about.

But to his great relief, the street remained empty. Either they were keeping their heads down or – Wallace glanced at his watch – most people were still at work.

Without wasting time, Wallace cut across the yard and down the street. He climbed into his truck and threw it into reverse. When he reached the bungalow, he bumped over the kerb and backed across the lawn to park with just enough room for the lowered tailgate to reach the lip of the porch.

With sweat dripping down his face and blood dripping down his side, Wallace slid out of the truck. Moving with purpose and determination, he grabbed the red wheelbarrow from beside the green dumpster and rolled it inside the house.

Wallace dumped the guard into the rear of the truck and double-checked the steel cuffs. The man was still unconscious, the brutal blow to his skull even more devastating than Wallace had realized.

Fucker deserved it, said his inner voice. *He wouldn't have hesitated to do worse to you.*

Wallace slammed the tailgate closed so that it pinched the loose end of the tarp and secured it tight. Breathing heavily, fearing he was pushing his luck, he ventured back into the house and down the hall to the bedroom. His left leg throbbed, the muscles cramping and making his limp more pronounced, but it was just another ache, another reminder that, despite everything, he was still alive.

In the doorway, Wallace surveyed the destroyed room. Plaster dust covered every surface. The guard's handgun was a distinct lump on the floor, while his uniform shirt hung from a bedpost. Wallace moved inside and grabbed both.

Finally, he took a moment to check on Petersen again.

He squatted down, wiped some of the dust away from the unconscious man's nostrils and mouth, and loosened the silk noose a little further. Even as he performed these tasks, Wallace wished he could be a different kind of man.

He wanted to press his knee against the detective's throat and push down until he heard that satisfying crunch as the windpipe collapsed. This bastard had helped put his family in peril. He didn't deserve to live.

But Wallace wasn't that man. At least, not yet. 'I hope this ends your fucking career,' he hissed.

Before leaving, Wallace picked up the bedroom phone and dialled 9-1-1.

CHAPTER 34

Marvin leaned forward and asked, 'What do you mean? He killed the wrong Indian.'

Crow rubbed at his eyes, wiping away tears. 'JoeJoe helped Wallace cross the border. I don't even know where he was headed.'

'You better explain.'

'I already did, remember? Last night.' Crow's voice turned hard, angry. 'Wallace's family is missing, but you didn't believe me, so my friend is out there by himself and now this crazy son of a bitch is after him, too.'

Marvin ground his teeth. 'I had no reason to believe you, Crow. You didn't see that house. The evidence was—'

'Bullshit!' said Crow. 'I know Wallace. I know what he's capable of and what he's not.'

Marvin flinched. 'Yeah, maybe.'

Crow noticed the change in Marvin's tone and pushed himself up on his elbows. He flinched slightly as pain flared from his freshly stitched abdomen.

'What does that mean?' he challenged.

Marvin flicked his eyes to the door and shrugged. 'I called in a favour at the lab. Asked them to take a quick look at the blood evidence. Just to see if there was anything that we could rule out.'

'And?' Crow pressed.

With a sigh, Marvin asked, 'Does Wallace have a dog?'

'No, Alicia's allergic. That's why he was being so soppy about that damn stray cat. Why?' And then it dawned on him. 'Son of a bitch. It's not even human blood, is it?'

Slowly, Marvin shook his head.

Crow practically growled. 'Is Cheveyo here?'

'Yeah, he's waiting out in the hall.'

'Get him in here. Now!'

CHAPTER 35

Six blocks from the detective's house, Wallace pulled into a side street and flipped open a brown leather wallet. From inside, he plucked out a Washington State driver's licence. The border guard's name was Desmond Morris.

Wallace punched the guard's home address into the truck's built-in GPS. Within seconds, the tiny computer calculated and displayed the fastest route. It was only a few miles away, outside of the city but still in a residential area.

Wallace felt the adrenalin drain from his body, causing him to shiver as a hollow darkness took its place. Judging by the address, the guard's residence didn't appear to be the kind of place where one could easily keep a woman and her two boys locked up and out of sight.

He leaned against the side window, his cheek touching the glass. His left arm was tight against his body, his hand gripping his stomach to lock the pain in place. He could feel the blood still leaking from the wound. His eyes were half-closed; breathing rapid but controlled.

He needed a place to talk to the guard. To get answers. He also needed to search his house. Leave no stone unturned.

Wallace put the truck in gear and drove down the street, following the GPS unit's turn-by-turn directions.

The guard known as Desmond Morris lived in the end unit of a three-storey condominium four-plex with peek-a-boo distant ocean views from the top two floors. The bottom floor consisted entirely of a private single car garage.

Using the guard's keys, Wallace entered the condo through the front door. He carried the shotgun, but kept it down by his side – out of sight of any curious neighbours.

He surmised that since Morris was single and his detective boyfriend owned his own home, the condo would likely be empty. He was proven correct as he conducted a quick search of the top two floors without interruption.

Unfortunately, neither did he find any locked doors or sign of forced occupancy. If Alicia and the boys had been here, they had left no trace.

The only thing that seemed unusual was an over-abundance of mirrors. Every room had at least one. Either the guard really liked to look at himself or he never wanted someone to sneak up on him.

Wallace suspected the former.

Moving down to the garage level, Wallace located and tapped the automatic opener. As soon as the folding door trundled open, he ducked under and rushed back to the truck. He drove the vehicle inside and slapped the button again. The door lowered smoothly, hiding the truck and its contents from prying eyes.

The garage was meticulously clean, but so narrow it was difficult for Wallace to shuffle his way around the truck without smacking into a wall. Every moist bump told him he needed to bandage himself and stop the bleeding, but a more primitive part of his brain told him he needed to secure the guard first.

Morris was just too dangerous to leave alone for too long.

Wallace opened the tailgate and grabbed the guard by his bound ankles. With a deep breath, he yanked hard, pulling the body to the edge of the tailgate. The man groaned and suddenly kicked his legs, narrowly missing Wallace's face and causing him to jump back in fright.

Without Wallace to hold him up, Morris slipped out of the truck and fell three feet to the floor. With his hands bound behind his back, he hit the concrete pad with a bone-jarring slap. The noise was akin to a cheap steak being tenderized by a steel mallet.

Morris immediately went limp again as Wallace's eyes darted to the cab of the truck where he had left his shotgun and the weighted baseball bat.

Wallace stood still, regaining his composure, and waited a full minute to be sure. When Morris failed to open his eyes, Wallace bent to check his pulse. Despite the fall and the beating, it still felt stronger than his own.

Remembering his gym days, Wallace bent his knees to take the weight, kept his back straight and reached down. He wrapped his arms around the guard's chest and slowly dragged him up the two short flights of stairs.

On the main level, Wallace dragged Morris through a stark and modern living room to an attached open-plan dining room. There, he heaved the man's limp form on to one of four matching high-backed chairs. The chair was incredibly heavy. Custom designed, its Gothic framework was solid iron that had been bent and shaped in a blacksmith's furnace and finished with a dense smoky paint.

After studying the chair's architecture for a moment, Wallace carefully unlocked one of the cuffs around the guard's left wrist, slipped the chain underneath an iron crossbar and then quickly reattached it. He did the same with the ankle cuffs; now Morris and the chair were solidly attached.

Although he felt physically drained, Wallace didn't trust steel alone to contain the guard – especially since the fur-lined cuffs appeared more novelty than professional. With a weary sigh, he returned to the truck and unravelled a long length of rope from the tarp. He also retrieved his shotgun and custom-made *Phineas* baseball bat.

Back in the living room, he placed the gun and the bat on the guard's high-end leather couch before putting his knot-tying ability to good use. By the time he was done, Desmond Morris was lucky to still be able to expand and contract his lungs.

Finally satisfied, Wallace returned to the couch and lowered himself into a comfortable position. The butter-cream leather was even softer than it had looked, but Wallace had only been sitting for a minute before he saw the armrest changing colour from his own leaking blood. Heaving the heavy guard up the stairs had made his wound open wider.

'Shit!' he said aloud.

He glanced around and saw a small washroom off the kitchen. He tried to get to his feet, but his muscles trembled in protest.

He needed five minutes. Just a little breather. And then . . .

His inner voice, barely audible through the cloud of pain and exhaustion, returned. *Call her.*

Cursing again . . . wishing he was stronger . . . more capable, Wallace dug into his pocket and pulled out a blank business card with a handwritten phone number on it. His inner voice was right. He needed help.

The guard's home phone was sitting in a charger within easy reach of the couch. Wallace dialled.

CHAPTER 36

The moment he cleared the border, Mr Black exhaled a rare sigh of delight. He was back in America; the land of the free, the strong, arrogant and proud.

To an outsider, the people to the north might resemble their mighty southern neighbours. In fact, everything about them – their food, clothing, entertainment, media – screamed USA, except for the single most important aspect: they didn't *want* to be American.

Brazen socialists, they celebrated pacifism without acknowledging the only reason peace was even possible was because their umbilically attached ally was the most powerful war machine on Earth.

Huddled in isolated pockets scattered across a resource-rich land ripe for pillage, Canadians were still locked in a delusional belief that politeness and fair play would keep the rapists from the door. Their naivety was laughable. They could never understand what it was to build a monument that pierced the sky, only to watch it burn to the ground out of petty rage and jealousy.

Where they might cower beneath such aggression, America would do what it had always done: raise its middle finger and build one bigger, taller, more impressive. One day.

And yet Carver hadn't cowered. In fact, he had proven far more resourceful than anyone could have anticipated.

Mr Black shook the thought away. His target had been lucky. That was all. And now his luck was running out.

Mr Black's cellphone chirped from its dash-mounted cradle. He scowled and tapped the appropriate icon. A short message appeared onscreen. The message contained no inflection of fury or even disappointment, but he felt its presence just the same.

He tapped a short reply before pulling off the interstate on a slip road that led into the drive-thru lane of the first Jack in the Box hamburger stand he saw. He had been thinking of an Oreo milkshake for days.

As he waited for the car in front of him to order, Mr Black studied the customers who had chosen to eat inside the restaurant. From the licence plates in the parking lot at least half the patrons were Canadian tourists. He found it disturbing that without hearing them speak, that subtle difference in phonetics, he couldn't immediately tell which were which.

It had been like that in the sand, too: enemies and allies too much alike to know who was on your side. And even when you thought you knew . . . things could change.

He ordered a milkshake and was just about to take that first, cheek-hollowing sip when his cell-phone chirped again. He placed the drink in a holder, wiped his hands on a napkin and touched the message icon.

He frowned as he read the short message before tapping the GPS co-ordinates contained within. His phone instantly switched to its mapping program and displayed the fastest route.

With milkshake in hand, he returned to the inter-state and headed south towards Bellingham.

CHAPTER 37

Wallace clutched the Defender shotgun by his side and nervously peered through the peephole set in the middle of the door. The wide-angle lens distorted the woman's face, but even in exaggerated detail her beauty was unmistakable.

With her dark hair pulled back in a fiercely tight ponytail, Laurel's face appeared more sculpted than ever. Sharp lines accentuated where her jaw met her chin and where prominent cheekbones curved in towards a strong, perfectly symmetrical nose.

Her mouth wasn't smiling this time and the creases on her lips were tight with concern.

Wallace unlocked the door and ushered her inside.

'Thanks for coming,' he said. 'I didn't have anyone else to call.'

'Men and guns.' She hefted a sturdy leather medical bag. 'Show me your wound.'

Wallace closed the door and led the way upstairs.

As Laurel reached the main-floor landing and moved into the living room, she glanced over at the blond man tied to the chair in the adjoining room. Wallace watched her eyes skim the bloodied and broken mess of the guard's face, but her demeanour didn't change. She was a woman who had seen worse.

'Did you do that?' she asked.

'The bastard took my family. Besides,' Wallace lifted his wounded arm to show the amount of blood soaked into his shirt, 'he's already paid me back.'

Laurel turned to face him. 'He's the border guard you were telling me about? The one who sent the photo.'

Wallace nodded. 'I still need to talk to him. Find out who else he's working with.'

Laurel frowned. 'You mean he looks that bad and you haven't even started yet?'

Wallace couldn't hide his embarrassment. 'It was more difficult to get him alone than I hoped.'

Wallace quickly filled her in on what had happened at Petersen's house.

When he was done, Laurel asked, 'Why did you call the emergency operator?'

Wallace shrugged. 'I couldn't bring him along and I didn't want the bastard to die. If things don't work out here, I might still need him. These two are the only leads I have.'

Laurel frowned again. 'The cops might come here.'

'I don't plan to stay long.'

'We better hurry then.'

Laurel placed a hand on Wallace's arm and led him to the couch. When he was settled, she sat beside him and lifted his wrist to take his pulse.

'You've made a mess of this beautiful couch,' she said.

Wallace looked at her through sunken eyes and grinned to mask the pain. He changed the subject: 'I wonder how many soldiers got themselves shot just to be treated by you.'

'Only one,' said Laurel. 'But I believe he was more relieved to be sent home to his mother than to have me digging a bullet out of his thigh.' She flashed the tiniest of smiles. 'We were low on anaesthetic and he was allergic to morphine. His screams scared the other boys shitless.'

Laurel released Wallace's wrist and moved to kneel in front of his left side. She produced a small pair of stainless-steel scissors from her medic's bag.

'Lift your arm,' she instructed. 'Put it behind your head and keep it there.'

She cut a large panel out of the shirt, removing the sleeve in the process but keeping the collar. Blood bubbled and oozed from a smooth puncture just below Wallace's armpit in the fleshy part of his side.

Laurel pinned back the flap of shirt, exposing a larger and more ragged exit wound. It was as though the bullet had punched its way in, but then chewed its way out. The exit wound was the size of a Bluenose dime.

Laurel made a clicking noise with her tongue before digging in her bag and returning with a pair of thin translucent surgical gloves.

Wallace winced and groaned as Laurel probed and palpitated his wound with her gloved fingers.

'It's clean,' she said. 'The bullet went straight through. No arteries nicked that I can see. No muscle damage. You're lucky. A few inches to the right and it would have pierced your heart. It just needs cleaning and stitches.'

'What about blood loss?' Wallace asked.

'Have some liver for dinner.' She winked. 'You're only down a pint or so.'

Wallace grimaced. Liver, fried in onion and bacon, with a baked potato on the side, was one of Alicia's favourite meals. But whenever she took the notion for it, Wallace managed to convince her that only the local family restaurant could do it any justice. That way he and the boys could treat themselves to something less revolting.

'I'll need hot water and towels,' said Laurel. 'Have you taken any painkillers?'

'No. I was going to look, but—'

'Good,' she interrupted. 'Most people think all pain medication is the same. It's not. In your condition, you need to avoid acetylsalicylic acid.'

'Avoid what?' asked Wallace.

'Aspirin,' said Laurel. 'It's an anti-coagulant. Not good when you're bleeding.'

'Oh. I was hoping you might have something

185

better anyway? A pill that takes the edge off but won't make me drowsy.'

Laurel smiled. 'I'll see what I can do.'

When Laurel returned from the kitchen with a basin of hot water and a small stack of fresh white towels that she had found in a hall cupboard, she quickly and efficiently cleaned Wallace's wound. When she was done, she dabbed it with a splash of peroxide from a small brown bottle.

Next, she held up a length of black thread and removed a curved needle from a sterilized pouch.

'I don't have any anaesthetic,' she said. 'So this is going to hurt.'

Wallace gritted his teeth in dreaded anticipation. 'Suddenly,' he moaned, 'you don't seem so attractive any more.'

Laurel laughed delightedly. 'That's not the first time I've heard that.'

She plunged the needle into his skin and began to sew.

CHAPTER 38

Desmond Morris opened his eyes and groaned as Laurel was tying the final knot on Wallace's exit wound and clipping off the stray ends of thread with her tiny scissors.

His first word was unrecognizable behind the ball gag, but its intent was clear enough. He followed the expletive with a vigorous testing of his bonds. The rope and cuffs held strong. The heavy iron chair barely wobbled.

Wallace swallowed two orange pills that Laurel said would help block the pain, and picked up the customized baseball bat.

'Thanks for your help,' he said to Laurel. 'But you might want to leave now.'

Laurel blinked. She didn't appear disturbed.

'I know what he's done,' she said. 'I'll stay. See what he has to say.'

Wallace met her gaze, preparing to argue, but knowing he didn't have the strength for it.

'Suit yourself,' he said. 'Just don't try to stop me.'

The guard watched Wallace approach with steely disdain. There was no fear. Not yet.

Morris's forehead had swollen into a Neanderthalian ridge. The skin was yellow and tender with underlying ripples of green, purple and dark indigo. Both eyes were bloodshot, the skin around them blackened to resemble a raccoon. His nose didn't look broken, but Wallace suspected the shotgun's blunt impact had cracked bone beneath the heavy eyebrow ridge. Concussion or brain swelling was likely, but Wallace didn't care.

He moved behind the guard and unbuckled the strap that held the gag. He reached around to—

'Don't go near his mouth,' said Laurel. 'He could take your fingers off. I've seen it happen.'

Morris shot Laurel a foul look, as if that had been exactly his intent.

Wallace nodded his thanks and held the leather strap off to the side of the guard's head. He tugged until the rubber ball reluctantly popped out of his mouth.

Morris immediately spat a thick wad of blood and saliva on to the floor, then moved his jaw from side to side, working out the kinks.

'Should've left it in.' His voice was hoarse. 'I ain't telling you a goddamn thing.'

Wallace didn't hesitate. He didn't have the time or patience for meaningless bravado. He gripped the bat in both hands and swung, letting his un-injured right arm carry most of the weight.

The loaded bat skimmed the surface of the guard's left knee, just catching the knob of bone in what a ballplayer would call a foul tip. There was a nasty crunch and pop as the kneecap seemed to separate from the rest of the leg before cartilage and tendons snapped it back in place. It was quickly followed by the guard's snarling bellow of pain.

'Fucking coward,' screamed Morris. 'Can't take me man-to-man so you gotta do it like this?'

'Where's my family?' said Wallace.

'Fuck you.'

'Why did you take them?'

'Fuck you twice.'

Wallace swung the bat again to the same knee. The crunch was louder this time, more contact, more pain, and Morris's face turned the colour of his towels. He growled more than screamed and his breath quickened like an angry bull about to be unleashed from its cage. His face flushed red and streams of pink snot flowed from his nostrils.

'Where's my family?' said Wallace.

'You'll never find them.'

'Who has them?'

Morris snorted to clear his nasal passages, but he didn't answer.

'Why did you . . . take them?' Wallace tried to be fierce, impervious, but his voice broke on the question.

The guard slid his lips open to expose bright red teeth. He had bitten his tongue or the inside of his mouth while containing his pain.

'For a murdering bastard, you're kind of a pussy.'

Wallace stared at the man in horror. 'Murder? What are you talking about?'

Morris grinned wider and shook his head.

Wallace hefted the bat in his hand. 'I'll fucking break you open.'

The guard practically laughed. 'You think I ain't had worse?'

Wallace swung the bat for a third time, harder. There was no crunch. This time it was a sharp, brutal *snap*!

Morris screamed so loud that Wallace felt it reverberate deep in his bones.

'Too noisy,' yelled Laurel. She tossed Wallace one of the bloody towels she had used to clean his wound.

Wallace snatched the towel out of the air and stuffed it into the guard's mouth, muffling him.

Morris's eyes were wide now, his nostrils flared. His swollen forehead was beaded in cold, clammy sweat. But despite everything, he still didn't look remotely afraid.

Wallace turned his back on the prisoner and threw the bat angrily to one side. It skidded across the floor and crashed into a wall. He went to rub his face and saw the dried blood that covered his hands.

His own blood.

But still . . .

How far was he willing to go?

He wiped his hands on his pants. He felt sick.

Yesterday at this time he had been sitting in a food court, eating a cinnamon bun and looking forward to a pleasant supper and some alone time with his wife while the boys played in the hotel pool.

And today? Today he was . . .

'Torture won't work on him,' said Laurel. 'You don't have the stomach for it and, unfortunately, it appears he does.'

Wallace stared into Laurel's eyes, sensing her inner strength, and wishing it was something he possessed.

'With time,' she continued, 'you could break him. Anybody can be broken, but you wouldn't be able to trust the information he gave you. Most tortured prisoners will confess to anything just to stop the pain.'

Wallace looked at Laurel helplessly, not wanting to believe but knowing that what she said was true. Who was he kidding? He was about as tough as an old banana – and Desmond Morris fucking knew it.

He rubbed his face; blunt, chewed-up finger-nails clawing pathetically at tired skin.

'What do we do?' His voice cracked under the strain. 'How do I find out what he's done with my family? I don't even care why any more. I just want them back.'

Laurel stood and walked over to him. She touched his arm – a brief, gentle caress – and moved on to the guard. She ignored the man's loathsome glare and walked behind him. Through the oval gap in the chair's iron back, she studied his inked flesh.

'He's definitely ex-military,' she said. Her finger stroked the man's bare skin, just beneath his muscular neck. Morris flinched as though her touch burned. 'See this large tattoo?'

Wallace had noticed the curving shape of a snake slithering over the guard's shoulder and around his neck to flick its forked tongue towards his left ear.

He moved to stand beside Laurel. She radiated calmness and he sucked it in like a vampire, every drop making him feel less likely to fall apart and tumble into a pile of broken jigsaw pieces. She reminded him of Alicia, and how much he depended on her.

It was Alicia's strength, wisdom and serenity that kept him going when he worried about unpaid bills or when the rehab on his leg seemed too much to bear. She was his rock, the foundation upon which everything else was built, and yet he now felt that he had never told her just how much that meant.

He studied the tattoo on Morris's back, fighting an urge to rip it from his skin with fingernails and teeth. The snake's scaly body curled around the guard's spine in a clever display of optical illusion. And although most of the snake was simply a black outline, dozens of the petal-shaped scales had been coloured in. Considering the intricate design, the hodgepodge of colours looked to have been selected at random; a strange mosaic created by a blind man.

'Those are kills,' said Laurel, pointing to the coloured scales. 'The different tones represent different types and rank of enemy combatants. He's obviously seen action in both Afghanistan and Iraq.'

She pointed to a series of numbers mixed in with the pattern of the snakeskin. The writing was so small that without a magnifying glass, the numbers were almost impossible to see. 'Those are likely GPS co-ordinates of his more memorable missions.'

Wallace pointed to the coloured scales. 'Why are there Xs in the middle of some, but not others?'

'Eye for an eye,' said Laurel. 'On those engagements he killed an enemy in retaliation for losing a member of his unit. I have seen them on quite a few of my patients. The markings were different, crosses mostly, even a series of dots, but the meaning is the same.'

Morris shook his head violently until he worked the towel free. He spat it out with a hoarse scream. 'Shut up, bitch! Do you know what this cowardly bastard did?'

Wallace darted in front of the bound man and grabbed hold of both his ears. He twisted them fiercely, feeling cartilage crackle and skin stretch as he thrust his face to within an inch of the guard's.

'What have I done?' Hot, angry spittle flew from Wallace's lips. 'Tell me what I'm supposed to have done?'

'*Semper fi*, bitch.'

Morris launched his head forward, his teeth snapping like a crocodile, aiming to grab and tear cheek, nose or lips. Wallace lurched back just in time, feeling the man's teeth skim the stubble beneath his lower lip.

Roaring in frustration, Wallace snatched the ball gag off the table and forced it into Morris's mouth before he had time to clench. He pulled the strap tight behind the guard's head, locking it uncomfortably in place.

'Sorry,' he said to Laurel before realizing how lame that sounded. It was something one would say if their conversation had been interrupted by a phone call.

He tried to shake away the panic, to control his too-rapid breathing and concentrate on what the guard had said.

'*Semper fi*,' he repeated. He had heard the phrase in war movies, but never really understood it. 'What does that mean exactly?'

'It's Latin,' said Laurel. 'Short for *semper fidelis*. Among other things, it's the motto of the United States Marine Corps. It means "always faithful".'

'Faithful to who?' asked Wallace.

'Country, naturally,' said Laurel. 'But out on the battlefield, it's being faithful to your unit. When you're outgunned and under-supplied, it becomes all about watching each other's backs. Leave no man behind. The bonds formed when patrolling on enemy soil are virtually unbreakable. You would have to live it to know it.'

Wallace pointed to the last grouping of coloured scales on the guard's back. A mass of mustard yellow, comprising close to a dozen scales, surrounded a linked cluster of six Xs. Beyond that cluster, the remainder of the scales were empty, uncoloured flesh.

'Likely his final mission,' said Laurel. 'He sought revenge for a lot of friends that day.'

'So he was telling the truth,' Wallace said quietly. 'He has had worse.'

Laurel nodded. 'The question, however, is why isn't he still doing it? Men like this live for the military. They don't just love the job, they *are* the job. His unit is his family; closer than blood. He would never quit to work the border. It's too much like being a cop rather than a soldier. That last mission must have cost him everything.'

'*Semper fi,*' muttered Wallace under his breath.

CHAPTER 39

Wallace dragged his fingers across his scalp in frustration. He needed to lash out, to hurt someone, but he had lost all taste for punishing the guard. If he wouldn't talk, what was the goddamn point?

'I'm a bus driver,' Wallace told Laurel. 'The furthest abroad Alicia and I have ever been is a rainy week in Mexico before the boys were born. We've never been to the Middle East, so what's my family got to do with a bloody US Marine?'

'I don't know,' said Laurel. 'But if he's sentimental enough to tattoo a memorial to the dead on his back, maybe he's kept other things, too. He wouldn't be this loyal to just anyone. Money doesn't buy *semper fi.*'

Wallace looked down at Morris, but the man simply glared back, disclosing nothing.

He turned to Laurel. 'I'll look upstairs. You should pack your things and leave in case the cops show before I'm done.'

Laurel took hold of Wallace's arm and led him into the living room, out of earshot.

'What are you going to do with him?' she asked.

196

'Damned if I know,' said Wallace. 'Like I said, I'm only a bus driver.'

'If he gets loose, he'll come after you,' she said. 'That one's not the type to forgive and forget.'

Wallace sighed and his frustration came to a boil. 'Yeah, well, he better join the goddamn line. I'm not giving up until I find my family.'

Laurel's eyes looked pained as she gave his arm a final squeeze. 'Go search upstairs. I'll see if I have something in my kit that will buy you some time.'

Wallace started in the smaller of the two bedrooms. Morris had turned it into a sparse office with a simple desk and chair in one corner. On top of the desk was a laptop computer.

Wallace lifted the lid, waited for the screen to brighten, and began clicking through the various folders saved on the hard drive.

He didn't know much about computers, but during his time off from work Alicia had shown him the basics on her own laptop. He didn't quite see the appeal – although he had wasted hours on a website with funny stories and jokes written by and for bus drivers – but he didn't want to be completely clueless when the boys were talking about iTunes and torrents and an online game they referred to as an MMORPG.

Wallace continued to click until he found one folder titled: *Wallace Carver*. Opening the folder, he saw it contained a collection of digital photographs.

The tiny icons were too small to make out any detail, but Wallace discovered that if he clicked on them, they instantly enlarged.

One of the photos looked incredibly familiar. It showed Wallace sitting alone in his green minivan, but the background wasn't the Peace Arch border. He recognized the edge of a neon sign in one corner. The photo had been taken in North Vancouver as Wallace was leaving his physiotherapist's office.

Wallace enlarged several more photographs. Most of them showed the same thing, but from different angles. There was nothing specific to indicate a date. The photo could have been taken days, weeks or even months earlier.

Someone had been following him, waiting for just the right moment to take Alicia and the boys. But why? How could he possibly have made such an enemy? He was nobody. And why target his family? It didn't make sense.

He clicked on the final image. Its icon was slightly different and it launched a separate program called Photoshop. When the program finished loading, it displayed the photograph that had been emailed to Detective Petersen at the mall: Wallace alone in the minivan as he drove across the border. But in this file, the photograph was in layers. A small menu on the right of the screen showed three separate layers had been combined to create the final image.

The top layer was a duplicate of Wallace leaving

the physiotherapist's office, except the background had been erased or cut away to isolate the van.

In the menu, the tiny symbol of an eye lay to the left of each layer. When Wallace clicked on the first eye, the top layer vanished to reveal the middle layer, which was some kind of digital mask used to obscure part of the bottom layer.

Wallace clicked the eye symbol again and the mask vanished to reveal the unaltered bottom layer. This final layer showed a blue Dodge van with California plates being inspected at the border crossing. Wallace recognized neither the van nor its passengers, but he instinctively knew they weren't important. This Dodge was simply creating a hole that his own vehicle would fill.

Wallace stared at the photograph, not knowing what to do with it. It was proof that he wasn't crazy, but after the Bellingham police found their detective strangled half to death on his own bedroom floor, would anyone even care?

He closed the laptop, unplugged its power cord from the wall and carried it with him to the second bedroom.

CHAPTER 40

Wallace turned the master bedroom and ensuite bathroom upside down. He shoved the mattress off the bed, pulled drawers out of the dresser and clothes out of the closet, dumping everything on to the floor.

The search came up empty. Apart from discovering Morris's affinity for expensive, custom-cut suits and imported silk boxers, he didn't find anything of a personal nature.

It didn't make sense. What Laurel said was true. Morris was both sentimental and loyal to an extreme. Why else would he tattoo a part of his body that he couldn't even admire without . . . ?

Wallace glanced at the full-length mirror mounted on the wall within a few steps of the walk-in closet. Morris was a bodybuilder. He liked fine clothes and had them tailored to fit his sculpted body. Big shoulders. Narrow waist. Arms like Popeye.

He was proud, vain, obsessed.

This mirror was framed in white oak. Thick. Solid. Wallace ran his fingers along each edge, feeling for a latch.

Nothing.

He placed his hands on its smooth reflective surface and looked at the old man staring back at him. He didn't recognize the tired face, nor the person cowering behind the eyes. Deep inside, it wasn't a man. It was a young boy. Weak, lost, desperate . . . scared. He shoved away in disgust, daring the glass to break, to curse his luck even further.

The sudden release of pressure made something click and the mirror swung away from the wall on invisible, silent hinges. Wallace quickly grabbed hold of the frame and swung it open all the way to reveal a secret space, no deeper than an average medicine chest, in the wall behind it. The hollow was lined with tempered-glass shelves.

The top two shelves were filled with money, stacks of it. Wallace picked up a bound package. American hundred dollar bills. So crisp and fresh, the corners crackled as he flicked through them. The printed band running around the stack told him the amount: $25,000.

There were other stacks, at least a dozen of them, all in various denominations and amounts. Wallace guessed it totalled over three hundred thousand dollars. He had never seen so much money.

Imagine what Alicia and he could do—

Fuck!

Wallace shoved the money back on the shelf, angry with himself and the creep of greed that distracted him from his mission. His *only* mission.

Wiping a sheen of sweat from his brow, he moved

down to the third shelf. This one was mostly empty, except for a well-thumbed Zippo lighter and a set of dull metal dog tags, rectangular with curved corners, on a beaded stainless-steel chain.

Wallace ignored the lighter and picked up the tags. They were stamped with the guard's name, blood type, social security number, Armed Forces branch, religion and gas mask size.

Desmond Morris was Catholic, and in case of chemical attack, he took a large.

Wallace slipped the tags into his pocket and moved to the last shelf. It contained a narrow metal cash box that was the length of a shoebox but only half as deep. Wallace removed it from the shelf. It wasn't heavy, but it was locked.

He shook it. The contents didn't make any sound.

He searched the shelves for a key. It would be small, easy to hide. But he didn't find one. He stepped back—

And froze in place at a sudden noise from downstairs: the protesting screech of metal. It came from the garage; the nails-on-blackboard noise bouncing through the heating ducts.

He tried to place the sound in context, but the only thing that made sense was that someone had forced open the garage door. Someone who didn't have a key and didn't want to be seen. He doubted it was the police. They wouldn't be so quiet. They liked their sirens, battering rams and jackboots.

Wallace swallowed nervously, picturing the

shotgun resting on the leather couch in the living room, and the baseball bat somewhere on the floor. He slid the metal box into the back of his pants, where a handgun would have been welcomed, and swung the mirror closed. It clicked into place, seamlessly hiding its secret once again.

He picked up the laptop and moved to the top of the stairs, wondering if, and hoping that, Laurel had already left.

He moved down the stairs, trying to be quiet but fearing that everyone within a two-block radius could hear his heartbeat. It thundered in his chest. He strained to listen over the rapid thumping. The house was silent.

He took three more steps, hovering two steps above the landing that led into the living room. He was about to call out, to see if Laurel was still there, when everything stopped.

A dark stranger stepped on to the landing, appearing as if from nowhere. The man was tall, thin and dressed from head to toe in black. Even his minimal shoestring tie and hollow piercings were black. His eyes, however, were incredibly bright. They radiated delight, like a cat that has just discovered its tortured prey is still twitching, game for a little more fun.

'Mr Carver,' said the man. 'Congratulations. You've been very busy.'

'Who are you?' Wallace kept a firm grip on the laptop, wondering how much damage its half-inch-thick aluminium edge could inflict.

The man reached into his pocket and produced a small handgun. He casually pointed it at the laptop's core . . . aiming through it to the palpitating heart of Wallace.

'You can call me—'

Blood sprayed from his mouth as the man crumpled to his knees and his bright eyes rolled skywards. A second crunch of metal against bone made him drop the gun before he pitched facefirst on to the floor.

'Come on!' Laurel tossed the bloodied baseball bat aside. 'We have to get out of here.'

As Wallace stepped over the unconscious man, Laurel ran back into the living room to snatch up her medical bag and the shotgun. She passed the gun to Wallace as they headed down the last flight of stairs and out the front door.

Wallace felt numb as he staggered down the pathway beside Laurel. A large black SUV was parked in the steep and narrow driveway, blocking any exit from the garage. The vehicle was big enough to carry eight people, but despite the tinted windows, it looked empty.

If there had been others, they would have stepped out to block their way. Laurel and he wouldn't have stood a chance. That meant the dark stranger had arrived alone.

'Who was he?' Laurel shouted.

Wallace shook his head. 'I don't know, but . . .' The blood drained from his face as he finished processing the thought. 'He knew my name.'

The third man. The thought stabbed into Wallace's brain with such force it almost took him to his knees.

Wallace reasoned there had to have been at least three men involved in the abduction of his family: the border guard, the detective . . . and the one who had actually taken Alicia and his sons from the mall.

Wallace stopped, his chest heaving, and looked back at the condo.

'Come on!' said Laurel. 'My car's right here.'

Wallace shook his head again. 'I need to go back,' he said. 'He must know where my family is.'

'Too risky. I don't know how hard I was able to hit him. He's armed and he's a professional. We have to go.'

Wallace stuck the shotgun between his knees to free his hand and pulled the metal box from behind his back. He stacked it on top of the laptop and offered both items to Laurel.

'Take these and wait for me. I'll get some rope and hogtie the bastard.'

'I don't—'

'We'll take him somewhere where he can scream as loud as he wants and no one will care. I have to get him to talk. I'm all out of options.'

'You're making a mistake,' said Laurel.

'I've no choice.'

As Laurel reluctantly accepted the items, Wallace turned and ran back towards the condo.

CHAPTER 41

Mr Black groaned as he rolled on to his side and opened his eyes. Instantly, he felt vulnerable, exposed and angry.

He forced himself to sit up, to lean his weight against the narrow doors of the hall closet. From this position, he could at least see any attack and respond with some measure of lethal force. His childhood had taught him to never sleep on his stomach; never to leave his back exposed.

Mr Black touched the back of his head and his hand came away bloody. He probed deeper, ignoring the pain as his fingers pressed into the swollen, torn lump. His skull felt intact. No loose shrapnel from shattered cranium. A lousy flesh wound, nothing more.

But inflicted by whom? That was the question.

He found his gun on the floor and slipped it into his pocket. Then, suppressing another groan, he grabbed on to the short decorative railing that edged the first three stairs and pulled himself to his feet.

His vision swam and his stomach churned in protest. His head was pounding and his ears felt stuffed with cotton wool, but the main source of pain was his tongue. He had given it a severe bite.

He spat a wad of fresh blood on to the floor, stretched his neck and rolled his shoulders, just as—

Wallace Carver appeared at the top of the stairs and froze in place. A deer in the headlights. *Roadkill*.

Mr Black grinned, showing bloody teeth. 'You should have kept running while you had the chance.'

Wallace couldn't disguise the nervous glance he cast over his shoulder, obviously calculating his chances of being able to flee, before he snapped the Defender hard against it. He had a white bandage, spotted with fresh blood, under his left arm and yet the shotgun's gaping muzzle was aimed unwaveringly at Mr Black's chest, centre mass, showing he meant business.

It was a good choice of weapon, too. Practically idiot proof *if* you had the balls to pull the trigger.

Mr Black studied Wallace's eyes. They were hard and focused into razor-edge slits. He was wounded and full of rage, but it wasn't enough to disguise his true fear.

'Where's my goddamn family?' Wallace seethed. 'Why are you doing this to us?'

And there it was. How could the man threaten when he didn't really want to kill? He wanted answers, not bloodshed. Never a good bargaining position.

Relishing the moment, Mr Black slipped the curved knife from his belt and settled it in his hand. He waved it slowly, allowing its polished surface to catch the light.

'Why don't I show you exactly where they are?' Mr Black grinned wider as he took a step forward.

'Fuck you!' Wallace yelled and squeezed the trigger.

The shotgun blast reverberated in the hallway and a deadly swarm of lead wasps tore giant holes in the walls and made chalk and pink-insulation clouds bloom.

Mr Black, although surprised, still had the lightning-quick instincts to abandon his attack and roll into the living room before the pellets could render his flesh.

A second violent blast quickly followed, tearing through the hall closet and removing a manhole-sized chunk of the doorway. The pellet spread was so wide that a large mirror above the butter-cream couch shattered into a million pieces.

Mr Black cursed and rolled deeper into the room to escape the flying shrapnel. In the same smooth movement, he slipped his knife back on to his belt and retrieved his gun.

He heard the distinct and guttural *click-clack* of a new round being chambered into Carver's shotgun and he waited, patiently giving his ears time to stop ringing and his full senses to return.

Aiming at the open doorway, elbows locked, he

focused on his breathing, bringing his pulse rate down to a calm level.

Carver just had to take one step into the room for it to be his last.

After a full minute had elapsed, Mr Black cautiously and silently made his way closer to the opening. With his ear to the wall, he listened for any movement, knowing the bus driver couldn't possibly understand the art of breathing. When he heard nothing, he rolled across the opening and aimed his gun down the stairs.

There was no need. Wallace Carver was gone.

CHAPTER 42

'You did the right thing.'

Inside the car, Wallace held on for dear life as Laurel pressed the accelerator to the floor. Her eyes were constantly flicking to the rear-view mirror, watching for any sign of the black SUV as she put as much distance between them and the condo as possible.

'He *would* have killed you,' Laurel continued. 'You know that, right?'

'Fucker moved like a ghost,' said Wallace. 'What the hell am I up against? This is madness.'

Laurel tapped the metal box sitting between them. 'Maybe this will have answers.'

Wallace glanced down at the box and then quickly looked away. It seemed too little for all he had endured.

'If it doesn't, I'll need to step up my game,' he said. 'Fuck baseball bats. If they want to play with knives, I'll need to come at them with something even worse.'

'You don't have the stomach for that,' said Laurel gently.

Wallace stared out the window. His face was hard. 'I do now,' he said.

CHAPTER 43

Mr Black stood in the living room and peered out the front window. His SUV was still in the driveway, which meant Carver's truck was trapped in the garage.

Curious.

No other vehicles were travelling on the quiet street and no nosy neighbours had rushed out to see what all the noise was about.

Desensitization of society, thought Mr Black, was a truly wonderful thing.

He removed his cellphone from his pocket, inserted the wireless earpiece into his left ear, and tapped an icon labelled *Scanner*. When the program launched, he opened the menu and double-checked that it was still monitoring Bellingham PD. When he clicked OK, the chatter of the local emergency band immediately came alive in his ear.

If anyone did report the gunshots, he would know instantly when the police were on their way.

An agitated thump drew Mr Black's attention away from the window. When he turned to face the dining room, the bound man in the wrought-iron chair eyed him warily.

Desmond Morris's normally handsome face was a mess: bloodshot eyes and a battered nose beneath a badly swollen and discoloured brow. He looked as though he had attempted to head butt an anvil.

Mr Black purposely ignored him a little longer as he crossed the room and snatched a discarded towel from the couch. He found a clean corner and pressed it into his mouth. The towel soaked up the blood from his lacerated tongue, but it was dry and uncomfortable.

He dropped the towel to the floor as he moved into the dining room and walked around the guard's chair. He examined the bonds and was amused by the pink fur-lined cuffs around the man's ankles. The cheap chain between the cuffs was broken, but his legs were still bound firmly to the chair by rope.

Morris's left knee was swollen to the size of a softball, battered most likely with the same blunt instrument that had been used on Mr Black's own skull. As a pain centre, the knee was an odd choice. There were larger nerve clusters in much easier-to-access places.

'This is quite a mess, Morris.'

His speech sounded slightly thicker, the edges of the consonants more rounded, less sharp, but he was relieved the injury to his tongue hadn't impaired his overall elocution. He had worked hard on his enunciation for years and prided himself on the clarity of his diction.

In his younger days, he had known a boy who spoke with a lisp. The boy had endured incredible torment from the other children before he set their foster home on fire and disappeared into the night. Everyone in the home died in their beds. Mr Black could recall their screams behind locked doors and bolted windows, but . . . strange, he could no longer remember the means of his own lucky escape.

Morris bristled and strained against the rope, making his muscles bulge and ripple. His lips were stretched so tightly over the red rubber ball that the flesh looked ready to split.

Mr Black flashed crimson teeth. He touched the back of the guard's head and flicked the steel buckle on the leather strap with his fingernail. 'Kinky.'

He loosened the strap and pulled the gag from Morris's mouth.

'Thank God,' said the guard. He moved his mouth in a circle and shifted his jaw from side to side. 'Untie me. We need to catch that fucker and peel the skin from his bones.'

Mr Black nodded agreeably. 'I love the sentiment.' He absently touched the back of his own bloody head. It was achingly tender. 'But there's one small hitch.'

'What?'

The man was irritated. Understandably so, but . . .

'I need to know what you told him first.'

214

Morris's face folded into a brutal snarl like a pitbull in the ring. He spat bloody phlegm on to the floor.

'I didn't say a goddamn thing. You know better than to ask me that.'

'I do, Morris, I do.' Mr Black couldn't keep the soft, condescending chuckle from his voice. 'But you know our friend? A stickler for details.'

'Fuck you, T-Bone.'

Mr Black sprang forward, his claw-like knife suddenly in his hand. The blade was turned around so that it curved downward and the needle-like tip quivered a fraction of an inch above the guard's wide, bulbous left eye.

'That name is dead,' he hissed through clenched teeth. 'You ought to know better.'

'Sorry, sorry, *Geesus!*'

The guard's eyes widened even further as Mr Black dipped the tip of the knife into his skin and carved a razor-thin line around his cheek.

Morris screamed, but more in anger than pain. 'What the fuck?'

'The cheek is the tastiest part of any animal,' said Mr Black casually. 'Did I neglect to teach you that?'

Morris bared his own bloody teeth. 'Cut me the fuck loose, you goddamn freak. You don't have the right to touch me.'

Mr Black guided the knife gently across the guard's face until he reached his neck. The man's thick carotid artery, pumped full of rich, oxygenated blood, stood out against his straining skin. The curved knife tip pierced the flesh above the artery. A tiny, opening incision. Morris barely flinched.

'What did you tell Carver?'

'Nothing. I told you already.'

'If you were uncooperative, why did he leave you alive?'

''Cause he's a goddamn civilian pussy.'

Mr Black tilted his head in contemplation. 'How did he even know you existed?'

'How the fuck should I know?'

Mr Black slowly moved his head in the other direction. 'Interesting question, though, isn't it? How *did* he know? You were not to have any contact with him.'

'I didn't. I swear.'

Mr Black glanced at the floor, distracted by another thought. 'Is that his blood on the towels?'

'Yeah, I clipped him when he nabbed me at Paul's.'

'Paul? The detective?'

'Yes.'

'Your lover?'

Morris wrinkled his nose. 'Just someone I was fucking.'

'Your lover?' repeated Mr Black. He pressed the knife a little deeper.

Morris sighed rather than groaned, more frustrated than frightened. 'Yes. OK? You happy?'

Mr Black nodded, but it wasn't in response to the guard's concession. 'He came back for the cop.' His eyes and voice drifted. 'That makes sense. Maybe the accident with the van . . . he guessed something wasn't right . . .'

His eyes flicked back to the guard. 'Is he still alive?'

'Paul?' Morris shrugged. 'I don't know. Maybe.'

'That could be a problem.'

'I can take care of it.'

'Really?' Mr Black emphasized his incredulity.

Morris sighed again, heavier. 'I *was* taking care of it before Carver busted in.'

Mr Black nodded. 'A lone bus driver against a United States Marine with how many kills to his name?'

Morris sneered. 'He laid you out, t—'

His words were cut off as Mr Black's knife sliced through his large artery and across his throat. The man's heart, sensing the massive trauma, pumped furiously in panicked response, a futile gesture to seal the fatal wound.

Mr Black jumped back to avoid the spurting arterial spray, angry at himself for the impulsive loss of control. Despite all his hours of meditation and inner reflection, he was still a helpless victim to raw emotion.

And he didn't even get to ask his last question: *Who was helping Carver?*

While Desmond Morris bled out, Mr Black walked through the condo. When one overlooked the bullet holes, blood spatters and shattered mirror, it was actually decorated quite beautifully. Sparse, yet comfortable.

In its own way, it was not unlike a barracks. Larger, naturally, but everything in its place. No clutter. No sentimentality. Clean, cold and efficient. Mr Black could see himself in just such a place if he ever settled down.

Upstairs in the master bedroom, he studied the mess. The room had been ransacked, but in a panicked frenzy rather than a controlled search. No part of the room appeared untouched, which meant Wallace hadn't found whatever he was looking for.

Mr Black smiled appreciatively. Morris must have played him.

It was the extension of an idea their sergeant had when they were all first in the sand. Morris had begun his obsession with tattooing the snake on his back and the Sarge had suggested he incorporate GPS co-ordinates into the design. That way, he reasoned, if Morris was ever captured and needed a break from the inevitable torture they all knew would be their due, he could break down and reveal that a set of co-ordinates pinpointed a secret stash of stolen treasure or weapons, whatever he deemed his enemy craved more desperately.

It became a game, something to occupy their down time and prevent boredom from finding a home. Morris's tattoo contained the co-ordinates to six secret locations across three countries, each one equipped with enough tripwire explosives to obliterate a small unit and blow a hole in the sand large enough to be noticed by orbiting satellite.

It was a pity, then, after all that effort, that Morris wasn't the one who ended up in the interrogator's chair. At least he had remembered the basics and tried to buy some time by leading the bus driver on a frustrating chase through his underwear drawer.

Mr Black was about to leave the bedroom when he caught a glimpse of himself in the full-length, oak-framed mirror. His face and hands were splattered with blood. He walked into the adjoining bathroom and washed. The bathroom was large with an oversized glass shower that could easily accommodate two people, and something you rarely saw outside of Europe – a bidet.

When he returned to the full-length mirror, Mr Black adjusted his tie, making sure the strings were of equal length. He could still see faint splashes of blood on his clothes, but that was one of the beautiful things about black cloth. You had to really look close for bloodstains to matter.

A pair of greasy handprints on the mirror bothered him. The rest of the house was kept so clean. He stepped closer to the mirror and examined the marks. The ring finger on the left hand showed an absence of smudge, precisely where a wedding band would sit.

Mr Black positioned his fingers on top of the handprints and pressed down. The mirror clicked and swung open.

Mr Black frowned. Morris had talked.

Inside the hidden compartment, stacks of money lined the shelves. But they appeared untouched. *Curious.* Surely, if the bus driver had discovered this, he would have been tempted? How could he not?

Perhaps Morris had told the truth after all.

Mr Black flipped through one of the stacks of bills and conducted a quick mental calculation. He nodded his approval. Morris had been frugal but not anal. That's something he wouldn't have expected.

He returned the bound stack of bills to the shelf. Morris wouldn't be needing it, but in the meantime it was in as safe a place as any.

He moved to the next shelf and picked up the Zippo lighter. He recognized it. It didn't belong to Morris.

Curiouser and curiouser.

He swung the mirror back into place, grabbed a T-shirt off the floor and wiped away the greasy handprints.

When he was done, he headed for the stairs. He still had work to do.

CHAPTER 44

Laurel drove Wallace out of Bellingham and into the country. Soon, they left the blacktop and bumped down a gravel road lined with trees. A few miles later, the road dead ended on the flat brow of a steep hill with an impressive view. Laurel tapped a button to engage the vehicle's four-wheel drive and turned on to a perilous dirt trail that wound its way into the bosom of a lush green valley.

At the bottom, a small log cabin sat atop a stone foundation near the banks of a narrow creek.

'It was my grandfather's,' said Laurel. 'I've always found it to be a peaceful retreat.'

Wallace studied the rolling hills surrounding them.

'No place to land your plane,' he said.

Laurel grinned. 'That's why it's peaceful. This is where I come when I'm not working.'

She parked in front of a detached garage and climbed out. Wallace followed her across a roofed porch and through the front door. The door hadn't been locked.

'Trusting,' he said.

'Good neighbours,' she replied. 'Robbing me would be the same as robbing them. We look out for each other here.'

Inside the house, Laurel placed the metal box and laptop on the kitchen table. Wallace followed with his silent offering of a lone pair of military dog tags.

'It's something,' Laurel said.

Wallace shrugged and shifted his gaze away from hers, not wanting to show his disappointment and dismay at having left the most valuable clue behind.

Laurel walked over to a nearby wall phone and reached out for it just as it rang. She smiled as she answered.

'It's OK,' she said. 'He's a friend. Yes, I'm sure. Everything is fine.'

She hung up and turned to Wallace. Her smile was wide and infectious with delight.

'Told you,' she said. 'Good neighbours.'

Wallace tried to smile back, but the corners of his mouth barely bent. Laurel moved back to the table and opened the laptop.

By closing the lid without shutting it down, Wallace had simply placed the computer into sleep mode. When Laurel opened the lid again, the laptop quickly returned to life and displayed the last thing Wallace had seen.

Laurel studied the manipulated photograph, clicking the eye icon to reveal and hide the top layer.

222

'This is nice work,' she said.

Wallace glared at her.

'I mean,' she added quickly, 'that it isn't amateurish. A lot of people fool around with Photoshop, but it's usually pretty easy to spot the fakes. Someone took their time with this one. Someone with skills.'

'Meaning what?' asked Wallace.

'Did the guard strike you as an artistic soul?'

Wallace shrugged. 'Too narcissistic. There wasn't a single painting in his house. Just mirrors.'

'Let me try something.'

Laurel moved the pointer up to the program's menu and down a long list of items until she found the one she was looking for. When she clicked it, a new window opened. It revealed detailed information about the image, including the name of its creator.

'Vanity, thy name is . . . J. Ronson.' Laurel looked up at Wallace. 'Does that name mean anything to you?'

Wallace bit back a curse. 'None of these people – none of these names – mean anything to me. Not a goddamn thing.'

Laurel's eyes softened, but as though she could sense that sympathy would only weaken his barely held together resolve, she pushed the laptop aside and picked up the metal box. She pursed her lips as she studied the small lock.

'I have some tools in the garage,' she said finally. 'Be right back.'

Wallace watched Laurel leave before he pulled out one of the sturdy kitchen chairs and sat down. He rested his elbows on the table and placed his head in his hands. He was so damn tired, but all he could think about was Alicia, Fred and Alex.

His loved ones needed him to find them. They were counting on it. Believing in it. And unless he died trying, he couldn't fail them.

CHAPTER 45

When Mr Black answered the text message on his phone, he was naked and glistening from the shower. Before rinsing in water as cold as the tap could deliver, Mr Black had cleansed himself in scalding heat, allowing the entire room to fill with steam and relax the wrinkles from the suit that hung on the bathroom door.

He had felt the blood and daily grime ooze from his pores, leaving him pure, untouched and alive.

He sat on the bidet and reinserted the earpiece as he tapped his reply. The condo was beginning to feel like home and he wondered what the presence of a dead man in the dining room would do to the selling price. He considered the hidden stash behind the mirror. Perhaps he could buy it with Morris's own money.

The thought made him smile.

Entering the bedroom, Mr Black studied the piles of silk boxers littering the floor. Despite his muscular bulk, Morris had a relatively slim waist. Mr Black had never worn silk, but it looked much too tempting to resist.

He picked up a pair of purple boxers with a button fly, slipped them on and gasped at the sensual caress of the material. It felt . . . wonderful.

Why wasn't everything made of silk?

He retrieved his suit from the bathroom. The material now felt rough in his hands and although the wrinkles were noticeably diminished, the stains looked worse – rehydrated and fresh.

His cellphone buzzed again. He read the message and frowned. This game was becoming tiresome. He wished Wallace Carver had stuck around so that he could have ended it once and for all. Not everyone would have been pleased, but at least it would have been over and they could start something new and lucrative.

Glancing down at the package on the bed, Mr Black appeased his disappointment with the knowledge that at least he wouldn't be arriving at his next destination empty-handed.

CHAPTER 46

They opened the box.

It was surprisingly easy. A heavy wood chisel, a hammer and a single solid whack in the right spot split the lock in half. If doctoring became too dull, Laurel had a future in safe cracking.

Inside, they found military discharge papers, a series of newspaper clippings and two photographs. Laurel opened the discharge papers first. She read them and frowned.

'What's up?' asked Wallace.

'These are for a general discharge.'

'So?'

'A Marine with his number of kills should have received an honorary discharge for meritorious service. A general discharge doesn't fit with his tattoo.'

'The tattoo also showed a large number of revenge kills,' said Wallace. 'Maybe they weren't all by the book.'

Laurel shook her head. 'If he stepped over the line, he would have been court-martialled and received a dishonorable discharge. He would never have been allowed to work for Border Patrol or any other government office. Even McDonald's wouldn't hire him as they're a government supplier.'

'So the papers don't fit the man,' said Wallace.

'Not even close,' said Laurel.

Next, Laurel laid the two photographs on the table. The first one showed a small platoon of young men. They were posed in full artillery gear against a background of desolate sand. All the men were scowling fiercely for the camera, but twenty of the faces were marked by a red X.

Wallace tapped the photograph. 'Morris had at least that number of crosses on his back.'

'Morbid keepsake,' said Laurel. 'His platoon obviously saw a lot of action and he lost a number of friends, but to cross them out like this . . .' She stroked each X with the tip of her finger. 'It's like a countdown. He was keeping track of the X, watching it creep closer to his own day of reckoning.'

'Don't romanticize him,' Wallace scolded. 'The man's a killer. My guess is he was just keeping score so that he knew how many insurgents to kill to balance the scales.'

Laurel allowed Wallace's reprimand to slide by without comment and turned to the second photograph. It showed a smaller unit of a half-dozen men gathered around an armoured Humvee. Desmond Morris was standing by the rear tailgate with sleeves rolled, muscles glistening, a big-ass, grenade-launching rifle in his hand. He was smiling, and unlike the pantomime warrior scowl of the other photo, this was a smile of pure joy. He was truly happy to be where he was.

'Like I said before,' said Laurel as she studied the photograph, 'men like him don't quit. He lived and breathed, ate and shit being a Marine. Trust me, I met lots of them. The Corps meant everything to him.'

'Could he have become disillusioned with how long the war was taking?' asked Wallace.

Laurel shook her head. 'Not a soldier like him. He does his duty regardless of who's giving the orders or who's in the White House. Each tour, if anything, serves to make him stronger and deadlier.'

'Christ,' said Wallace wearily. 'How did my family come to cross his path?'

Laurel opened the newspaper clippings and began to read. They were reports from Afghanistan and Iraq, most of them mentioning casualties from landmines and ambushes. Like most articles concerning the war that made their way into the mainstream press, they were so light on details you could practically see the government censors' red pen.

The most recent articles were at the bottom of the pile. Laurel showed one *Washington Post* clipping to Wallace.

BAGHDAD, 26 April – Five American soldiers were killed in a roadside ambush

Saturday in Iraq. A report that three soldiers were also taken captive has been denied by the US military.

The five soldiers were killed during routine patrol outside the volatile northern city of Mosul, the military said in a statement.

An Iraqi police lieutenant-colonel in Mosul, who declined to be named, said he had received reports that al Qaeda rebels captured three American soldiers during the attack.

In Washington, a Marine Corps spokesman at the Pentagon denied the claim.

'We take such allegations very seriously,' said Maj. Douglas Armstrong. 'But nothing has been substantiated at this time. We're mourning our dead and continuing our investigation.'

Mosul and the surrounding Nineveh province are the last remaining bastion of al Qaeda and other Sunni Arab insurgent groups.

The soldiers' names were withheld pending notification of their families, officials said.

'The last cluster on Morris's back had six crosses,' said Wallace. 'But this report says five were killed.'

Laurel handed him the next clipping. It was shorter than the first.

WASHINGTON, 2 May – Two captive American soldiers were rescued from an al Qaeda encampment in Hamam al-Alil on Friday, the US military said.

'An elite squad raided the encampment shortly before dawn,' said Maj. Derek Chang, a spokesman for the US military in Mosul and surrounding Nineveh province.

'Initial reports have verified the classified operation was a complete success.'

Maj. Chang was unavailable to provide more details on how these soldiers came to be in the hands of al Qaeda. All calls to the Pentagon were also met with a refusal to comment.

'Two were rescued,' said Laurel. 'That leaves one from the initial three unaccounted for.'

'So the mission wasn't a complete success,' added Wallace.

Laurel picked up the discharge papers and looked at the date.

'Desmond Morris received his discharge papers six weeks later.'

'Which means what?' asked Wallace.

'I would guess some kind of cover-up,' said Laurel. 'I don't think that rescue mission was authorized.

The military doesn't usually downplay its successes. Daring rescues are a recruiter's wet dream. Morris and what was left of his unit must have gone rogue. In doing so they rescued two of their men, but probably cost the life of the third. The military couldn't let them get away with disobeying orders, but at the same time they would have admired the bravado of the mission. How could they admit they didn't have the balls to launch a rescue for their own men? It probably seemed best to have the offending soldiers kicked out on a general discharge instead of a public court martial and the brig.'

Wallace rubbed his face in his hands. 'OK, so he's a disgraced hero. How does that help us?'

Laurel held up the group photo. 'We now know who he was most loyal to and would refuse to name under torture. When it came to backs against the wall, it wasn't his country or the Corps. It was his unit. We just need names.'

'You can find them?' asked Wallace.

Laurel's mouth twitched and her eyes hardened in concentration. 'I think so. We know Morris didn't carry out this rescue mission on his own. The members of his unit who joined him would have likely faced the same discipline and been discharged at the same time, probably the same day. I'll make some calls. I still know people who owe me favours.'

'What can I do?' asked Wallace.

Laurel's eyes softened again. 'Get some rest,' she said. 'I'll wake you when I have what we need.'

'Maybe I should make coffee,' Wallace suggested.

Laurel placed a hand on his arm and squeezed. 'Try to get some sleep,' she said. 'You've lost blood and you'll need your strength. Trust me.'

Wallace didn't think sleep was possible as he made his way into the living room. A wood-burning fireplace was nestled in the corner, ghostly remains of ancient soot trails curling from its mouth to climb up a face of wonderfully mismatched river rock. However, in place of a roaring log fire, Laurel had filled the cold hearth with a small electric heater. Its three coiled-wire bars glowed red and gave off just enough heat to combat the chill.

Wallace lay down on an old threadbare couch near the fire and pulled a woollen blanket up to his neck. His eyelids had barely brushed each other before he was lost to slumber.

CHAPTER 47

The private five-acre parcel crowned the summit of a steep hill within a mile of the Pacific Ocean. A partially constructed, two-storey house sat in the middle, surrounded on three sides by dense clusters of windswept and rain-battered cedar.

The front side had been logged a quarter way down the hillside to open up the spectacular westerly view. The logs had been milled on-site and used to build the house. Two benefits in one.

On Mr Black's cellphone, the satellite image of the clearing resembled an old-fashioned keyhole.

The house's sprawling front deck was designed for lazy afternoons. A place to settle into your favourite Adirondack chair, share a drink with a lover or friend and take the time to absorb the sheer majesty of nature's ever-changing canvas. From this vantage point, panoramic sunsets, more spellbinding than any Fourth of July fireworks, were enough to make even a devout atheist believe in God.

Today, however, the ocean was invisible beneath a heavy blanket of fog. As the Lincoln crested the hill and bounced along a slippery dirt road in four-wheel drive, a cold dampness splattered it's windshield like fat, skinless bugs. Behind the wipers, Mr Black studied the house. It was definitely in worse shape than on his previous visit, a mere eight months before.

The main floor showed the concern and attention to detail that its owner had planned to lavish on the whole structure. The lower half was finished in natural red cedar with large picture windows and matching trim. Anchored beneath every window was a cedar flowerbox so that from inside the house, no room would be missing the sight of nature's ever-changing colour and ever-lasting life.

The owner had completed the ground-level first, so that he and his family had a place to live while he worked on the upper floor.

The construction was solid, but now the flower-boxes sat unattended and barren. The entire second storey was unfinished. Bare, unprotected walls were grey with damp and streaked with menacing fingers of black and green mould. Large holes covered in rotting particle board marked where additional windows and sliding glass doors had been intended to be installed.

The ribs of an upper deck, offering an even superior view to the lower, protruded from the walls. But they were simply rough beams with no supporting slats to allow anyone to stand or sit.

Mr Black shook his head. Too much time had passed. The whole floor would have to be stripped back to its studs and started again. Even that might not be enough if the damp had seeped down to the lower quarters. What a waste.

He parked the Lincoln beside a burgundy clone in front of the framed skeleton of what had once promised to be a detached double garage. Without a roof, the garage couldn't even keep off the rain.

When he climbed out, the screen door at the rear of the house clattered with the wind. Loose. Unsecured.

The owner must have been watching him drive up, but didn't bother to wait and make sure he was alone.

Mr Black shook his head again. In the sand, the man had been paranoid about security. It was one of the things he admired most. Locks and bolts and a well-oiled gun. Lessons of survival. Lessons to live by.

He stomped up a small flight of wooden stairs. Blistered paint flecked off under his boots to expose rot underneath. He scraped the mud off his soles on a jagged metal grate anchored to the top step and opened the door.

Sergeant Douglas Gallagher sat at a round kitchen table, a mug of coffee cradled in his distinctive right hand. The middle finger had been severed at the second knuckle; the ring finger beside it, at the first; the pinkie was missing entirely.

'Fuckers missed the most important one,' Gallagher had said when Mr Black first found him. His hand had been bloody and raw with stark white bone jutting from ripped flesh. He had wiggled his trigger finger. 'Give me a fucking gun.'

Gallagher's left hand was now out of sight under the table, but his arm was moving restlessly back and forth, giving his nether regions a nervous scratch.

Mr Black barely recognized him. He had lost too much weight. His hair was thinning in an odd, clump-like pattern and had turned a shade closer to puddle grey than the smooth coal black he was known for. He wore a two-inch square adhesive bandage on his neck and his face was puffy, retaining water, the skin riddled with an unhealthy pallor.

Mr Black sniffed the air; tasted a sour whiskey tang.

His sergeant looked old and tired – except for those eyes. Blue-green glacial ice and nearly as hard, they challenged him to comment.

Mr Black said nothing as he removed a package from under his arm and tossed it on to the table. Wrapped in brown butcher's paper and tied with string, it was a flat square the size of a large pizza.

'What's this?' asked Gallagher.

'A present.' Mr Black placed the Zippo lighter on top. 'This, too.'

Gallagher brought his scratching hand up from beneath the table to reveal a massive .44 Magnum Desert Eagle pistol. The Israeli-made weapon had enough stopping power to make regulation-issue body armour as useless as plastic wrap.

Mr Black smiled thinly. *Still paranoid.* The eyes didn't lie.

Gallagher laid the gun on the table and picked up the lighter. He rubbed its smooth gunmetal surface between his fingers before flicking it open and thumbing the flint wheel. It sparked and flared with a gentle orange flame.

'I lost this during the last mission,' he said. 'Where did you get it?'

'Morris's.'

Gallagher's eyes narrowed. 'Huh.'

'He always was a sentimental bastard.'

'Was?' asked Gallagher.

Mr Black nodded at the brown package.

Gallagher's eyes narrowed further as he tugged the string's neatly tied bow. The waxed paper opened in slow motion like a blossoming flower.

'Jesus Christ!'

Gallagher leapt to his feet, spilling his coffee as he scrambled back from the table.

'Morris's tattoo,' explained Mr Black.

Gallagher's lips curled into a snarl, but he remained mute. His eyes were wide and angry and, if possible, even harder than before.

That alone was worth it, thought Mr Black. His old sergeant looked alive again.

He produced the guard's cellphone from his pocket. It was a perfect match to his own. He laid it on the table beside the ragged patch of skin, careful to avoid the spilled coffee.

'Nothing to lead back to you,' he said. 'Clean. Unsentimental. What I do best.'

Gallagher swallowed, his gaze transfixed by the tattoo. It had shrunk since Mr Black removed it from Morris's muscular frame. Headless and without the bony ridges of the man's spine to wrap around, it now resembled the severed tentacle of a mythical sea monster rather than a snake.

'Yeah.' Gallagher swallowed drily. 'What you do best.'

Mr Black smiled. That's all he ever wanted. A simple show of appreciation.

Gallagher moved back to the table and righted his coffee cup. He couldn't take his eyes off the slab of rendered flesh.

'I can't believe that bloody driver not only made it back across the border, but bested Morris, too. He was a damn fine Marine.'

'Wallace Carver had help,' said Mr Black.

'Oh? Who?'

'I don't know yet . . .' Mr Black reflexively reached up to touch the back of his head. The bump was prominent and still tender. 'But I will.'

Gallagher snorted, but it was less out of disgust than an effort to clear his nasal passages.

'How did this fucker even find out about Morris? He was ordered not to have contact.'

Mr Black told Gallagher about the police detective and his theory that Wallace must have tracked Petersen down only to arrive at the same time Morris was attempting to tie up loose ends. While monitoring the scanner, he had heard some interesting information. He knew it was only a matter of time before the police arrived at the condo and discovered what was left of its owner.

'So what's his next move?' asked Gallagher.

'Someone called 9-1-1 from the detective's house and left the phone off the hook. I assume it was Carver. He wanted Petersen alive. That's his only lead.'

Gallagher nodded and reached out a hand to hover a fraction of an inch above the frightening square of flesh.

'Morris loved that fucking tattoo,' he said. 'Hate to think of him being buried without it.'

'He should've held on tighter, then,' said Mr Black.

A reluctant smile fluttered across Gallagher's dry lips. 'You're a sick bastard.'

'You should know.'

Gallagher's smile vanished. 'I don't want Carver hanging around down here. He's already caused too much trouble.'

'I could stake out the hospital,' said Mr Black. 'He's bound to—'

'No,' said Gallagher sharply. 'We make him go where we choose.' He furled his brow and curled his lips into a sneer. 'It's time to get him back on to the path we set. I want him rotting in jail. Alone and without hope. I want him to fucking suffer. To never know—'

A noise from the other room made Gallagher blanch. He pointed at the parcel. 'Put that the fuck away. Quick.'

Mr Black carefully refolded the brown waxed paper and retied the string. He had just finished when a strikingly handsome woman entered the kitchen.

Mr Black had seen her before, but never up close. She had long curly hair the colour of a sunset.

CHAPTER 48

Wallace stood alone in the middle of the deserted shopping mall. His voice was hoarse from shouting; his ears rang from the devastating hollowness of no reply.

A giggle. Footsteps. The shadow of two boys running down an empty corridor.

'Wait!'

He raced after them, reached the end. T-junction. Two more corridors. He swivelled his head. Left and right. Both deserted.

Another giggle.

Behind him.

He turned.

He was no longer in the mall.

Two boys, not his sons, were sitting together on a familiar vinyl bench seat. They had some kind of comic book in their hands. The interior illustrations were black and white. The writing on the cover was Japanese.

Other seats were filled with passengers: tourists, mostly, but also daily commuters returning from work.

Wallace turned around. He was driving the bus.

The windshield wipers were moving rapidly. An unexpected storm had stripped leaves and branches from the ancient cedars in historic Stanley Park and turned the gutters into churning rivers.

He had been reassigned from his usual route in North Vancouver to help with increased summer traffic across Burrard Inlet. He didn't mind the change, although he was always nervous during the first trip on an unfamiliar route.

He drove the #257 Horseshoe Bay Express that shuttled commuters and tourists from downtown Vancouver through Stanley Park and across Lions Gate Bridge to West Vancouver. After a quick stop at the popular Park Royal Mall, he would carry a full load to Horseshoe Bay where BC Ferries would sail his passengers to either the tranquil Sunshine Coast, nearby Bowen Island or across the Strait of Georgia to distant Vancouver Island.

He drove past the turn-off to Vancouver Aquarium and headed into a narrow three-lane tunnel of trees that led to the seventy-year-old suspension bridge. As one of only two routes across Burrard Inlet, the centre lane of the bridge needed to change direction several times per hour to accommodate traffic patterns. At its most congested, it could take over twenty minutes to cross the five-thousand-foot span. When traffic was light, it took less than two.

Wallace kept to the right as traffic was heavy and the rain was fierce. The green light above the centre lane was flashing, indicating that direction of traffic was about to change. Wallace checked his mirrors.

Cars in the centre lane were begrudgingly falling in behind him, clearing the way for the imminent rush of oncoming traffic.

The light in the centre lane turned red and for a moment there was some elbow room. An entire lane empty of traffic on his left. While to his right, a narrow sidewalk, short concrete barrier and metal railing were all that separated him from a deadly two-hundred-foot drop to the busy shipping lanes below. Yellow phone boxes blurred past – a recent pilot project that offered direct access to a Crisis Centre for those dozens who annually considered the final leap.

Wallace glanced in the mirrors again. His heart skipped and began to race.

A small red car was roaring up on his left, taking advantage of the empty lane, its windshield wipers moving so fast they were a blur. Behind it, a dark SUV had made the same dangerous move, egging the little car on and giving it no room to fall back.

Wallace quickly glanced forward. Two lanes of bumper-to-bumper traffic were bearing down like an invading army of snarling, super-charged mechanical beasts.

The little red car wouldn't make it. It didn't have the muscle to fight the wind, the rain and the rapidly narrowing gap.

Wallace couldn't brake. In this weather, with a hundred impatient drivers chewing each other's bumpers, a multi-car pile-up was a certainty.

Wallace shoved open his side window and stuck

out his arm. He waved his hand frantically, trying to warn the car to brake and pull in behind him. The driver didn't notice or couldn't see him through the blinding rain.

Suddenly, the driver downshifted and the little car's engine squealed in protest as it attempted a final burst of speed to squeeze by Wallace's massive front bumper.

'Hold on!' Wallace screamed to his passengers.

He pumped his brakes and felt the bus lurch, but it was too late. He saw the two occupants of the car as it swerved in front of him. For a moment the picture froze in high-definition clarity. A woman, her face as white as death itself, clutched the steering wheel. In the back seat was a young, dark-haired girl, her mouth stretched in a terrified scream, pink tonsils vibrating at the back of her throat.

The small red car crunched against his front bumper, but it didn't have the momentum to stop from being swallowed whole. The front of the bus lifted off the ground, its tyres bursting and massive rims spinning like buzz saws as the two vehicles crashed through the barrier and slid over the edge of the ancient bridge.

Wallace woke up screaming – the nightmare, the too-real memory, still playing in his head.

CHAPTER 49

The redhead didn't acknowledge Mr Black. With her head held low, chin tilted to bosom, she glanced at the table, walked to the sink and rinsed a cloth under the tap.

When she returned, she wiped the spilled coffee and lifted the brown paper package.

'Don't open that,' said Gallagher. 'It's private.'

'I'll put it by the sink,' she said. 'Does your friend want coffee?'

Mr Black tilted his head, trying to see the woman's face beneath her long, curly bangs. She wasn't young, but time had been kind to her. The wrinkles around her eyes appeared to be mostly from laughter and her delicate pale skin had been jealously protected from the sun. Her lips were a cupid's bow of pink rosebud and yet something about them appeared unyielding and distractingly fierce. He glanced over at the fresh bandage on Gallagher's neck and decided that although the woman hid her teeth behind a coral veil, he imagined they could be deceptively sharp.

Suddenly aware that the woman was studying him with the same intensity, Mr Black smiled. Not to be friendly. And he could tell from the slight tremor in the soft square of skin between her eyes, that she understood.

Her eyes were as green and untrusting as a cat's.

'If you don't want coffee—'

'I do,' he said. 'Black.'

The woman retrieved a fresh cup from the cupboard and filled it to within a hairline of the brim. Despite its fullness, none of the coffee spilled over the lip when she placed the cup in front of him.

A challenge?

Mr Black lifted the cup to his lips and took a long sip. He didn't spill a drop either.

The woman filled Gallagher's cup – her fingers gripping the handle of the glass decanter so tightly, the knuckles turned white – before returning the pot to its burner. Mr Black admired her murderous restraint, but found it curiously up-setting that his old sergeant didn't seem to notice, or care, just how dangerous this woman could be.

'Leave us,' said Gallagher.

The woman hesitated. 'I was hoping to—'

'Later!'

Gallagher's lips curled and he made a noise in the back of his throat that reminded Mr Black of a feral dog that had attacked them during a mission in the sand. The dog had sprung from nowhere and savagely ripped out Corporal Andrew Penner's throat before Mr Black had done the same to it.

The woman left the room with her head hung low once more.

Mr Black raised an inquisitive eyebrow.

'I don't know,' said Gallagher irritably. 'She keeps moaning on. The sooner I get rid, the better.'

Mr Black sipped his coffee, his gaze drifting across the table. Something was missing.

He glanced over to the sink. The brown package was there. He had watched the woman move it and sensed her concern over the uncomfortable feel of what lay within.

He hadn't noticed her pocket Morris's phone.

Her hands had been steady. She wasn't scared. She was cunning.

CHAPTER 50

Laurel rushed into the room, her eyes wide with alarm. Wallace sat on the edge of the couch, his back hunched, wiping a sheen of cold sweat off his brow.

'Are you OK?' she asked. 'You were screaming.'

Wallace looked up. 'Yeah, sorry. Bad dream.'

'Your wife and sons?'

Wallace shrugged. 'That was part of it.'

'It'll be the stress,' said Laurel. 'It digs up our darkest stuff.'

'And it does a damn fine job, too.' Wallace sighed and rubbed the sleep out of his eyes. 'You find anything?'

'Come into the kitchen,' she said. 'I got what I could.'

On the kitchen table, Laurel spread out five sheets of paper fresh from the printer. Each one showed a grainy black-and-white mug shot of a former Marine, along with discharge dates and other relevant details.

She slid one of the printouts to the side. It showed the border guard they had left tied up in his condo.

'That's Desmond Morris,' she said. 'We already know his story. He was part of a three-man unit that went rogue.'

'Only three men?' Wallace asked. 'Against an al Qaeda encampment?'

'That's how we know it wasn't authorized,' said Laurel. 'The military brass can't do anything small scale. This trio had guts.'

'Or insanity.'

Laurel shrugged and slid a second sheet to the same side. It showed a young man with a head so round it could have been a soccer ball. 'Michael Shepherd, explosives expert. He and Morris were close friends, but he died on a construction site in New Jersey six months ago. The official investigation ruled it an accidental detonation during a demolition, but my contact says he wouldn't be surprised if Shepherd triggered it on purpose. He took the discharge hard.'

Laurel slid a third sheet over to join the other two. The man's face was so densely black, and the quality of the printout so poor, it was difficult to make out anything but the whites of his eyes.

'Tennyson Bone was the third member of the rogue unit and, from all accounts, its main instigator. His list of confirmed kills is impressive, although I'm told that's not the whole story. My source tells me they shouldn't have cut this one loose. He even scares the generals.'

Wallace pulled the sheet closer and took a hard

look. 'This could be the man who showed up at Morris's condo. Does he live around here?'

'His address is listed as Chicago, but mail has been bouncing back to the Corps. They have no idea where he is.'

Laurel pointed to the two remaining printouts.

'These are the Marines who were rescued. On the left is Lance Corporal James Ronson. He was a communications specialist. More geek than killer, but essential. Without him, your unit is deaf, dumb and blind. He would have made a prize catch for al Qaeda.' She paused. 'On the right is the unit's leader, Sergeant Douglas Gallagher. He would have taken his capture as a personal insult. From what I could gather, he sounds like the type of man who would save the last bullet for himself rather than be taken alive.'

'Why were those two kicked out of the Corps?' asked Wallace. 'They couldn't have disobeyed orders if they were being held prisoner.'

'It's what happened after,' said Laurel; 'the part that didn't make the newspaper.'

'Which was?'

'My contact says everything is sealed away, but he skimmed the reports before they were buried.' She grinned. 'The generals treat him like a butler, but there's not much he doesn't see or hear. During and following the rescue, unofficial estimates put the number of dead in the encampment at close to fifty. Unfortunately, not all of them were combatants.'

'What does that mean?' asked Wallace.

'These men went on a killing spree and it didn't matter who crossed their path. If you weren't a Marine, you were dead. Men, women and children were slaughtered, even livestock. My source estimated that less than a dozen of those killed were al Qaeda. There is no official estimate since some of the bodies were rigged with explosives to take out anybody who tried to move them later.'

'Christ,' said Wallace. 'They pissed off the wrong Marines.'

'Nobody would weep for the insurgents,' said Laurel, 'but the villagers don't have a choice. Most of them aren't protecting al Qaeda because they want to. It's purely a matter of survival.'

'And none of this made the papers,' said Wallace.

'Not a peep. If it did, those five men would never have been discharged. The Corps buried it fast and deep and as quietly as possible.'

Wallace moved the five sheets of paper around. He placed the dead man and the border guard to one side. They didn't have a current address for Tennyson Bone, but Wallace was fairly sure he had to be the armed man who appeared unexpectedly at the foot of Morris's stairs.

He tapped the printout of Lance Corporal James Ronson.

'J. Ronson,' he said. 'He created the fake photo.'

'Looks like it,' said Laurel.

'But Gallagher's the unit leader? The one they're all loyal to?'

Laurel nodded. 'Does *his* name mean anything to you? Anything at all?'

'Nothing,' said Wallace. 'I wish to hell it did.' He sighed wearily. 'Do we have an address for either of these two?'

'Sergeant Gallagher has a post-office box. It's in Washington state, so we know he's nearby. I'm still trying to track down a residential address. It must be rural.'

'And the geek?'

'Less than five miles away. He inherited a house from his parents in Happy Valley, but my contact says he's pretty messed up. If he hadn't been kicked out with the others, he likely would have been eased out on a medical discharge.'

Wallace bristled. 'I need to fill in the gaps and find out where Alicia and my boys are. This geek's involved and he may be an easier nut to crack than that bastard Morris.'

'Not necessarily,' said Laurel. 'He was being held by al Qaeda, remember? My contact says both he and Gallagher were tortured – quite brutally.'

'Then he'll be softened up,' snapped Wallace.

He pushed back from the table, his features sharpened by an angry scowl. He scanned the table and picked up the hammer and chisel that Laurel had used to open the metal box.

'This time,' Wallace said angrily, 'I'll do more than bruise bones. And if this one doesn't talk, I'll carve out his fucking heart.'

CHAPTER 51

Mr Black excused himself from the table and headed to the lone bathroom which was set off a narrow corridor at the rear of the house. He passed through the living room with its large picture windows positioned to take advantage of the view.

A floor-to-ceiling stone fireplace with a polished redwood mantel dominated one corner of the open area. In pride of place on the mantel, a silver-framed photograph showed a smiling woman and a beautiful baby girl. The photo was black and white, but both females shared the same large, baby-seal eyes.

Before the hallway, a wide open-riser staircase travelled nowhere, its climb blocked by an over-sized trapdoor in the ceiling. The hinged door was made of rough, unpainted plywood and secured with a padlock.

Mr Black walked around the stairs to reach the bathroom. He knocked on the door. A sharp intake of breath from inside was followed by the sounds of frantic shuffling.

Mr Black leaned against the jamb. Calm.

Relaxed. A visiting shadow. Player of games. Nothing more.

'That phone won't work,' he said through the door. 'The keypad is secured by a password. Pain, really. I prefer biometrics, myself.'

The woman didn't answer.

Mr Black thought about the phone, about what the woman could do with it. Without the password, she couldn't dial out, send email or texts. She could access some of the applications, but a GPS module or police scanner wouldn't do her much good trapped in a bathroom.

He hesitated.

The phone had a browser for the Internet. It used a touchscreen keyboard, which was separate from the keypad. The virtual keyboard wasn't secured.

Mr Black stepped back and kicked open the door. It didn't take much.

The woman was sitting on the toilet with the phone in her hand.

No pretense. No apology.

Mr Black snatched the phone away from her and glanced at the screen. It showed the keypad, locked and useless.

Disappointment was etched on the woman's face despite a defiant attempt at concealment.

'Worth a try,' he said. 'But Gallagher is the paranoid sort.'

The woman flicked her long hair to one side and glared at him. For the first time, he got to view the full impact of what she had suffered. The side of her neck was mottled in angry bruises that retained the imprint of mutilated fingers. Two heavier, thumb-sized marks formed a V directly over her windpipe. The bruising was deep.

She nervously moved her hair back to cover the marks, but as she did so, Mr Black also noticed her arms. Dark purple and yellow bruises ran the length of them, made more prominent by her fair, lightly freckled skin.

She had struggled, but her enemy had superior strength and a depth of cruelty non-combatants could never fully understand – until it was too late.

'Why are you alive?' he asked.

The woman's eyes widened in horror, as if the thought of her demise hadn't entered her mind. Or if it had, she had buried it, pretending it wasn't the only conceivable outcome.

Curious.

'What you doing, Bone?' Gallagher called from the kitchen. 'It's turning dark out there. We have to go.'

Mr Black cocked an ear. There was an unsettling slipperiness to Gallagher's words, as though he had taken Mr Black's short absence as an excuse to relubricate his tonsils. This newfound dependency would also explain his disappointing lack of interest when his own bathroom door was kicked in.

In the sand, Gallagher would have crippled a

256

soldier for less. This wasn't the same leader who had stared deep into a troubled man's heart and saw the misaligned cogs within the feral machine. That man hadn't asked to be obeyed, he had led by example to show why he must be.

Mr Black slipped Morris's cellphone into his pocket and turned his back. As he walked away, the woman's bravado collapsed and she wept into her hands. She tried to be quiet, not wanting to give him the satisfaction of her defeat.

She didn't.

There was no satisfaction simply because he didn't care. In his mind, she was already just another ghost.

At the rear door, Gallagher was breathing heavily as he bent over to pull on a tall pair of rubber boots. When he looked up, his eyes were noticeably bloodshot.

'You got boots?' he snarled.

'I'm fine,' said Mr Black.

'This shit is worse than sand. It sticks to everything and hardens like cement. Fucking rains all the time, too.'

'We should go to Africa,' said Mr Black. 'Money to be made with our skills.'

Gallagher scowled and held up his mutilated hand. 'You think anyone would hire this?'

'You can still shoot. They missed the most important finger, remember?'

Gallagher grinned and lifted a metal flask from

his back pocket. He unscrewed the top and held it up. Amber liquid splashed over the rim. Freshly filled.

'Fucking sand niggers,' he toasted before taking a deep swallow.

Mr Black bristled as his former sergeant returned the flask to his pocket. He understood the need for any soldier to unleash the shadow within. And although he found his release in other ways, he had spent many a dark night watching over the sergeant and his flock as they lost their minds to alcohol and opium.

On duty, however, he would rather slit their throats than serve beside them in that state. That was a line drawn in the sand, and served up one night in graphic detail, by Sgt Douglas Gallagher. How could such a lesson be forgotten by its own teacher?

'You comin'?'

Without a backward glance, Gallagher tugged on a battered oilskin hat and threw open the kitchen door. He staggered down the wooden stairs and squelched noisily into the mud.

Reluctantly, Mr Black followed.

Dark, rain-filled clouds drooped low enough to make both men hunch their shoulders as they walked deeper into the clearing behind the house. Beyond the mud, on a small grassy knoll, they came to a circular stone well.

Hand-built with thick mortar and rough-hewn stone, the well looked like the kind of postcard-friendly attraction that tourists drop coins into in exchange for false hopes and imagined blessings.

'It's fed by a mountain stream,' said Gallagher. 'Runs clear most of the year, but it can get blocked and full of silt sometimes. When I first bought the land, we drank straight out of the bucket. Then, one spring we got sick with fucking Giardiasis.'

Gallagher laughed. Throaty. Coarse. 'Beaver Fever they call it here. You should have seen us. This was before Katie was born, mind you, which was a blessing. One bathroom and there's the two of us with stuff pouring out either end. I thought we were going to die and one of you lot, or a bloody MP, would eventually find our dehydrated husks curled up together on the bathroom floor.'

He shook his head with exaggerated force. 'It wasn't fun at the time, but when you go through something like that, it can bring you closer together as a couple, you know? Kinda like the Corps. Sometimes you have to fall into hell to discover how quickly your friends are willing to rush in and pull you back out.'

Gallagher tried to laugh away the darkness that had entered his voice. He covered it with a quip. 'I'd rather take on a whole platoon of ragheads than endure it again.'

Bending down, Gallagher grabbed hold of a rusted iron handle bolted in the middle of a large circular stone lid.

'I stopped using it after that,' he said. 'Give me a hand.'

Together, the two men pulled the lid aside. Gallagher switched on a flashlight and pointed it straight down into the deep, dark hole.

Mr Black leaned forward and stared into the abyss. The water level was high and for a spine-tingling moment he wondered if he had carelessly allowed himself to be delivered to the edge of his own grave.

Wallace Carver had slipped through his grasp. Desmond Morris had already paid a price. What more fitting reprimand could there be than a bullet to the back of the head?

He turned slowly to peer over his shoulder. Not willing to go peacefully, his hand was already reaching for the knife on his belt. But Gallagher wasn't staring back from behind the cocked hammer of his Desert Eagle. Instead, his gaze was completely focused on the depths of the well, and from his disappointed expression, whatever he had expected to find down there was missing.

CHAPTER 52

Lance Corporal James Ronson had inherited an ugly house in a simple neighbourhood that showed its age with liver spots and varicose veins. An architect's designed-by-committee nightmare, the early 1970s split-level had been built with sawdust and chewing-gum before it was marooned upon a high concrete basement with undersized windows.

Its cracked stucco siding and overgrown front lawn reminded Wallace of homes in his own North Shore neighbourhood that – on a double-dog-dare to prove adolescent bravery – he used to throw eggs at or cover in toilet paper when he could sneak enough rolls out of the house.

Neglect often invited youthful imaginations to assume such homes must be either haunted or lair to a cannibalistic witch. The truth usually wasn't much better than the fiction: an alcoholic bachelor or lonely widow whose children were now too busy with their own lives to ever stop around.

Or in this case, a soldier. Kidnapped, tortured and dismissed. If he had kept to himself, Wallace could have mustered some pity. But Ronson

261

hadn't. He had left his cave and attacked innocents, which made him nothing short of a monster.

Wallace glanced over at the empty passenger seat beside him. He found being alone difficult. With no one to watch his back and nobody to tell him he was doing the right thing. Not that he doubted himself – he was doing what he must – but when the chips were down, that's when true friendship meant the most.

Laurel had told him she was sorry but she couldn't take part. The risk was too high. She gave him a clean shirt that had belonged to her grandfather and said he was welcome to borrow her car.

'If you get caught,' she added, 'I'll tell the police you stole it.'

It was a fair trade.

Wallace picked up his shotgun. The Defender felt warm in his hand, even comforting. Reloaded and only a little worse for wear, it gave him strength. And even if that fortitude was false, even if all he held was an inanimate tool, he took whatever he could get.

'Let's do this,' he said to himself.

Gun in hand, Wallace slipped out of the truck and moved up the weed-infested garden path at a brisk pace. Four concrete steps to the front door. He tried the handle, but this wasn't Canada. It was locked.

No time to waste.

Wallace knocked and pressed his ear to the door.

When he heard footsteps approach from the other side, he took two steps back. As the handle began to turn, his foot lashed out. The door smashed open, knocking whoever stood behind it flat on his ass.

Wallace rushed inside.

The man on the floor was barefoot, wearing baby-blue boxers and a thin white T-shirt. Blood spotted the front of the shirt from a dripping, freshly flattened nose.

Wallace pumped the shotgun, letting the man hear the anus-puckering *click-clack*, while he kicked the door closed behind them for privacy.

The man lifted his hands to cover his face. He was already trembling. A good start.

'I ain't got nothing worth stealing, man. A few old computers maybe, some small tools. You'd break your back moving the TV. It's a bloody dinosaur.'

'James Ronson?' Wallace asked.

The man peered out from beneath splayed fingers. 'Yeah, that's me.'

'My name is Wallace Carver. That mean anything to you?'

'No.' His forehead crinkled into deep furrows. 'Should it?'

'My wife and sons are missing. I think you're involved.'

Ronson lowered his hands and looked up at Wallace through intelligent but muddied chocolate-brown eyes.

'You're the bus driver,' he said.

A surge of anger made the shotgun tremble against Wallace's shoulder. 'That's me.' His voice cracked. 'What have you done with my family?'

'Hold on, hold on,' Ronson blurted. 'I wasn't involved OK? I mean, yeah, I know about it, but, man, I just handle the comms, do a little computer work, you know? I set up the phones, it's what I do, but I didn't want nothing else to do with it.'

Wallace snarled and kicked at Ronson's legs. 'Get up.' He waved his gun in the direction of the living room. 'You're going to tell me everything you know or I'm going to make al Qaeda look like a fucking babysitter.'

Ronson blanched and rolled over to push himself to his feet. He was skin and bone, with a two-day growth of beard. Clusters of scabbed-over needle marks and tiny symmetrical cuts that could have come from a razor blade ran along the insides of his arms and the backs of his legs. But there was also enough muscle definition to let Wallace know he hadn't completely given up on himself. Not yet.

As he walked, Ronson tilted his head back and lifted his T-shirt to press it against his bloody nose. His exposed back was etched in raised scar tissue.

Wallace looked closer. The scars formed a familiar grid pattern: a game he played with his sons; a game they loved because Wallace concentrated hard on losing nearly every turn. Someone had carved a game of X & Os on the man's flesh.

A large C cut deeply across the grid, showing the game had ended in a tie.

Ronson turned and dropped on to an ugly couch in the middle of an even uglier room. Asparagus-green shag carpet covered the floor and continued inexplicably halfway up the walls. The walls, in turn, were painted a lighter shade of mint, as though the designer had thought a slight contrast would make all the difference.

The shag was beaten down from years of shuffling feet and featured several prominent burn marks. The ceiling was yellow from cigarette smoke and streaked with ghostly tentacles of soot from a gas fire in the corner that had likely passed its last inspection more than three decades earlier.

'I know,' said Ronson. 'Hideous, ain't it.'

'Suits you,' said Wallace.

Ronson sighed resignedly. 'Yeah, you could be right.'

He lowered his T-shirt as the blood in his nostrils began to clot. More scars, in a similar pattern to the ones on his back, vanished beneath the thin fabric.

Wallace resettled the shotgun in the crook of his shoulder. 'Who's got my family?'

Ronson glanced nervously at a small table beside the couch. A blown-glass pipe and several tiny nuggets of crystallized cocaine sat on a ceramic pie plate that celebrated America's 1976 bicentennial.

'You mind if I smoke?' he asked.

Ronson's hand was already reaching for the pipe when Wallace smashed it to bits with the blunt end of his shotgun.

'Fuuuck!' Ronson yanked his hand back and stared at his fingers to make sure they hadn't been mangled.

'Answer the fucking question,' Wallace snarled.

'I was gonna. I was gonna,' protested Ronson. 'I just . . . just needed a little.' He scraped fingers through his greasy hair, digging the nails into his scalp as bubbles of spit foamed upon his lips. 'Fffuuuck. Fuuuckers. You have no fffucking idea who—'

Wallace slammed his shotgun down on the side table again, splintering the wood and sending any remaining shards of pottery, glass and drugs spilling into the deep-pile carpet.

He glared at Ronson. 'Next time, it's your fucking hands. Both of them. Then your feet. I'm sure you know exactly how many bones are in your feet? Al Qaeda may have used you for sport, soldier, but you have no fucking idea how serious I am!'

Ronson held up his hands in surrender. 'OK, OK, but they'll fucking kill me, man.'

'Fast or slow?' asked Wallace.

Ronson looked up at him, confused. 'What?'

'Will they kill you fast or slow?' Wallace repeated. ''Cause I'll damn well make it slow.'

Ronson began to chew the nails of his right hand. 'You're fucking scary, man.'

Wallace scowled and leaned his face closer. 'Who's got my family?'

Ronson sighed heavily and spat out a few shards of fingernail. 'That would be Sergeant Douglas Gallagher. He was my unit commander. Hell of a Marine.'

Wallace ground his teeth. 'Why?'

Ronson's eyes widened in surprise. 'Why did he take them?'

'Yes,' Wallace snapped.

'To punish you.'

'Why?' Wallace repeated.

The surprise left Ronson's face to be replaced with genuine puzzlement. 'Because of what you did, man.'

'And what was that?' asked Wallace.

'Come on.' Ronson smirked nervously. 'How could you not know?'

Wallace stepped forward and jammed the barrel of the shotgun against the man's temple. The cold steel cut into flesh as Ronson strained his neck muscles to stay upright.

'OK, OK. FUCK!' Ronson fixed a fierce glare on Wallace. 'You killed his wife and daughter. They were all he had left after he was kicked out of the Corps. You took them away. He's not the kind of man who could ever let that go.'

Ronson was unable to disguise a look of un-bridled disgust as he added, 'And who could blame him?'

CHAPTER 53

Sgt Gallagher dragged his disbelieving gaze away from the dark, empty hole.

'Where the fuck are they?'

He turned to glare at the house where the red-haired woman was silhouetted in the kitchen window. From this distance, her expression was unreadable.

Mr Black frowned, relaxed his grip on his curved knife, and peered back down into the well. Gallagher's flashlight beam was moving across the walls in a random, useless pattern.

Something glistened and was gone. It had looked like—

'Go back,' said Mr Black.

'What?'

'Move your flashlight back to the left. I saw something.'

Gallagher swung the beam across the slippery stone wall.

'There,' said Mr Black.

Gallagher froze in place, his light illuminating a crack in the wall where several large stones had been pulled out. Two small boys were huddled in the crevice a short distance above the icy water. They were pale and frail, frightened and starved. The cold and damp had sapped their strength to the point where they barely had enough left in reserve to shield their eyes from the flashlight's brutal white glare.

'Resilient little buggers,' said Gallagher. 'I wasn't sure they'd survive.'

And wouldn't that have been for the best? thought Mr Black.

CHAPTER 54

Wallace took a step away from the couch and wiped a sheen of nervous sweat from his face. He moved his tongue around the inside of his mouth, trying to get rid of a bad taste.

It still didn't make sense.

'How did I kill this man's family?' he asked.

'How?' Ronson blurted. 'Fuck me! You have to know that.'

'Pretend I don't,' Wallace snapped. His voice was sharp and tinged with violence. At the same time, his finger quivered above the trigger, so close it could easily slip. A simple spasm; an accidental twitch.

Ronson gulped and a wash of panic rippled in a wave from forehead to chin. He glanced to the side table where his pipe had been smashed to powder.

'M-maybe we could have a drink? I've got—'

Wallace lashed out with his foot, sending the small table crashing into the wall.

Ronson winced. 'OK. OK. It was a bus crash. Last year in Canada.' He looked up at Wallace.

'You were driving the bus, right? Gallagher showed me—'

'What?' Wallace practically snarled. 'What did he show you?'

'Photos. Clippings from the newspaper. There was one of the crash on the bridge and another of you receiving some medal from the mayor. Christ, all the medals stripped from us, how you—'

'Did you read it?' asked Wallace.

'The story. Uh, no. But Gallagher told us exact—'

'FUCK!'

Wallace spun the shotgun around in his hands and slammed the butt into the wall above Ronson's head. Brittle chunks of plaster sprayed over the seated man as the gun smashed through to the studs. Smaller chunks littered the air when the gun was yanked back out of the hole and retrained on Ronson. Wallace's trigger finger trembled as he fought an overwhelming urge for carnage.

Ronson held up his hands. Chalky dust stuck to the sweat beading his forehead and the twin trails of blood dripping from his nose.

'Look . . .' He tried to sound calm despite the quiver in his voice. 'I know it was probably an accident. Fuck, if I don't know about that . . . but Gallagher went through a lot in the sand and he didn't adjust too well to being back home. Not that it was easy on any of us, especially with the

Corps turning its back, but hell . . . his wife and daughter were everything to him, man. He was trying to adjust, trying to win them back, and then you—'

'Win them back?' said Wallace. He shifted uneasily on the balls of his feet.

'Yeah. Carly left him. Said she couldn't live with his moods any more. Took their daughter, Katie, with her. If Gallagher was dark before she left, Christ, he really plummeted after. The Sarge was always a scary motherfucker, but . . . anyway, he had his old unit track her down. We didn't know she had gone to Canada until, well . . . Bone found her, but by then it was too late . . .'

Ronson let the rest of the sentence drift, as if sensing that Wallace was no longer listening. The shotgun barrel had slowly tilted down, aiming away from his face to hover at the centre of the scar-tissue grid that marked his ruined stomach.

Wallace stared out the living-room window, his focus adrift. He had forgotten to draw the curtains. *How could he have been so careless?* He saw his own face reflected in the glass. The fear in his eyes reminded him of the woman. Her features had been sharp, almost skeletal, with high cheekbones above deep hollows; plump, determined lips, and a prominent, almost-mannish chin. In photographs, she likely would have been stunning. In person, however, it took a sprinkle of light freckles across the bridge of her nose to soften the effect and elicit a sense of vulnerability.

Her hair was auburn and it fell away from her face in tendrils, reaching past the broken glass, dangling towards the watery abyss . . .

Wallace blinked, not wanting to remember, but unable to shake the morbid hold the memory had on him.

The woman's daughter was also thin, but not to the same anaemic degree. She had darker hair and a rounder face, but like her mother, she possessed amazingly large and expressive eyes.

As they hung over the edge of the bridge – steel cables snapping, glass popping, metal twisting and groaning, with their crushed car miraculously and tentatively locked in the bus's front bike carrier – both sets of eyes were focused entirely on him.

Pleading.

Despite the blood. Despite his injuries. He was their world. Their only hope. And he had been terrified.

Wallace blinked again. For a moment he was unsure what was memory and what was real.

A shadow moved beyond the window.

A figure approaching. Running. Fast.

'Fuck!'

Wallace pivoted with the shotgun tight against his shoulder as the front door was flung open.

'Don't shoot,' a familiar voice called.

Ronson looked up from the couch in confusion as Wallace instantly lowered his weapon.

A rugged, calfskin leather face with deep-set eyes and sharp cheekbones emerged around the corner and Wallace's heart swelled with gratitude and relief. Crow's face was disturbingly bruised and swollen, but the damage did nothing to diminish the size of his grin.

'How did you find me?' Wallace asked.

'I called Laurel as soon as I could. She sent me straight here.' Crow's eyes flicked apologetically to the floor. 'Sorry it took so long.'

'Your timing's perfect,' said Wallace. The flood of emotion reflected on his face vanished as his gaze returned to Ronson. 'This son of a bitch was just starting to talk.'

Crow moved deeper into the room. In one hand, he clutched a matching Defender pumpaction shotgun. In his other, he held up a glowing mobile phone.

'You'll want to take this call,' he said. 'It's for you.'

CHAPTER 55

Mr Black anchored his feet on either side of the stone well, gripped the nylon rope tightly in both hands, and descended into darkness. When his right foot slipped over the crevice and found purchase on the narrow ledge, he was able to stop.

He squatted down and peered between bent knees at the two boys. At first glance, they didn't look much like brothers. The younger one had ginger hair and a mass of freckles that covered his forehead, nose and cheeks, as though a jar of peanut butter had exploded through a colander. The slender nose and bright eyes, however, clearly showed which parent he favoured.

The older one had dark hair, large protruding ears and a longer, more adult face. It was a face he still needed to grow into. And despite being just as terrified as his brother, his small hands were curled into protective, fight-ready fists. *Like father, like son.*

Mr Black didn't know how to look unthreatening and he imagined his fierce coal-black face was exactly what little white boys feared most of finding in the dark.

275

He smiled, but that elicited a squeal of fright.

'M-m-make him g-g-go away.' The younger boy buried his face in his older brother's chest.

'If I go away,' said Mr Black, 'you'll die down here. Both of you. In the dark and the wet and the cold. Do you want that?'

The older brother attempted to lift his chin and steel his gaze, but fear made his lower lip quiver and courage lost its way in the inky folds of Mr Black's shirt.

'We want to go home.' His voice barely reached a whisper.

'Only one way to do that.' Mr Black glanced skyward. 'You must rise.'

The older brother gulped and lifted his gaze slightly higher, but he still fell short of Mr Black's stare. 'How can we trust you?'

'I haven't said anything about trust,' said Mr Black. 'But I will make you a promise.'

The younger brother lifted his face. 'W-w-what's th-th-that?'

Mr Black inexplicably smiled wider, but the exposure of that many shiny white teeth made the young boy clamp his eyes shut and bury his face again.

'Have you always stuttered?' Curious. A flicker of memory; the smell of smoke and burning children.

'It's getting better,' said the older brother. His voice had become less tremulous, like the first flutter of a hatchling's wing. Not yet strong enough to fly and yet tempted by the possibility. 'Fred goes to a speech therapist after school.'

Mr Black cocked his head to one side and sized up the older boy. Despite everything, he still had fight. Perhaps he took after his mother after all.

The younger boy, Fred, opened his eyes again. 'Wh-wh-wh-wh . . .' His face turned red, but he couldn't get the words out.

'He wants to know what your promise is?' said the older boy.

Mr Black cocked his head to the other side. 'How do you know that's what he wanted to ask?'

'Because I want to know, too.'

'And will you believe me?'

'If you promise.'

Mr Black straightened his legs and swung away so that his head and upper torso vanished from the cone of artificial light being shone from above. In the darkness, he ground his teeth and refocused his energy. His curiosity about the children was unhealthy. Their trust and naivety stirred an anger that constricted blood vessels and made his head start to pound. He inhaled deeply. Remembered who he was. The shadow. The ghost. The killer.

He bent his knees and dipped back into the light.

'I promise to take you and your brother out of this dark place. Nothing more.' He didn't smile or attempt any expression of friendliness. 'I can take one at a time.'

'Take Fred,' said the older boy. 'I can wait.'

Mr Black snarled at the growing bravery in the boy's voice. He swung in close until his face was inches from the boy's alarmingly large eyes.

'Don't get the wrong idea,' he growled. 'I made a promise to get you out of the hole. That's where the pact ends. Understand?'

The boy's eyes filled with tears. 'I'll wait here,' he repeated in a shakier voice.

'Yeah,' said Mr Black. 'Like you've got a choice.'

The younger boy screamed hysterically as Mr Black snatched him off the shelf, threw him on his back, and climbed the rope.

When they broke the surface of the well, Sgt Gallagher grabbed hold of the boy and untangled his locked arms from around Mr Black's neck.

'What kept you?' Gallagher barked. 'It sounded like a bloody UN debate down there.'

'They're alive, aren't they?' said Mr Black.

'So?'

'They'd be less trouble dead, but more awkward to carry.'

Gallagher snorted and tightened his grip on the squirming boy's wrist. 'Get the other one.'

When both boys were finally out of the well, Gallagher and Mr Black headed back to the house. They were only halfway across the clearing when the woman burst through the kitchen door and came running towards them.

The boys saw her and instantly transformed into

278

squirming, mewling vermin with jagged teeth and sharp, dirt-encrusted nails.

Gallagher cried out in pain and let the younger boy go.

'Little prick bit me,' he snarled.

Mr Black held on to his captive for a short while longer, just to prove a point, before finally relenting.

The boys ran across the muddy yard at breakneck speed before tumbling into their mother's waiting embrace.

Mr Black turned to Gallagher. 'What are you planning to do with them?'

'Not me,' said Gallagher. 'You.'

Mr Black slid his tongue across his teeth in an attempt not to show his true reaction. 'And what do you want me to do?'

'Take them to Canada,' said Gallagher. 'Drop them at that friend of Carver's. The Indian.'

Mr Black was puzzled. He hadn't told Gallagher about his encounter with Crow.

'Why?' he asked.

'It'll draw Carver back there pronto. Once he's across the border, you'll tip the cops and that'll end this.'

'End it?'

Gallagher grinned. 'The Mounties are looking for a man who may have killed his family and dumped the bodies, right? We give them two of the bodies. Only they're stored in the basement of his best friend's house.' Gallagher laughed. 'Let Carver explain his way out of that one.'

Understanding dawned.

'You don't want the boys alive.'

'Fuck, no,' said Gallagher. 'Like you said, they're less trouble dead. Be as messy as you like.'

CHAPTER 56

Wallace was dumbfounded as he accepted the phone from Crow and placed it to his ear.

'Hello?'

'Wallace? It's Delilah.'

'Delilah?'

At the mention of his wife's name, Crow winked at Wallace and snapped the shotgun to his shoulder. He pointed it unwaveringly at Ronson.

'Is everything all right?' Wallace tried to control a rising panic.

'We're fine,' said Delilah, 'but listen. Alicia posted an update to her Facebook page.'

'When?'

'Within the last half-hour.'

'How?'

'I don't know.' Delilah became flustered and her voice rose in pitch. 'It doesn't tell me—'

'OK,' Wallace blurted, angry at himself for the question. 'What did she say?'

'It's kinda strange. Here, I'll read it out: "SOS. SOS. High hill. Ocean visible. Trees. 2 men. Military? Afraid. Name Douglas. Boys are—"

That's where it ends. She must have been interrupted.'

Wallace's head spun and the locking ability of his knee joints suddenly began to fail. He shoved the phone at Crow before staggering to the corner and dropping into an old armchair. His stomach churned as he buried his face in his hands and allowed tears to flow unabashedly.

SOS. *Save Our Souls.*

Alicia and the boys were still alive.

'You OK?' asked Crow.

Wallace looked up and wiped his eyes. 'Yeah. Sorry. It's just a relief to know she's still fighting, that I'm not too late.' His voice broke and he struggled to get the words out. 'All this time, I didn't know.'

'How could you?' said Crow. 'Nobody else even believed you.'

Wallace looked up through puffy eyelids. 'You did.'

Crow shrugged. 'Even then, I could've done more.'

Wallace shook off the suggestion. 'You're here now and I wouldn't be this close without your help. Laurel only trusted me because you did.'

Crow smiled at the mention of Laurel's name. 'She's a hell of a woman, ain't she? Hope my girls turn out as good as she has.'

There was a hint of sadness in his friend's voice that troubled Wallace. Almost as though he thought he might not be returning home to watch his daughters grow.

'They will,' said Wallace. 'They're being raised by two of the best people I know.'

Crow slipped the phone into his pocket. When his gaze returned to Wallace, his smile was gone and his tone had returned to business.

'Alicia's message only mentions two men.' His voice became iron. 'We can take them.'

Wallace drew on his friend's strength. He wiped at his face again, took several deep breaths and stood up.

'OK.' He tried to sound strong. 'I'm ready.'

They turned their attention to Ronson who hadn't moved an inch from his spot on the couch. His eyes darted around the room at a frantic pace and his tongue slithered across his lips like a serpent.

'Is Gallagher's place on a hill overlooking the ocean?' Wallace asked.

Ronson gulped and nodded.

'Do you know how to get there?'

'I've been up once when he was first starting to build. Most of the time when he wants something, he just calls or—'

'Who's the second man?' interrupted Crow.

Ronson sucked air through his teeth. 'Probably Bone.'

'Tennyson Bone,' said Wallace, remembering the computer printouts. 'A tall black man? Shaved head?'

'Mean as hell and good with a knife?' added Crow.

'Yeah,' said Ronson warily, 'that's him.'

Wallace caught Crow's eye. 'Did Laurel fill you in?'

'Best she could over the phone.'

'If this Bone character is the same one who surprised me at the guard's house, he may have that blond bastard Morris with him, too. He's injured, but still . . . that makes three.'

Crow didn't blink. 'I still like our odds. This Bone and I have unfinished business.'

Wallace turned, curious. 'Why's that?'

Crow reflexively smoothed his shirt against his stomach to reveal the ridge of a heavy bandage underneath. 'He killed JoeJoe and put me in hospital for a short while.'

'Christ,' said Wallace. 'Why?'

Crow's eyes glistened. 'He was looking for you.'

Wallace's face drained of blood. 'God, Crow, I'm so sorry.'

'Not your fault, but I aim to make him pay.' Crow turned his attention back to Ronson. 'And you're going to help.'

Ronson threw up his hands in frustration. 'I only set up the phones, man. I didn't get involved in any revenge shit, but you don't want to mess with Gallagher. He's the bravest motherfucker I ever served un—'

'Brave?' Wallace sneered. 'Is that what you call abducting an innocent woman and two young boys?'

Ronson lifted his shirt, exposing his scars. 'You see these? Just fucking games, man. Sergeant Gallagher kept those al Qaeda bastards off me as long as he could. They were cutting him to pieces and he was spitting it right back in their faces. Every time they moved on me, he found some way to bring the focus back to him. I wouldn't be alive today if—'

'Who fucking cares?' snapped Wallace. 'If this is what you do with your life, you don't bloody deserve it.'

'I agree.' Crow lowered his shotgun and removed a large knife from a leather sheath on his belt. He held it up to the light. 'I say we finish what they began.'

At the sight of the glistening knife, Ronson began to shake uncontrollably and the front of his boxers darkened with urine.

Wallace had heard people say that what doesn't kill you makes you stronger, but in his experience, the opposite held more truth. Ronson had been tortured to within an inch of his life and now it merely took the threat of violence to bring the nightmare flooding back.

Wallace held up one hand. 'We don't have time for this. We need to get to where that son of a bitch is holding Alicia and my boys.' He pointed at the cowering man on the couch. 'He knows where that is.'

CHAPTER 57

When Sgt Gallagher reached the reunited family, Alicia threw the boys behind her back and bared her teeth.

'You son of a bitch,' she snarled. 'You said that well was dry. My boys are soaked to the bone, starved and frozen. You promised that if I—'

'They're alive,' said Gallagher. 'Be fucking grateful.'

Alicia pounced like a bobcat, her nails sinking into the man's cheek and drawing blood as her teeth reached for his throat to finish what they had started beneath the bandage . . .

She howled in pain as Gallagher's companion clamped a hand on her shoulder and squeezed the nerve cluster. The entire left side of her body went numb and she hung limply, powerlessly, in his grip.

Then the real pain came—

Gallagher slapped her back-handed. Callused knuckle and sandpaper skin. His wedding ring, a simple platinum band, split her lip and rattled teeth.

She was torn loose of the tall man's

nerve-deadening grip and spilled to the wet ground, gasping and spitting blood.

Her first instinct was to curl into a ball, but Gallagher wasn't done. His booted foot found her soft centre before she could protect it.

Air exploded from her lungs and her eyes bulged. The pain was crippling, but the only thought that flashed in her mind was a primal need to protect her children. She tried to roll over, but became trapped on her back in the mud, her neck at a perilous angle as Gallagher's foot began to descend again.

The heavy sole was aimed at her head. A killing blow.

Fury had overtaken sense, her defiance triggering something dark and monstrous within him.

Alex, her oldest but still just a child, charged forward and threw himself at Gallagher's leg. The top of his tiny skull smashed into the large man's knee and yet he still found the strength to coil his arms and legs around the powerful limb and hold on for dear life.

Gallagher twisted in the air, his balance suddenly off kilter. His redirected foot missed Alicia and hit the slippery ground at an awkward angle. It skidded out from under him, causing his arms to windmill uselessly as he fell ungraciously on his backside into the mud.

But Gallagher didn't stay there. He was a soldier, a fighter whose only rules were maim or be maimed, kill or be killed. He roared in anger and grabbed the young boy by the hair. Yanking Alex off his leg, he shook him by the roots until the boy howled in agony. Then he pulled back his other fist—

'Don't!' screamed Alicia. 'He's just a child.'

Gallagher flashed a cruel smile. Then he launched his crippled fist and smashed it into Alex's face.

The loss of his fingers weakened his punch, but he could still hit hard enough to snap the boy's head back and deliver a man's dose of pain. The boy's eyes rolled in his head before his body slapped the ground.

Alicia howled and curled her body around her oldest son. The younger one held on to her back, weeping so hard that streams of snot flowed down his chin.

Gallagher rose to his feet and angrily shook off the mud. Embarrassed, he wanted to continue the hurt, but the woman and her children were too soft a target, too easy to break and destroy.

He stepped forward and pressed his muddy face as close to his soldier's as a drill sergeant at boot camp.

'What are you doing just standing there?' he hissed. 'You let that kid blindside me.'

'I figured you could handle him,' said Mr Black.

Gallagher snorted. 'Don't get fucking smart. You're not paid to think.'

'I'm beginning to wonder if I'll be paid at all,'

Mr Black retorted. 'If I had known you planned to keep the family, I would have expected you to ask for a ransom.'

Gallagher winced. 'This isn't about money.'

'It should be,' said Mr Black. 'Gold is the only currency we can count on. The only one that won't stab us in the back. You do the job, you get paid and you get out. Didn't you teach me that?'

Bristling with red-faced fury, Gallagher extended the only whole finger remaining on his right hand and pressed it into the centre of his soldier's forehead.

'Do you think this is a partnership?' he asked.

Mr Black didn't flinch as the sharp nail bore into his flesh, the disfigured hand turning clockwise until its upraised thumb resembled the hammer of a gun.

'You're my soldier,' Gallagher roared. 'I'm your sergeant. Don't . . . ever . . . fucking . . . forget.'

Mr Black didn't say a word as Gallagher withdrew his finger and walked around the weeping, huddled mess of bodies onthe ground.

'Bring them inside,' he ordered. 'We'll deal with it there.'

CHAPTER 58

They travelled in Crow's vehicle, a white Yukon Hybrid borrowed from Cheveyo.

Ronson had been given thirty seconds to change clothes before his hands were tied behind his back and he was bundled into the vehicle. Crow chose to sit beside him in the middle row of seats, the business end of his shotgun pressed into the man's side.

'If he tries to escape,' Crow explained to Wallace, 'I'm angry enough about JoeJoe to pull the trigger. You might hesitate and that's all the time a guy like this needs to fuck us both up.'

Wallace didn't argue. From the driver's seat, he glanced in the rear-view mirror, catching Ronson's eye.

'What can we expect at Gallagher's place?' he asked. 'It sounds remote.'

'Yeah, the Sarge don't like civilians much. Never has. He liked to say that if you weren't following orders, specifically *his* orders, you were just in the way.'

'What about security?'

Ronson attempted to shrug, but his bonds were

290

so tight that he could barely move his shoulders. He wet his lips instead.

'He's a paranoid son of a bitch, always has been. But the only time I was ever invited to his new place was when he first started construction. He held a small beer-and-barbecue lunch to show off the view. Carly and Katie were there; Bone and Morris. The only one missing was Shep and this was before . . . well . . . before he blew himself to fucking pieces. Poor bastard. Anyways, I didn't see any electronics and Gallagher didn't ask my advice. If he wanted to secure the perimeter, I'm pretty sure he would have asked for my input.'

'What about weapons?' asked Crow.

Ronson grinned. 'Oh, there'll be weapons. Count on it. Gallagher always kept an arsenal.'

Wallace's eyes narrowed. 'Why didn't we find weapons in your house?'

'Me and guns are over, man,' said Ronson. 'Don't get me wrong, I could probably still shoot the ball sack off a housefly if I needed to, but I'm just as happy to never hold steel again. Let me rot my chops in cyberspace. Less painful for all concerned.'

'What about this other soldier?' asked Crow. 'Bone.'

Ronson rolled his tongue into his cheek and his eyes flickered across Crow's face. 'What did he do to your boy in Canada?'

Crow had trouble masking his anger. 'Sliced his throat without blinking. He was also planning to gut me like a fish before we were interrupted.' His eyes locked on Ronson. 'Just like your friends in the desert.'

Ronson swallowed uneasily, but nodded as though he expected nothing less. 'I've never seen anything like him. Sergeant Gallagher can be mean, especially if he doesn't like you or you go off task without permission, but Bone is a stone-cold killer. Whenever we got in a tight spot, it was usually Bone who pulled us out.'

Ronson shook his head, remembering. 'One time we were pinned down in the middle of fucking nowhere and that black ghost just up and disappeared. Then, before we knew it, the enemy starts screaming. Made the hair stand up on the back of our necks to hear it. By the time we scrambled out of our hole and reached their camp, every last one of them was dead. Bone was just squatting on the ground, picking his teeth with his knife and covered from head to toe in blood. He scares everybody except the Sarge.'

'We should kill him first,' said Crow.

Ronson snorted. 'Yeah, good luck with that.'

'You think he's unkillable?'

Ronson shook off the question. 'I didn't say that. He's human, I think, but it'll take more than you to do it.' He snorted. 'To put it in perspective, Sergeant Gallagher and I were being held by al Qaeda in a secure bunker in the middle of an Iraqi village. The situation was so FUBAR that the entire United States military had thrown up its hands. But you know what? Even when it looked hopeless, the Sarge kept saying over and over that Bone was coming. I mean, I figured he was just trying to give me some hope to keep me alive, but he really believed it. And when that door burst open, I thought I was dreaming. Bone, Morris and Shep did what the most powerful army in the world was afraid to do: kicked major ass and said to hell with taking names.'

Ronson laughed on the brink of hysteria. 'And what do you have?' He jerked his head in Wallace's direction. 'He needed a goddamn bus to kill a woman and child.'

Wallace's face instantly flushed with anger and his hands gripped the steering wheel so hard it threatened to snap in two.

'You son of a bitch,' Wallace growled. 'I don't know what this is about, but I didn't kill anyone. You didn't even read the goddamn story.'

The bus groaned and tipped further over the edge of the Lions Gate Bridge. A heavy bolt snapped and the bike carrier shuddered, its tentative hold strained to the breaking point, making the car slip deeper into the abyss.

The woman's terrified gaze locked on Wallace.

'Save my daughter,' she pleaded. 'Please.'

Wallace forced his eyes to look away. He carefully pulled his crushed foot out of the tangle of twisted metal where his brake pedal used to be. His trousers were sliced open from the knee down, exposing flesh, bloody and raw. He could even see bone, white amidst the throbbing purple of torn muscle and yellow fat. But despite the alarming pain, the tibia hadn't snapped.

Gritting his teeth, he unclipped his safety harness. Gravity pulled him hard against the oversized steering wheel, but the belts had done their job. His chest wasn't crushed. He could breathe. He was alive.

Wallace turned to stare back at his passengers. They were crying, frightened, bruised and battered, but they were all alive and their collective injuries appeared minimal.

'Move to the back,' he ordered. 'Open the rear exit door and help each other out.'

Forty faces stared back at him. They were frozen; in shock. Nobody moved.

Wallace peered through the crowd, separating wheat from chaff, until he spotted a young Indo-Canadian businessman near the back. The cut of his suit suggested he could be a junior manager, but the shaved head and stainless-steel earring said he hadn't yet given up his identity for a company car.

Wallace pointed a finger at him and raised his voice. 'You, sir. You're in charge. Get that exit door open and help these people out of the bus and on to the bridge. Help is on its way, but I need you to do it now.'

It took a second, but the young man accepted the challenge and headed to the rear of the bus. He glanced at the instructions printed beside the red emergency handle and gave it a yank in the correct direction. The door swung open and, as if the air was suddenly filled with pure oxygen, the other passengers snapped awake and began to scramble towards escape.

'Don't panic,' Wallace yelled after them. 'Look out for each other and everyone will be OK.'

With his passengers safely departing out the rear, Wallace returned his attention to the front. The bus's massive windshield had shattered in the crash and been ripped away, leaving nothing but strips of flapping rubber to mar the view. Beyond the long hood and the dangling car, there was only dark sky and darker water.

Wallace fought his panic and tightened his focus. He locked in on the woman and child. They badly needed help and he was all they had.

'I'm coming,' he said. 'Hold tight.'

Wallace inhaled deeply before climbing out of his seat and over the dashboard. A powerful wind whipped at his uniform as he lay on his stomach and slid headfirst out the broken windshield.

'I know it was an accident,' said Ronson, 'but that doesn't—'

Ronson's words became trapped as Crow wrapped a hand around his throat and squeezed. Ronson's eyes bulged and his face turned from veiny red to deathly blue. Crow showed no signs of letting go.

'We still need him,' said Wallace, although his heart wasn't fully vested in his words.

Crow continued for a few seconds longer before letting go. The ex-Marine rocked forward, gasping for air, his chest wheezing.

'Fuck,' he cried. 'You've got issues, man.'

'Don't you get it?' Crow hissed. 'Why do you think the city gave him a goddamn medal? Nobody died. He rescued the girl and her mother just seconds before their car dropped into the sea. He's a genuine A-plus fucking hero.'

'That's not possible,' said Ronson. He sat up straight again, his throat as scarlet as a baboon's ass. 'Gallagher told us—'

'He lied,' said Wallace.

Ronson paled. 'Why would he do that?'

Wallace stared straight ahead. His voice was low and cold. 'That's something we'll be sure to ask.'

CHAPTER 59

In the kitchen, Alicia sat on one of the chairs and held her two boys close. She kissed their muddy cheeks and made comforting noises in their ears. The older boy was shaken but awake; he trembled and mewled, while his younger brother sniffled and whimpered.

Gallagher was sickened by the sight. Weakness was a disease and children had to be taught at a young age how to stand alone, how to listen and obey without question. For these two, it was already too late. Discipline hadn't begun soon enough and irrational fears had been allowed to fester.

There are no monsters in the woods. Switch off the light and go to sleep.

If we want to eat, we kill. Animals aren't pets.

Nightmares are for babies. You're not a baby, Katie.

Gallagher shook his head, chasing noisy memories away, and focused on Alicia. She refused to look at him.

Women are like that, he had discovered. When a man is angry, he'll never lower his gaze. But women like to hide the knife until your back is turned and they are sure its point will stab deep.

A man had never wounded him so.

Alicia's face was bruised; her lips bloody and swollen where his ring had cut her. He wouldn't apologize, but still he wished he hadn't lashed out. He never wanted to hit. Never planned to choke or punch or kick.

He had marred her beauty, that pale skin and copper hair . . . *she was so much like his Carly.*

He had noticed the resemblance the first time he saw her. In that photo. The photo with him. The false hero.

He had only wanted to talk to her. To find a voice that wasn't full of anger and fear. She would see beneath his scarred and blistered skin to the place where his heart still beat.

Carly had stopped looking, stopped trying to understand. She had told him to his face that she wished al Qaeda had finished the job. She had become a traitor, deserting him when he needed her most.

After the crash, just as he finally had a chance to bring her back home, she had taken Katie and vanished from the hospital without a trace.

No note. No goodbye. Nothing.

The only thing he knew for sure was that she couldn't have done it alone. She had help. She must have. And there was only one person she would have trusted: a lousy bus driver who reached across a watery abyss. He made her a ghost, just as if she never made it off that damn bridge.

Gallagher had searched for months, but Carly had learned well. She stayed off the grid. She never contacted the driver, nor anyone from her former life. For all he knew, she was no longer even on the continent.

The driver, however, was easy to find.

As was his wife.

Alicia had welcomed him into her life with the click of a mouse. All it took was a Facebook account under a false name and a friendly female face with an interest in a hobby called felting. It had been so easy; he didn't even need Ronson's help.

In this chatty cyber world, Alicia shared her daily excitements and frustrations, her dreams and desires, the little secrets her husband was too busy to pay attention to. She even posted snippets of poetry. Sappy little verses about loss and longing that never seemed to rhyme.

He came to know her intimately, to understand her better than the bus driver ever could. She yearned for something new, something adventurous. A life away from kids and housework, where each day was different, exciting and bold.

She called out for someone to stop the world, just for her. In short, she had yearned for him.

'What are you going to do with us now?'

Gallagher lifted his head and stared across the

table, as awareness dawned that Alicia was talking to him again.

He placed his hands on the table, showing they were empty, and tried to look pleasant. It wasn't an expression he was good at.

Bone stood beside the sink, silent and observant.

'I have a proposal for you,' said Gallagher.

Alicia's face was tense, her eyes wary, but still she showed remarkable strength. She was worth saving.

'I'm listening.'

That was good. That was a first step.

'I'm willing to let your boys go. In the morning, after you've cleaned them and fed them and said your goodbyes, my . . .' He looked over at the sink, trying to decide on just the right word. He needed one that emanated a sense of trust. He had always considered Bone to be a soldier, but that word didn't hold the same weight with civilians. 'My *friend* will return them to Canada.'

The boys whimpered again and clung tighter to their mother, but Alicia's eyes never wavered from his. She was listening, understanding. Connected.

'In exchange for me?' she said.

Gallagher nodded. 'You stay here. With me. You do what I ask with full obedience and have no contact with your husband or your sons ever again. In short, you become dead to them just as my wife and daughter are now dead to me. If you do that, no harm comes to them. That's my pledge.'

Gallagher's eyes flicked over to Bone. His expression was blank, betraying nothing. The perfect soldier.

Alicia swallowed. 'Where *is* my husband?'

'At home. He couldn't find you and gave up trying.' Gallagher tried to sound sincere. 'I'm sure it was difficult, but life goes on.'

Alicia shook her head. 'You don't know my husband.'

Gallagher fought against a sudden ignition of anger, hiding it behind a furrowed brow.

'I know men,' he said bluntly.

'Not this one.' Alicia's voice broke with emotion and her eyes filled with tears. 'He can surprise even me.'

Gallagher slapped the table with such force the boys jumped and went completely silent.

'You forget that I know you.' Gallagher's voice became a growl. 'I followed. I listened. I understood. I know when the boys drove you crazy and when your husband let you down. I know when you felt lonely, disappointed and frustrated.'

Alicia snorted with disgust. 'You saw snippets. Silly things I felt like sharing with people I thought were my friends. You don't know me at all. Not even close.'

Gallagher rose to his full height and fingered the massive handgun stuck in his belt.

'If that's the truth,' he said, fighting for control, 'then there's no point making the deal.'

Alicia pulled her boys tighter to her bosom

and stared defiantly into Gallagher's cold, dead eyes.

'No,' she said, 'there's not.'

Gallagher flared his nostrils and sucked in a deep breath, but his response was cut short by a sharp electronic squeal. It was followed instantly by a series of continuing low-level chirps.

He spun to face his soldier. Bone hadn't moved from his place by the sink. The only sign that he'd even noticed the alarm was the hint of an ungenerous smile upon his lips.

'Arm yourself,' Gallagher commanded. 'Somebody's at the outer perimeter.'

CHAPTER 60

The white Yukon pulled off to one side of the road and stopped below the crest of the hill.

With the engine idling, Wallace turned around in his seat to face Crow. 'You ready for this?'

Crow's eyes remained hard, but his lips twitched as he answered. 'Nope.'

Wallace returned the frail smile, knowing his friend was trying to ease the tension, but still . . .

'If you want to turn around and go home, I won't stand in your way. You know that, right? You've already done more than I could ever ask.'

Crow's smile vanished and a spark of anger flashed in his eyes. 'Don't even go there. Those boys have always known that if they get into trouble and can't go to you, they come to me. What kind of godfather would I be if I didn't live up to that promise now? I've seen up close exactly what you're up against. You need me and I'm in it till the end, you hear?'

Wallace choked back a lump of emotion and nodded his appreciation. Now wasn't the time.

'OK,' he said. 'We have to make sure my family

is here. If they are, maybe we can arrange an exchange.' He indicated Ronson. 'Him for Alicia and the boys.'

Crow raised an eyebrow. 'You think he has value?'

Wallace shrugged. 'His friends threw their careers away to rescue him once before.'

'Not just me, though,' Ronson piped up nervously. 'If Sergeant Gallagher hadn't been with me, I don't know if they would've bothered.'

'What about *semper fi*?' said Wallace.

Ronson smirked. 'Some people think that kind of loyalty comes sewn on to the uniform. It doesn't. It's earned. In the sand, Bone was Gallagher's pet, but I knew he always looked at me as just another morsel waiting to be chewed up and buried.'

'Let's hope you're wrong,' said Wallace.

Ronson shrugged. 'Do what you gotta do, man, but just remember, they're born killers. And from what you've told me, you're not.'

The lone white SUV rolled over the crest of the hill and bounced along a rutted path to enter the clearing.

Staring at the unfinished house in the centre of the muddy yard, Wallace wondered how the scariest/stupidest/bravest thing he had ever done had ended up saving the lives of two strangers while placing his own family in such peril. It didn't seem fair.

He had risked everything to climb out that bus window, and this was his reward?

He swallowed and felt guilty. There he went again, thinking life owed him. This wasn't about reward, or punishment, or even about him. This was about Alicia and the boys.

After the accident, he should have embraced life, embraced his family. If he had paid more attention, been a better husband, a better father, perhaps . . .

Light blinded him as a bank of high-intensity halogens snapped to life on every wall of the house. The powerful security lights created a perimeter of at least sixty to seventy feet around the entire house, illuminating every rock and weed. Anyone attempting to sneak across the clearing would have been exposed instantly.

Crow tensed in the seat beside Ronson. The only sound was the sucking squelch of fresh mud under the tyres, a patter of rain on the windshield and roof, and the hard, steady breathing of three nervous men.

Wallace kept the wheels rolling through the encroaching dusk towards the light. Slowly. Steadily.

With sweat beading his upper lip, he glanced in the rear-view mirror at Ronson.

'You're sure there isn't any way to contact them? Let Gallagher know that I want to talk?'

'Landlines and cellphones can be monitored and tracked,' said Ronson. 'Gallagher had me build three secure phones. Real beauties, custom software, the works. They can call out to anywhere, but only receive calls and texts from each other.'

'You sure there's only three?' said Crow.

Ronson shrugged. 'If I did build a fourth, I don't have it with me. Same difference, right?'

The vehicle's broad monochromatic nose breached the outermost shell of artificial light as though pushing aside a sheer curtain—

The ground erupted and the SUV bucked as the night air was torn asunder around them.

Automatic gunfire sprayed from the house, sending a Kamikaze horde of steel-jacketed slugs to cripple the vehicle. Metal puckered and buckled, rubber and plastic blew apart, headlights exploded and the radiator hissed and screamed in agony.

Wallace threw himself flat across the front seats as the windshield shattered, spraying his back with blunt pebbles of glass. The noise was deafening as the vehicle disintegrated before his eyes and death whizzed over his head.

He reached up and yanked on the wheel in an attempt to turn away, but the front tyres shredded into useless strips and the metal rims sunk into the mud. When the engine stalled, the steering wheel went stiff and unresponsive in his hands before locking up completely.

Wallace kicked on the parking brake to prevent the vehicle from rolling closer to the house. If it wasn't for the solid density of the Yukon's massive

306

V8 engine, he knew everyone in the cab would already be dead.

Alive, he couldn't get over the noise. There was an unending stream of bullets and every one made him flinch. He knew the expression 'nerves shot to hell', but had never fully understood it until now. How soldiers kept their wits together conflict after conflict, he didn't know.

When the shooting finally stopped, Wallace lifted his head and peered over the lip of the riddled dash.

Steam billowed from uncountable holes stitched across the dying vehicle's long hood. The hot mist momentarily blocked his view, but it also blinded the shooter.

'Told you he was paranoid,' said Ronson.

Wallace tried to hold his frustration inside, but couldn't. He slammed a fist into what remained of the dashboard and released an agonized wail. He had needed to hear his own voice, to reassure himself he was still alive. His ears rang, but he wasn't yet deaf.

'I know how you feel.' Crow's voice was hoarse and crumbling at the edge. He sat up and shook pieces of glass and plastic from his hair. 'What the fuck was that?'

'A warning,' said Ronson drily. 'If they wanted you dead, you would be. Wouldn't surprise me if Gallagher had an RPG in there. Take out this vehicle in a heartbeat.'

'It didn't feel like a fucking warning,' Wallace snarled.

With a vicious kick, he forced open his door. He waited, expecting more gunfire, but none came. Despite the reprieve, Wallace didn't exit.

'Get him ready,' he said to Crow.

As Crow worked on Ronson, Wallace scrambled between the seats to join them. He pushed open the passenger door directly behind the driver's to create a buffer of two doors between him and the house.

After taking a deep breath to control the panic that filled his chest like a mass of expanding foam, Wallace turned to Ronson. Despite his seasoned bravado, Wallace knew the former Marine had to be just as scared as they were.

'You ready for introductions?' he asked.

Ronson couldn't nod or shake since Crow held his head rock solid, one of the shotguns attached to his right temple with thick bands of duct tape. Before he could voice his answer, Crow sealed a fresh band of industrial grey tape across his mouth.

'He talks too much,' said Crow.

Wallace took another deep, calming breath and nodded. 'OK, let's do this.'

Wallace took a tentative step outside, keeping his head low to stay out of sight behind the door.

Inside the vehicle, Crow pushed on the gun's barrel, forcing Ronson to scuttle over in the seat and join Wallace.

Crow handed off the gun.

'Be careful,' he said. Then to Ronson, 'Don't

even think about it. Putting you down is the easiest and smartest thing we could do.'

Crow picked up the second shotgun and chambered a round. Wallace flinched reflexively; Ronson didn't. His eyes had already taken on a hundred-yard stare.

Slowly, Wallace pushed Ronson out into the open beyond the doors.

After another deep breath, he shouted towards the house. 'My name is Wallace Carver. I've come for my family and I'm willing to make an exchange.'

CHAPTER 61

Alicia lifted her head at the sound of her husband's voice and released an astonished cry of joy. The unrelenting gunfire in the confines of the tiny kitchen had sounded like the end of the world, but she never imagined for a moment it was Wallace being shot at.

Despite everything she had said, those goading words of defiance, she never actually believed that Wallace would find her. How could he? She didn't even know where she was. The creep had used a woman's profile to befriend her on the Internet and she had unknowingly given him everything, every detail that he needed to snatch her and her boys from the Bellingham mall.

Wallace didn't even use the computer, had no interest in it, but she had hoped beyond hope that someone – a *real* friend – would read her urgent SOS and get a message to the authorities.

Alex and Fred, however, never shared her doubts. Even in the cloying darkness of the well, when the man had come to separate her from her children with false promises and rough hands, when Alicia thought her screams would lead to madness, the boys never stopped believing. To them, their father – the man who could wrestle them both at once, snap his fingers and whistle, and drive an enormous transit bus – had always been a hero.

Upon hearing his voice, the boys instantly began screaming in unison. 'Dad! Daddy! Dad!'

'Shut them up,' Gallagher shouted.

He turned from the window and snapped a fresh magazine into a lethal-looking automatic weapon, black steel designed by a madman for one reason and one reason only: massive carnage.

He pointed the weapon at the boys, but Alicia immediately rose to her feet and stepped in front of them.

'It's over,' she said. 'Why don't you just let us go?'

'I can't do that,' said Gallagher.

Alicia firmed her jaw. 'We won't tell the cops. We won't tell anyone. We just want to go home.'

Gallagher tried to smile, but it didn't quite work.

'Your husband is a piece of work. He's got a shotgun fastened to the side of my soldier's head. How the fuck does a bus driver get the balls to do that?'

'He loves his sons,' said Alicia proudly. 'What father would do any less?'

Gallagher's upper lip curled into a sneer.

'I've killed lots of fathers and lots of sons. Your man is nothing special.'

Alicia swallowed and her eyes softened as she

squeezed the shoulders of her sons. 'Maybe not to you, but he means the world to us.'

Gallagher glared at her and turned to his companion. 'Lock them in the bathroom till this is sorted.'

Alicia considered defying him, but there was something fiercely unsettling about the black man's demeanour that stifled any rebellion. She grabbed her boys and hustled them out of the room.

Mr Black closed the bathroom door behind the woman and her two children. The door hung loose on its hinges from when he had forced his way in earlier and he didn't see a way to lock it from the outside.

Instead, he removed a spare cartridge from his pocket and pressed his forehead to the hollow door. With careful aim, he dropped the shell on to the fringe of hard tile that peeked out from under the door. The brass pinged beautifully.

'That was the pin to a fragmentation grenade,' he said through the door. 'If you try to open this door, it will explode. Neither you nor your children will survive. Do you understand?'

He heard a frightened whimper from inside.

'Do you understand?' he repeated.

'Yes,' said the woman.

'Good.'

Back in the kitchen, a canvas bag filled with weapons and ammunition had been dragged out of a cupboard and unceremoniously dumped on the table.

Gallagher knelt by the open window, still cradling his favoured M4 assault rifle. A crude but effective weapon capable of firing up to 950 rounds per minute, the M4 was a solid choice for close-range work. And although it suffered from an annoyingly inferior ballistic performance beyond three hundred yards, Mr Black had found it rarely let him down when a high body count was the main objective.

He studied the remaining weapons cache and selected an M39 Enhanced Marksman Rifle with an attached Leupold Mark 4 scope. He flashed Gallagher a look of annoyance. The M39 was not the sort of weapon one normally dumped in a canvas bag and hid in a kitchen cupboard.

Gallagher didn't notice Mr Black's scorn. He was too busy peering out the window at the puzzling scene beyond as the bus driver continued to plead for contact while threatening the broken shell of what was left of Ronson.

Not that Ronson had ever been much of a Marine. He was the kind of bleating modern soldier who preferred to kill anonymously from the safety of a monitor and joystick than to meet his enemy face to face. And if that was the military's future, Mr Black was glad to be out.

With reverence, he carried the rifle to an adjacent window beside Gallagher and peered through the scope. The range was ridiculously short for such a weapon. He quickly dialled down the scope to 8X magnification, but even then he could still select which sweat-glistening pore or blackhead he wanted to plug.

The bus driver was attempting to shield himself behind the vehicle's open doors, but tempered glass and lightweight aluminium weren't much of an obstacle for a 170-grain bullet moving at 2,837 feet per second.

He moved the scope to the left and caught sight of a second man huddled behind the front seats. He frowned when he recognized Crow. This man shouldn't be here and there was no possible way that he had been the one who knocked him out at Morris's condo.

Were there others?

Mr Black quickly surveyed the surrounding area through the scope. He didn't see anyone else, but suddenly he felt less comfortable with his situation. His instinct for self-preservation was tingling.

'The second man is Crow,' he told Gallagher. 'Wallace's bus driver friend.'

'How the fuck did they find us?' Gallagher asked. 'You said Morris didn't talk.'

Mr Black shrugged. 'I took him at his word. That was a mistake.'

Gallagher's face twisted into a scowl. 'You talked to Morris? He was still alive?'

'For a short while.'

'Christ, did you even try to call an ambulance?'

'He died in my arms,' said Mr Black. 'He

314

couldn't be saved. Besides,' he nodded out the window at the white SUV, 'he obviously couldn't be trusted either.'

Gallagher snarled. 'He saved my life.'

Mr Black flared his nostrils in anger. 'I saved your goddamn life. Morris was little more than a pack mule.' Before Gallagher could respond, Mr Black stabbed his chin out the window. 'Are you going to talk to Carver?'

Gallagher licked his lips and looked away. 'Don't know yet,' he said. 'Hate to give the fucker false hope.'

'Fine.'

Mr Black returned to the scope, selected his target and squeezed the trigger.

At the edge of light and shadow, a spray of blood blossomed and expanded to resemble an exploding poppy.

'Jesus Christ!' yelled Gallagher. 'What did you do that for?'

'Time to end his misery,' said Mr Black calmly. 'As you pointed out, why give him false hope?'

CHAPTER 62

The shotgun was torn out of Wallace's hands as the world exploded and a bloody wave slapped across his face and chest.

One second he was looking directly at Ronson, praying he still meant something to the armed men inside the house, and the next he was neutered, unarmed and blind.

A hand gripped his shoulder, pulling at him.

A voice. Crow's. Yelling. Screaming. Frantic.

Get inside! Get inside!

Wallace numbly dragged a limp hand across his eyes, swiping away a blindfold of gore. He staggered, his knees buckling as he gripped the door and struggled to stay upright.

A fresh corpse lay at his feet. Hands bound behind its back. Executed. Without mercy or warning or reason.

The top of Ronson's head flapped open like a greedy child's Easter egg, unwrapped and bitten before being tossed aside for another.

Crow's hand squeezed Wallace's shoulder with more urgency. His voice still yelled the same instructions.

316

Get inside! Get inside!

Wallace was frozen. Unable to move. Unable to think.

Strong fingers pinched, grabbing hold of shirt, skin and unyielding muscle. A second hand gripped his other shoulder. It hurt. Wallace registered the pain, but it was as if it was happening to someone else.

He felt himself being lifted, dragged backwards, his heels skidding across the ground. He smacked the side of the SUV and then Crow's hands wrapped around his chest and hauled him inside the vehicle.

Huddled on the floor, using the leather seat-backs as a shield, Crow stared at him in shocked disbelief. His eyes were larger than Wallace had ever seen; that noble, fearsome glare replaced with true horror and fright. Spatters of someone else's blood dripped down his face and his mouth opened and closed like a surprised goldfish scooped out of the bowl by a determined kitten.

'Holy fuck!' he screamed when the words finally took flight. To Wallace's ears, the expletive sounded no louder than a whisper.

Glass shattered and both men ducked as a renewed burst of automatic gunfire smacked into and through the doors that Wallace had thought could protect him. The metal became confetti; the tinted glass vanished as though returned to sand.

The shots were a mockery. A final *Fuck you* from a foe that knew it held the upper hand.

Wallace felt his anger return. An agonized heat coursed through his veins and thawed his frozen limbs. He wiped his face on his shirt, pinched his nose and blew to make his ears pop. He gave his head a shake to restart his brain and turned to Crow.

'I think I heard them,' he said.

'Who?' asked Crow.

'My boys,' said Wallace. 'I'm sure I heard them cry out for me.'

He glanced out the door at his shotgun tangled in a nest of bloody tape around the gaping skull of a dead man.

'We have any more weapons?' he asked.

Crow handed Wallace the remaining shotgun and pulled a Glock handgun from his waistband.

'That's it?' Wallace tried not to show his disappointment.

'Hold on.'

Crow scrambled over the seatback and into the rear cargo area. As he moved, Wallace noticed a fresh patch of blood spreading across his friend's stomach.

He pointed at it worriedly. 'Are you hit?'

Crow looked down and touched the spot. He shook his head. 'Stitches must have torn.'

'We're way over our heads, aren't we?'

Crow shrugged. 'This might help.' He pulled back a colourful Hudson Bay blanket to reveal a small cardboard box. 'Cheveyo had me stop by Randolph's on the way down.'

Crow dug into the box and held up a half-dozen grey cylindrical canisters marked with a bright yellow stripe and yellow markings that read: SMOKE WP. 'He convinced me to take a box of these. Paleface Barbecue Lighters.'

Wallace blanched. 'I don't want to set the house on fire. Alicia and the boys are inside.'

'We'll throw short,' said Crow. 'These puppies can create a real thick blanket of smoke. That'll give us time to either get the hell out of this mess or go deeper in without getting our asses shot off.'

'I'm not running away,' said Wallace bluntly. 'Not now.'

'Then let's get close.' Crow's mouth was grim. 'I want to look these motherfuckers in the eye.'

CHAPTER 63

The rear hatch of the white SUV popped open and slowly drifted above the roofline on silent air-filled struts. Immediately, the door's heavy glass was shattered by a rapid three-bullet burst.

When he looked over at Mr Black, Gallagher's grin had returned, his moment of mourning for two dead soldiers already in the past.

'They must be shitting themselves,' he said. 'Think they'll run?'

'It's a long dash back to the woods,' said Mr Black.

'What other choice do they have?'

'None.'

Mr Black scanned the perimeter of light again, trying to sense if there was movement in the dark woods beyond. The two men appeared to be alone, but he knew there was at least one other person working with them. And where there was one, there could be others.

He didn't like the feeling.

Gallagher was oblivious to the threat. His senses had been dulled by too much time away from the inherent paranoia of combat. He was over-excited by this skirmish, his actions more like a patriotic greenhorn with his first taste of blood than a battle-hardened salt who understood the enemy was mere vermin and they were the exterminators.

His former sergeant's eyes were lit up like sparklers and he inhaled deeply though his nose, drawing in the cordite fumes from over a hundred spent shells, as though the brass carcasses released pure oxygen.

Mr Black disliked the smell of burnt gunpowder, it reminded him too much of too much, but Gallagher was a man born for war. He was the type whose blood is meant to stain the sand, his body returning in silence and secret under a folded flag. The unsung hero. The martyr. The mourned husband and father.

Stripping him of his medals had been like flaying a layer of skin.

Not so Mr Black. He preferred more visceral trophies. Like Gallagher, he wasn't born for civilian life, but neither, as had been made abundantly clear, was he meant for uniform. At least not one that was afraid of a little senseless bloodshed.

The others had mourned their military discharge and closed their eyes to just how much freedom there was outside the government yoke. Morris had even traded one uniform for another. And now Gallagher. Instead of embracing the possibilities – Africa, Central America, wherever the highest bidder wanted to send them – he had moved the war inside his mind and become lost to it.

Pity. He had been a ruthless killer once. A man worth following.

Mr Black looked down at the rifle in his hands and pondered where Gallagher might have secreted his own ill-gotten reserves. The war had treated them well in many ways. Cash would be kept close, readily available, but unlike Morris, it wouldn't be behind a mirror.

He glanced up at the ceiling as though seeing through the wood and plaster to the unfinished area beyond. *Why was there a lock on the trapdoor?*

He grinned behind thick, plum-coloured lips as he came to an inevitable and bondage-breaking conclusion. This was no longer his battle. It was time for a new path. A new beginning.

'When they run . . .' Gallagher's words rolled off his tongue with the dreaminess of a junkie on the brink of a fresh fix. 'I'll stitch a few rounds right behind their heels, get their blood really pumping, make them think they're Superman. When they're at full gallop, you take a knee. One each.'

'I could just take them out,' said Mr Black, wanting it over, wanting it done. 'Back of the head. Easy.'

'Nah, let's make them crawl. Give them a little glimpse of hope. See how far they get before we switch out the lights. We could make it interesting.

A wager? Which one do you think will crawl the furthest?'

'It's a sucker's bet.'

Gallagher looked over, annoyed. 'Huh?'

Mr Black sighed quietly. 'I can take out a knee cleanly or I can blow it apart. The choice is mine.'

Gallagher considered this. 'If you did them both clean, who would you pick?'

He didn't hesitate. 'The Indian.'

'Why?'

'More to live for. He's got a wife and family back home, but you've already taken everything from Carver. Dying here is no different than dying elsewhere.'

'He could start over.'

Mr Black offered a cruel smile as he shook the words away. 'You couldn't.'

Gallagher rocked back on his heels as though he had been punched. 'I'm trying to.' His voice was a growl. 'That's what this is all about.'

'No.' It was time to speak his mind. To put his exit strategy into play. For all he knew, the woods could be crawling with Indians. 'This is war. Plain and simple. You needed a distraction to stop from sticking a gun in your mouth and pulling the trigger.'

'Fuck you,' Gallagher snarled. 'You know what he—'

'It's bullshit,' said Mr Black calmly. 'I know what you told the others, but I know better. You don't care about this woman. She's not here to replace your wife. She never could. She hates you. Just look in her eyes. She'll always hate you.'

Gallagher flinched, but Mr Black continued.

'You saw a man, a civilian no less, who risked everything to save *your* wife and child after you drove them away. You wanted to punish him because it wasn't *you*. Your obsession was an excuse to go one-on-one against the man who did what you couldn't. He set your family free. You needed to break him. To bring him down to your level.' His eyes blazed with challenge. 'But you didn't. Wallace Carver didn't give up. He's here and that really pisses you off.'

'How fucking dare you?' Gallagher pointed his weapon. 'You don't challenge me.'

Mr Black peeled back his lips and showed all his teeth. Glorious. This was a glimpse of his old sergeant, but it was too late for resurrection now.

'The enemy is not in here or out there.' He stabbed a finger into his chest at a point above his heart. 'It's here. I oughta know. Killing doesn't dull the pain unless you *really* embrace it.'

'You don't know me,' said Gallagher. 'Don't think you know my fucking pain.'

Mr Black rested his rifle against the window sill, stood tall and stretched his back. He stood unarmed and unafraid. The decision made, he felt wonderfully free, like the time he had walked down the midnight street as a child, the perfume of gasoline and smoke clinging to his clothes, the sound of screaming fading in the distance.

He loomed above Gallagher, his teeth flashing like silverfish in the dull light.

'You always believed I was your obedient dog,' he said. 'But I was the bug in your ear, whispering dark thoughts. *Let's take the village . . . Let's kill every motherfucker in the whole motherfucking world.*' He laughed huskily. 'We burned that camp to the ground, littered the dead with explosives, and you still thought it was *your* idea. Why do you think I rescued you? Who else would give me such freedom to kill? You thought you held a leash, but it was you who turned me loose.' He laughed again, making it shrill and sharp as he reached for his knife. 'Trouble is, al Qaeda took more than your fingers. They also took your fucking balls.'

Gallagher's finger tightened on the trigger of his M4 just as the window behind him blew apart and white smoke flooded the room.

CHAPTER 64

Wallace ducked behind the SUV as the grenade detonated with an explosion powerful enough to shatter glass and spread white phosphorous particles for dozens of feet. The particles ignited, burning at 5,000 degrees Fahrenheit and releasing a thick cloud of smoke.

'Shit,' he cried. 'That was too close.'

'Let's hope it stunned them.'

Crow stepped out and lobbed two more grenades towards the house. They both exploded a second after he was back behind the vehicle. A dark shadow fell over the two men as the security lights became diffused, their intensity lost in the dense, sputtering smog.

When no gunfire followed, Crow chanced a second look. The house was barely visible behind the eerily distorted glow. The cool night air and damp weather, however, was quickly ruining their plan.

'The smoke's rising too fast,' said Crow. 'We have to move now if we want cover.'

Wallace pointed to the two large Lincolns parked a short distance from the house's rear door.

'We get between those,' he said. 'Regroup. That's one step closer.'

Crow lifted his handgun. 'I'll cover you.'

Wallace shook his head. 'We do this together.'

Crow handed Wallace one of the last three remaining grenades. He slipped the other two into his pockets.

'We should have stolen a couple of buses,' said Crow. 'Showed them what we're really made of.'

Wallace grinned. 'You ready?'

Both men ran.

CHAPTER 65

Gallagher screamed in surprise as a tiny particle of white phosphorous sizzled through his sleeve and became embedded in his skin.

He ran to the sink and slapped a soaking-wet cloth over the smoking hole while he frantically squeezed and pinched the burning flesh until the tiny grain finally popped loose. He dropped the cloth in the sink and cursed aloud.

He knew what that stuff did to flesh. It didn't just burn you, it burned *through* you. He had witnessed it first hand . . . hell, oftentimes it had been *by* his hand . . . and it was one of the worst ways to die he could imagine.

Maybe Bone was right to kill Ronson, he thought. Stupid fuck had obviously kept a stash of military-grade weapons at his house. And not only had he handed them over to Carver, he had also led the driver directly to this door.

Smoke filled the room, blinding him, but it was dissipating through the house and disappearing almost as quickly as it had arrived. A phosphorous grenade only burns for sixty seconds. Plenty of time for a trained man, but the drivers were pussies. They were probably still awestruck by the pretty smoke.

Gallagher grinned and reached for his weapon. He frowned. The weight was off. Too light. Six pounds, practically on the nose. He cursed himself, cursed the rust and the drink. In the sand he was a force not to be messed with, but out here, with nothing but woods and silence and *fucking rain*, his edge had dulled.

That's why Bone hadn't been afraid. Black bastard was keeping track; knew his magazine had run dry.

Gallagher moved effortlessly through the smoke to the kitchen table. A blind Marine was still a deadly Marine. He didn't need sight to do what had to be done. He knew the workings of his weapon better than the curves of his own wife.

At the table, he rummaged in the canvas bag for a fresh magazine. There were only two left. He had already gone through four. He dumped the spent magazine on the floor and snapped in a fresh one. He enjoyed the sound as it clicked home.

Locked and loaded, motherfucker! You scared now? You fucking should be.

Gallagher squatted down and scanned the room. Hot smoke rose as cool air rushed in through the broken windows to restore balance. From beneath the table, the room was dim but smoke free. Gallagher inhaled deeply. The air was sweet, fresh, a tang of salt and cedar.

Bone's discarded sniper rifle lay on the floor surrounded by an abstract puddle of broken glass. No blood. No body. He would be in his element. In close quarters, Bone always used a knife.

Gallagher checked his M4 was set to fire rapid three-round bursts rather than single-shot semi-auto. Naturally, it was. His ingrained soldier's instincts and training were still moving faster than his conscious mind. The difference, as any drill instructor would tell you, between life and death.

He moved through the doorway beside the broken windows that separated the small kitchen from the larger dining room and connected living area.

The high ceiling lifted the smoke skyward, allowing him to stand. The living room had been Carly's favourite: the tall picture windows looking out over the ocean, the log fireplace for those winter nights when it was just . . . He shook his head, not wanting to remember, not wanting to admit. Carly always said it was never just the three of them. The Corps was always present.

Before she took their daughter and left, Carly told him this was her favourite room when it was just the two of them . . . *Katie and her* . . . when he was gone, away from them, fighting a war . . . fighting for—

He wanted to believe it was *for them*, but deep down he knew it was for himself. He needed war as others needed air. Carly understood that better than anyone, she just couldn't live with it anymore.

But Carly was gone now. That was fact. There was nothing to stop him from embracing exactly who he was always meant to be.

Gallagher gripped his gun tighter and stepped into the open room just as a woman screamed.

He twisted around. Carly?

NO! It was almost a relief. Bone, damn his eyes, was right. This woman didn't hold any true value.

Alicia stood in the doorway of the bathroom with one son clutching her leg. His eyes were closed, terrified, while his mother screamed at Bone.

Bone was at the base of the unfinished wooden stairs. He was holding the younger boy under his arm – the one with ginger hair like his mother's. The boy was squirming, afraid, lashing out with tiny fists, but his blows were completely ineffectual.

Gallagher had watched Bone hold red-hot coals in his bare hands without flinching. The impact of a young boy's fist would be like the fluttering of an eyelash.

'We can sort this out, Bone,' Gallagher called.

'Too late,' Bone replied. 'Carly and Katie had the right idea. I don't need you, either.'

Gallagher's face burned as he brought his M4 to bear, but Bone's little black handgun was faster. The lone bullet smacked Gallagher in the chest, breaking two ribs and burrowing deep into meat inches from his heart.

The ex-Marine gasped and reflexively squeezed

the trigger of his own weapon. Bullets stitched the floor and walls, forcing the woman and her remaining son back inside the bathroom. He tried to readjust his aim as he pumped the trigger again and again, but by the time his last bullets found the steps, Bone wasn't there to meet them.

Sgt Gallagher watched the last surviving member of his unit run up the stairs to nowhere.

Bone fired his handgun again, but this time he aimed up and the bullet chewed wood and buckled the lock's hasp. The trapdoor sprang open as Bone hit it full bore with his shoulder, then he and the boy vanished into spider's webs and darkness.

The sound of more wood splintering came from the direction of the kitchen as the rear door was forced open. It was followed by the stamping of heavy, clumsy feet.

Gallagher knew he had to move. Live to fight another day. He snapped his last magazine into the M4 and heaved himself to his feet. Sucking air deep into his lungs, he heard and felt some of it hiss from the oozing hole in his chest. A fucking suck wound. Bone's parting joke.

Gallagher fought the pain and ran, heading straight for the last place Bone had been. The place where two human shields still cowered in fright.

CHAPTER 66

Wallace kicked open the kitchen door and rushed inside with his shotgun at the ready. Crow followed close behind, his handgun in a solid two-fisted grip.

The house reeked of war, anarchy and *blood*.

Wallace scanned the empty kitchen, looking for any sign of Alicia and the boys. Nothing.

He swallowed and moved on, knowing that if he stopped for even a second, fear would catch up and whisper its cold words of logic in his ear, make his muscles freeze and his courage vanish. He had faced that once before when he hung above the ocean and reached out his hand to a terrified young girl who likely imagined he was Death itself.

He had fought it then. He would fight it now.

Two archways led off the kitchen. The one on the far side of the table opened near the first rise of a wooden staircase that climbed to the upper level. Anyone perched near the top of the stairs would have a perfect spot for ambush.

Wallace turned to his left and took the doorway beside the two broken windows. He moved cautiously into a formal dining room that connected to a large, open-plan living area with floor-to-ceiling windows.

Keeping his back to the wall, his stomach churning, Wallace moved closer to the corner where a wide hallway led back to the stairs and the second kitchen archway.

He stopped at the corner and looked down at several large puddles of fresh blood on the floor.

'Fuck!' Crow swore behind him.

A sudden scream. Alicia!

Wallace had no choice. He took the corner.

No one was waiting on the stairs, but an unfamiliar face was vanishing into a small room further down the hallway. Behind him, Crow instantly fired off three shots from his handgun, stitching the plaster.

'Stop!' Wallace yelled. 'He has Alicia in there.'

'Good call,' a man shouted through the wall. 'You almost gave the boy a lobotomy.'

Wallace sucked in a deep breath and exhaled heavily.

'Alicia,' he called out, 'are you OK?'

Wallace heard a heart-wrenching sob, followed by his wife's tremulous voice.

'Alex and I are OK.'

Wallace hesitated. 'What about Fred?'

'The other one took him. I don't know where he is.'

'I can tell you,' said the man. 'You let me leave. I'll tell you where.'

'He's badly wound—' Alicia's words were cut off by a howl of pain.

Reacting on pure instinct and adrenalin, Wallace rushed headlong down the hallway and kicked open the flimsy bathroom door. With the shotgun pressed hard against his shoulder, his eyes locked on his target. The stranger sat inside the bathtub with the barrel of his weapon sunk into the soft underside of Alicia's chin.

Alex sat on the other side of his mother. His face was sickly pale and tears ran freely down his cheeks.

'Let them go.' Wallace's voice broke. 'You can have anything you want. Just please let them go.'

The stranger sucked in a deep breath and his chest gurgled. The act of breathing caused him noticeable pain.

'You're not supposed to be here.' The stranger laughed ruefully. 'You're supposed to be suffering in a jail cell, not knowing if your family is alive or dead. I had everything planned. It was perfect.' He paused and his tone lost any trace of humour. 'But then you have a knack for ruining perfect, don't you?'

Wallace blinked away a sudden arrival of tears at the sight of his wife and oldest child. So close and yet . . . The shotgun grew heavy in his hands until all he had left were words.

'You're Gallagher, right?'

'Sergeant Gallagher.' A defiant brightness returned to his eyes.

'I talked to your wife in the ambulance before we were taken to hospital,' Wallace said. 'She told me she had been running away. She was scared. So scared she thought she could outrun a bridge full of oncoming cars.' Wallace locked eyes with the man, attempting to burrow inside his brain, to make a connection. 'If you loved her so much, why was she so scared?'

Gallagher swallowed and sneered. 'I'm a bad man, I guess.' Sarcasm dripped like venom.

'You chased her,' continued Wallace. 'Sent her driving in front of a bus and off a bridge. Your child was in the back seat.'

Gallagher flinched. 'I didn't chase her. I was looking for her; I wanted to talk, to fix things. I didn't know she was in Canada until . . .' He hesitated.

'*Someone* was chasing her,' said Wallace. 'She was terrified and driving like a madwoman to escape him. She told me.'

Gallagher's face fell. 'Bone,' he said. 'Always too eager. He located her. But by the time I got to the hospital, she was gone again.' His eyes went cold. 'You were in the same hospital. You helped her disappear.'

Wallace swallowed. 'What do I know about running away?'

'Yeah,' Gallagher said wearily. 'A real fucking hero, huh?'

Wallace shook his head. 'No. Just a man.'

Gallagher shook his head. 'I could have made it

right. If you hadn't interfered and helped her vanish, I could have convinced her to come back. You ruined that.'

'Wallace didn't even know.' Alicia's wounded voice cut through the tension like a razor across skin. 'He underwent four surgeries on his leg. They kept him doped up or asleep for the better part of a week.'

Both men turned to her.

'I helped Carly and Katie,' she said. 'I saw them at the hospital when I was visiting Wallace. I wanted to meet the women who were so import-ant that my husband foolishly risked his own life. They were both so frightened that it broke my heart. I pried. I listened. And then I finished the job that my husband started when he pulled them off that bridge. I helped them begin a new life.'

Gallagher snarled and pressed the gun barrel deeper into Alicia's chin. Her neck stretched to an extreme angle until her head seemed on the edge of ripping free. She groaned but remained defiant.

'You can't keep someone by force,' she cried. 'That's not love. Carly and Katie were on that bridge because of you. Not us. It's time to let them go.'

Gallagher recoiled as though slapped and seemed to deflate before Wallace's eyes. His grip eased and his eyelids lowered to half mast. His tongue darted out from his mouth and ran circles around dry lips. It was obvious that he had lost a lot of blood.

Nervously, Wallace took a chance. He moved his gaze to his oldest son.

'Come here, Alex. Quickly.'

Gallagher flinched again, but he didn't resist as Alex scrambled out of the tub and rushed to his father's side. Wallace hugged him tight, but kept his eyes on Gallagher.

'Go to Uncle Crow,' Wallace said.

Alex resisted, but suddenly a pair of strong hands swooped in to pull him out of the doorway and into a massive, bone-crushing hug.

'That's all you're getting,' said Gallagher. His momentary daze had faded and his voice was filled with renewed strength. 'Until I'm clear of here.'

Wallace lowered his shotgun and laced his own words with venom. 'Need a hand?'

Gallagher grinned, showing bloody teeth. He spat on the floor. Thick and arterial red; signs of a critical wound.

'Just keep your distance,' he said. 'Your wife and I can manage.'

Wallace watched Gallagher struggle to his feet, the barrel of his gun never slipping from beneath Alicia's chin. His wife's stare was cold, calculating and so far away from the eyes that Wallace knew that he almost felt afraid.

When Gallagher was standing, he signalled for Wallace to move out of the way. Wallace stepped back, moving slowly down the hallway and into the living room. He raised his arms and rested his shotgun on his shoulder. Crow had moved off to one side, keeping Alex safely behind him.

Gallagher stepped into the hallway and stared at Crow.

'Loyal friends you have,' he said to Wallace. 'I used to know some, too.'

Keeping his gun pressed against Alicia's flesh, Gallagher turned and walked backwards through the doorway to the kitchen. Wallace followed, his hands still raised.

'Where's my other son?' Wallace asked.

'Where's my wife?' asked Gallagher. He moved around the table and edged towards the back door.

Wallace swallowed again. 'Alicia told you, I don't know.'

'I don't believe you, either of you.'

'Don't you think I'd tell you if I knew? I'm not that good a liar.'

'I think you are,' said Gallagher. 'Your wife didn't tell me about her involvement. And I asked her quite vigorously. You're both fucking liars.'

Wallace looked into Alicia's eyes. There was no hate or mistrust, only love. He sighed in resignation. 'Tell me where my son is and I'll tell you where your wife and daughter went.'

Gallagher smiled thinly. 'I fucking knew it. You sure you're just a bus driver?'

'No.' Wallace's voice was scratched and raw.

'That's just my job. I'm a father and a husband who loves his family. Now where's my son?'

Gallagher shrugged as if deciding it no longer mattered. 'Bone scurried upstairs with him.' He raised his eyes to the ceiling. 'You've cornered a fucking monster there. If you think I'm bad, you haven't seen a goddamn thing.'

Wallace blinked and released a long, slow breath. They were in the middle of the kitchen. The night was dark and still. Behind Gallagher, Crow had moved silently through the dining room and now stood in the other doorway. He raised his handgun in both hands and aimed it at the back of the man's head.

'You can let Alicia go now,' said Wallace. 'Last chance.'

Gallagher's brow furrowed in confusion.

'I think you're forgetting—'

'Mom!'

Alex rushed past Crow and sprinted into the kitchen, obviously misreading Crow's intent.

Gallagher released Alicia and spun around. As he pivoted, he aimed his M4 towards Crow.

'Get down!' Wallace screamed.

Alicia and Alex crumpled to the floor as Wallace's shotgun boomed.

The gun dealer had been right about what happened when your aim was high.

Scrambling off the floor, Alicia took one glance at Gallagher's headless corpse before running into her husband's arms. Wallace squeezed her, but no matter how hard he tried, it just didn't seem to be enough.

When Alicia finally released him, her eyes were dry and her voice unwavering. 'We need to get Fred.'

Wallace glanced behind him at the unfinished staircase and nodded. It wasn't over yet.

CHAPTER 67

Wallace stood at the base of the stairs and looked up at the trapdoor.

'He could pick us off one by one,' said Crow. 'It's too narrow an opening for the both of us to go in at once.'

Wallace reached into his pocket and lifted out the white phosphorous grenade.

'This is too dangerous.'

He dropped the canister to the floor, but as he moved to kick it away, Crow stopped him by trapping it with his own foot.

'Maybe not,' said Crow. 'We could ignite it in the back bedroom. The smoke will head straight for the ceiling. Bone won't stay up there if he thinks the house is going to burn down around him.'

'What about Fred?' asked Wallace.

'Bone will still need a hostage to leverage his escape,' Crow reasoned. 'He won't harm Fred until he's no longer useful, but we stand a better chance of rescuing him out in the open.'

Despite the obvious danger, Wallace didn't see any other option. He turned to Alicia who stood in the kitchen with Alex. Alex had his head buried in his mother's stomach and Wallace felt his heart crack. His son should never have witnessed what he had had to do in the kitchen.

'Hide in the woods,' said Wallace. 'If it all goes to hell and this bastard gets past us, I want you to get out of here. Don't stop. Steal a car and drive straight to Canada if you need to.'

Alicia opened her mouth to protest, but Wallace was one step ahead of her.

'You've already done your part,' he said to his wife. 'You kept our sons alive for this long. I'll get Fred, but you need to get Alex home where he belongs. I need you both safe.'

Alicia nodded and leaned down to whisper in Alex's ear. After a moment, they both headed outside.

When they were gone, Crow picked up the grenade and headed down the hallway to the master bedroom.

'You ready?' he called.

Wallace stood back from the staircase, his shotgun levelled at the trapdoor. He nodded.

Crow pulled the pin and tossed the grenade into the room. He closed the door to keep the phosphorous contained and hurried back down the hall to join Wallace.

The grenade exploded with a deafening boom that splintered wood and shattered glass. Smoke leaked out of the buckled bedroom door, but it quickly headed for the ceiling.

Wallace wiped his brow as he concentrated on the trapdoor above.

'Aim for his knees or ankles,' said Crow in a tense whisper. 'Your gun can take a leg or foot clean off, then I'll scalp the motherfucker while he bleeds out.'

Wallace gulped, but nodded his agreement.

They waited.

The smoke rose higher, thick and hot. It stung their eyes and scratched their throats. The crackling sound of burning could be heard from the bedroom and sweet wood smoke joined the chemical garlic stench of phosphorous.

A heavy thumping sounded above them, followed by the breaking of more wood. A clang of metal and then—

Two bullets pierced the trapdoor and chewed into the stairs, driving Wallace and Crow back a few paces. But the shots weren't aimed, the noise and hot lead serving as a warning to keep away.

Wallace glanced at Crow. 'He's not coming down.'

'He will,' said Crow. 'He's not the kind of man to martyr himself.'

'The smoke's getting too thick for Fred.' Panic thickened Wallace's throat. 'He'll be choking to death.'

'Patience. He'll come.'

Wallace tried, but his youngest son was in too much danger. Gritting his teeth, he broke rank and pounded up the stairs. Crow screamed at him to stop, but it was too late. Wallace raised his left arm above his head and smashed through the trap-door. The door crashed over on its side and Wallace immediately dived to the floor.

The room was thick with clawing smoke as Wallace rolled on to his stomach, desperately searching for a glimpse of the man's feet.

Instead of feet, Wallace saw smoke pouring out of a large hole in the wall where a sheet of rotten plywood had been torn from its anchors and tossed aside.

Yelling for Crow, Wallace ran to the hole. The smoke was too thick to see through. It was like standing in the middle of a toxic cloud with your shoes on fire.

Wallace had no choice. He leapt out into a blanket of weightless air and plummeted like a stone.

CHAPTER 68

When he hit the ground, Wallace attempted a paratrooper roll, but he wasn't a trained Marine. His knee smacked him on the chin, breaking two teeth, and his shotgun tore loose from his hand to vanish into a deep puddle of mud.

Roaring with a heady cocktail of anger, fear, pain and adrenalin, he spat out the broken teeth and scooped mud from his eyes just as—

Red taillights flashed a brief warning before the massive tailgate of a large SUV hurtled straight towards him.

Wallace didn't have time to blink. He threw himself back to the ground, desperately trying to bury himself deep in the mud as the SUV drove over the top of him. He could feel the hair-singeing heat of the muffler and exhaust as it passed over his head, but the raised under-carriage and four huge tyres missed him completely.

Wallace scrambled to his feet as the large black Lincoln pulled a smooth one-eighty and roared out of the clearing towards the road and escape.

He glanced to his left and spotted a second vehicle, nearly identical to the one Bone was fleeing in. Praying the keys were in it, he ran to the red SUV and hopped inside. He was covered in so much mud, he had to quickly grab the door handle to stop from sliding off the seat.

The key was in the ignition.

Without waiting for Crow to catch up, Wallace threw the vehicle into gear and tore across the yard in hot pursuit. The SUV bounced and slid as he pressed the accelerator to the floor in a desperate attempt to close the gap. Bone's vehicle had already left the clearing and disappeared over the hill.

Wallace slammed his fist into the steering wheel, trying to coax more speed from the powerful engine. He hadn't come this far only to lose one of his sons now.

Before reaching the road, the front wheels hit a trough so deep it almost caused the vehicle to flip and Wallace was smashed hard against the roof. Grimacing in pain, Wallace glimpsed Alicia and Alex within the circle of floodlights. They were frozen in place, staring at his retreating vehicle. They still looked terrified, but at least they were safe. He glanced in the rear-view mirror and saw Crow's silhouette running from the burning house.

For them, the danger had fled. But, he swore to himself, it wouldn't get away.

Wallace fishtailed around the first corner and

felt his wheels leave the ground at every bump. The ground was wet and slippery, but he had driven buses through slick BC winters when every other vehicle was trapped in its own driveway. White-knuckle driving was his specialty. And he was damn good at it.

When the road made the first horseshoe turn of an S-shaped bend, Wallace caught a glimpse of Bone's black SUV. It was only a short distance ahead.

He had closed the gap. Slightly, but it was something. He pressed his vehicle to its limit, praying that Fred had thought to fasten his seatbelt just as Alicia and he had always told him.

Please, he projected, *have that belt on.*

Wallace snapped on his own belt and took the last turn at breakneck speed. His vehicle practically slid around the curve on only two wheels—

And then his heart stopped beating.

Time froze solid.

There was no air. No light.

No reason. No God.

Standing in the middle of the muddy road, directly in the path of his out-of-control vehicle, stood his son.

Fred was screaming. Rooted to the spot. His mouth opened wider than even seemed possible as his eyes bore witness to the onrushing glimpse of his own mortality.

Once again, Wallace was Death in the eyes of a terrified child.

He didn't have time to curse or even to think. Everything was reflex. All four limbs worked in tandem for one impossible move.

Wheel.

Brake.

Accelerator.

Handbrake.

And prayer.

More prayer than he had ever said in his lifetime, all compressed into three small words: *Let him live.*

The vehicle snapped to the side, its rear fishtailing wildly one way and then the other. Tyres slipped and gripped and slipped again.

The huge SUV skimmed past the boy, barely ruffling his hair, before its momentum became too much to hold the road.

The vehicle flipped and rolled. Inside, Wallace held on for dear life, knowing he had no reason to expect survival and perfectly willing to accept the consequence. Both his sons were alive. Alicia was safe. Their lives in exchange for his; it was an easy deal to make.

The vehicle slammed on to its roof and was sucked deep into the mud, its velocity decreasing at an alarming rate. But then, as if found distasteful, the earth disgorged it again. This time the vehicle left the road and flew into the trees.

The forest was thick and deep. The vehicle smashed a brutal path before finally coming to a wheezing halt and collapsing in a nest of scraggly pine.

Metal hissed and cooled. Air bags wilted and flaky white dust settled over everything until all that was left was silence.

CHAPTER 69

Wallace sneezed and clutched at his neck. There wasn't a single muscle that didn't ache. The massive vehicle had taken one hell of a beating and yet its core integrity remained intact.

He wiped mud, cloying white dust and fresh blood away from his blurry eyes. A sudden movement outside the broken side window made his stomach lurch.

A large dark shadow was running towards him. The shadow held a knife, long and sharp.

Wallace grabbed his seatbelt, desperately trying to break free. The mechanism was jammed.

He was unarmed, injured and trapped.

Something slammed into the driver's door, but it refused to budge.

Wallace tensed, grimacing at the pain in his neck, and made a futile fist. It wasn't much, but it was all he had left.

'Christ,' said Crow, panting heavily. 'You gonna fight me, too?'

Wallace blinked his eyes into focus. Saw his best friend with a knife in his hand.

'I was going to cut you free,' said Crow. 'Unless you're fine where you are?'

Wallace grinned. Even the muscles in his face hurt.

'No,' he said. 'Get me the hell out of here.'

After Crow cut the belt, he helped Wallace slide through the broken window and out into the cool, wet air. Both men sat on the ground, catching their breath, allowing time to restart.

'Alicia and the boys?' Wallace asked.

'Everyone's OK,' said Crow. 'I asked Alicia to keep the boys behind in case . . .' He paused and looked away.

'In case I was jello?' finished Wallace.

Crow turned back and grinned. 'Something like that, yeah.'

'Gallagher may have been a crazy fuck,' said Wallace, 'but he had good taste in vehicles.'

'You OK to walk?' asked Crow. 'You've got some anxious people waiting to see you.'

Wallace struggled to his feet, stumbled and reached out to grab on to Crow's shoulder.

'I may still need some help,' he said weakly.

Crow wrapped an arm around Wallace's waist and held him upright. 'I'm here.'

Using his friend for support, Wallace limped out of the woods and into the waiting arms of his family.

CHAPTER 70

ive days later

Mr Black hadn't been able to enter Desmond Morris's condo until the local police finally grew bored of twenty-four-hour surveillance and moved on to more pressing matters.

Their interest had been his own fault, he knew. If he had disposed of the body rather than leaving it on display upon the dining-room table, he would likely have only had to wait a day or two at most.

But still, Morris had always enjoyed attention. Who was he to deny him one last show?

Mr Black waited until it was dark, then slit the crime-scene tape and broke the lock. The narrow house was eerily quiet as he crept up the first flight of stairs. The living room, once so perfectly neat and sterile, looked as if it had hosted a teenage rave. The carpet was trampled, holes had been cut into the walls to remove interesting blood spatter, and messy fingerprint powder covered nearly every surface. All that was missing was discarded condom packets, broken plastic cups of juice and a stoned DJ with his finger glued to the repeat button.

Mr Black returned to the stairs and climbed up to the master bedroom. It was in a similar state of dishevelment, but it actually looked slightly tidier than after Wallace Carver had ransacked it looking for . . .

Mr Black paused.

He had never actually known what Carver was after, but now he could guess. Morris had left information around that led Carver to Ronson, and Ronson had led the two drivers to Gallagher.

He paused again.

Did either of those men have information that led back to him? If so, he would need to visit the bus drivers again. Pity. He didn't care for Canada and the crossing had become so tedious. Still, Gallagher had been good to him once. Perhaps he owed him this one last favour.

Two birds. One stone.

Mr Black moved to the full-length mirror and pressed it with the tips of his gloved fingers. He had discovered in just the last few days that, like silk underwear, he enjoyed wearing gloves. They softened every sensation, made him feel less a part of the everyday world and more in touch with the only person who never let him down. Himself.

The mirror clicked and swung open.

The money was untouched. A nice little bonus.

He froze. A ripple in the air. Silent and yet—

He turned around.

A large Indian stood in the doorway. Naked to the waist, his face and chest were decorated in some kind of war paint. Blood red ochre and charcoal black. Primitive designs, but also deeply disturbing.

Mr Black stepped away from the mirror.

'Do I know you?' he asked.

'I am Cheveyo,' said the Indian. 'You knew my brother. JoeJoe.'

Mr Black frowned. 'The name doesn't—'

'You cut his throat. Left him to die on the road.'

Mr Black smiled thinly. 'Ah, yes. I remember now. It was over quickly. He didn't suffer.'

'But you will.'

'Ah.'

Mr Black reached down to his belt and removed his small, curved knife that reminded him of a bear claw.

'I find it's not size that matters.'

Cheveyo curled his lip and puffed out his chest. Muscles rippled as he reached behind his back to withdraw a large, glistening knife with a carved bone handle.

'Sometimes, it is.'

EPILOGUE

The woman and child laughed together as they walked out of the ocean and made their way across a large pile of cedar logs that cushioned the fragile shoreline from the persistent and ever-present surf.

Most of the beach was rocky, but here, in the heart of the tiny hamlet of Roberts Creek, a wide patch of silky sand hid beneath the waves. The sandbar only revealed itself at low tide and the knowledgeable locals knew to check their tables before heading down for a day of fun and relaxation.

Beyond the logs, a path led to a small parking lot decorated with a colourful mandala. Every year, the locals painted a new geometric scene in celebration of the universe. Everyone was invited to participate, regardless of age or skill. It was just one of the many wonderful delights that the newly blonde woman and her daughter had discovered in this little slice of paradise no more than a forty-minute ferry ride from where they had almost lost their lives.

Hand in hand, they walked across the parking

lot, over the bridge that allowed the fresh-water creek to meet its salty mother, and up the hill towards the General Store. The little, family-run store sold everything one could want for a perfect day: ice-cream, magazines, water toys, sandwiches, even cold beer and wine.

At the moment, it was ice-cream. A mother's promise to a loving child who had, at long last, rediscovered her laugh and her beautiful smile.

They reached the top of the short but steep hill, wiping sweat from their brows, child laughing at mother who wanted a second to catch her breath.

A man stood in front of the store. A man the woman recognized.

Her breath caught and her heart fluttered nervously.

The man looked up, but before his gaze could pass over them, two boys rushed out of the store with frozen drinks in hand and two new water pistols still attached to their cardboard backings. The boys ran around the man, giggling and using him as a shield as they pointed the packaged toys at each other and made *pow ping pow* noises.

A woman joined them. Laughing. She was beautiful, with long, curly red hair and a sunburned nose. She shooed the boys away and kissed the man on his stubbled cheek. The man hugged her and returned the kiss with passion.

They looked relaxed and happy.

The blonde woman turned away, not wanting to disturb, not wanting to interfere.

If anyone deserved a little peace and happiness, it was them.

Her guardian angels.